Heavenly Deception

Truth

By

T. L. Crain

DEDICATION

Dedicated to the unfortunate who have suffered at the hands of the powerful. Power is a lure to those who want to control the lives of others. That supreme control is harmful no matter if it's government or religion.

Table of Contents

ACKNOWLEDGMENTS

I'd like to thank those who patiently listened over the years as I talked about this trilogy.

Chapter 1

"Our father, who art in heaven, hallowed be thy name," the girl prayed as blonde hair fell forward as her head bowed in reverence before the the makeshift shrine, "Amen."

She walked to the window and stared up in amazement at the stars her god had created. Somewhere in the darkness, a gunshot rang out, destroying its solemn quiet. The gunshot, and violence in general, seemed to threatened her world and the sanctity of her bedroom.

Janice backed away from the window, climbed into bed, and pulled the covers close to her chin as if for protection against the world. Her mind replayed the violence that she saw on the nightly news. The girl was sure evil ruled a portion of the world. Every night she prayed for the violence of the world to end, yet it seemed to grow more powerful with each passing day.

When the world was dark and Janice was alone in her room, she sometimes had doubts about her beliefs because God had let this reign of evil continue. Then she would pray, begging for forgiveness, and cry because she had questioned God's will. The last of her conscious thoughts before falling asleep were to wish for all violence to end.

The girl awakened to a morning that was brighter and warmer than usual for early spring. Janice sprang from the bed and sniffed the clean morning air that drifted through the open window. She was optimistic about the coming morning. Janice shuttered her earlier trepidations in a hidden spot of her mind until another night when she lay scared in bed. It was Sunday and she looked forward to attending church with her mother. In God's house the world world be right again and she would feel safe.

As she stepped from the shower, a familiar sound came from below and her mood crashed. Her hands trembled as she listened to the sounds that flowed up the stairs, through the hallway, and into her room. Words that had not been meant for her ears, said in distant, violent voices, "For the last time, I'm not going to waste my Sunday going with you to that damn, silly church," her father shouted.

This had been followed by the usual words from her mother, "I'm only concerned about your salvation. It's time for you to give yourself to God—If for no other reason, do it for Janice."

Janice stepped back into the shower and turned the water on full to drown out the sounds. Water droplets crashed onto her trembling body as she said a silent prayer for her parents, especially her father. The girl knew he was a kind and gentle man, even if he wasn't as firm a believer in God as was she and her mother.

That morning in church, something seemed to be different. It could have been the sermon, because it had been about Lucifer and Hell. Those types of sermons usually gave her chills and left her wondering how someone could risk Hell by being an unbeliever. Janice felt confident in her belief, but that morning something had left her wishing to be anywhere other than church. There was an underlying feeling, one that for months had been creeping into her thoughts.

Once again, she tried to push those feelings away, but on this day they were almost overwhelming. The light shining through the multicolored panes of the stain-glass windows seemed brighter than usual that morning. Janice was sure that the coming day would be a good one. Something deep inside told her this day was going to be special and her mood began to lighten.

That all changed when she turned her attention back to the minister to find Ralph Laski turned around smiling at her. Janice immediately turned away to look back to the windows.

Ralph only attended church because he was forced by his parents. The devout girl hated people like him and wished they would stay away from church. Janice had always

3

believed that church wasn't a place for unbelievers. Ralph was nice looking, never caused trouble, and did well in school, but for that one reason, she wouldn't ever be friends with a nonbeliever. The minister had said many times that true Christians never associated with non-believers.

The sermon ran longer than usual and even Janice was glad to be out and on her feet. When the weather was warm, as it was that day, she usually walked the short distance home alone. Her white with pink trim spring dress played in the evening breeze. Because it was such a delightful day, she decided to take the long way home. This would take her through the park, which was usually safe enough during the day.

Near the middle of the park, she sat on a rock that partially sat in a bubbling creek. Janice had just closed her eyes to revel in the warmth when she was startled by the voice of a man. The frightened girl quickly turned her head to see a boy, slightly older than herself, standing to her right. He was tall for his age and had the aura of someone much older. She had wondered if it was, maybe, his eyes that made him look older. Whatever it was that set him apart from others, she felt no threat from the strange boy. He calmly asked, "Hi—may I sit with you?"

Janice slid over without answering. The boy sat, but avoided getting too close. This pleased her and she smiled. His clothes were simple jeans with a light blue t-shirt. This wasn't the usual church attire, but since she was late getting out of church, he could have, by now, gone home and changed. Janice wanted to question him about his beliefs, but hesitated since some thought it rude to ask such personal questions.

To her amazement, the boy asked, "Did you just get out of church?"

"Why yes. Do you go to a church near here?" She questioned.

The boy looked thoughtful and replied, "I normally don't go to church, but I did visit yours this morning."

Images of the morning's congregation reeled through her mind, but among those images she couldn't see the boy's face. She couldn't understand how she might have missed such a pleasant face. "I don't remember seeing you there." Janice said, a little puzzled.

The boy smiled and said, "My clothes don't fit the standards of your church, or most churches for that matter. I stayed back and out of sight."

Janice felt embarrassed, lowered her head, and meekly said, "I'm sorry, I shouldn't…"

The boy interrupted, "Don't be embarrassed, I could have worn better, I just chose not to on this day."

Glad that she hadn't insulted the boy, she asked, "I'm Janice—what's your name?"

The boy offered his hand and replied, "Lucifer," just as Janice touched his hand.

She immediately jerked her hand away after hearing his name, and asked with bewilderment, "Why would a couple name their son Lucifer?"

The boy asked with mocked offense, "Something wrong with my name?"

Janice stuttered and searched for the right words as to not offend any more than she had already. She replied, "Well, it's the same name as Satan—you know?"

"Oh yes, so it is. I sort of like the name, myself. I'm sorry if it bothers you. You can call me Stan if you like."

She nervously smiled and said, "Yes, Stan is better—I think."

They sat talking about mundane topics when there was a loud noise in the distance. Two men stood arguing when a gun suddenly appeared. The men fought as the gun waved wildly in the air, when suddenly, it fired. The sound of the bullet tearing through the warm, spring air gave no indication to its direction. The bullet no longer belonged to the turmoil of the two men that had caused its flight. The bullet was alone and was guided only by fate. The bullet had its own destination and no force on Earth could have stopped it as it tore into Janice's chest.

She slumped backward over the rock and screamed in pain. Blood flowed freely from the torn artery. Her life was running onto the rock and dripping into the stream behind her, turning the water a bright crimson everywhere it landed. Janice thought of her mother and father, and screamed aloud, "Oh God, help me," and then her world went black.

She gasped for breath as her eyes opened. The blood flow slowed and finally stopped. Janice sat up, still in shock, and looked at the blood stained hole in her dress where the bullet had struck. Memory of the impact and the searing pain played repeatedly in her mind. Janice finally dropped to her knees, clasped her hands under her chin, and prayed.

A hand touched her shoulder and a soft voice that could have only belonged to God, said, "Stand, my child, there is no need for prayers."

The prayerful girl opened her eyes and looked toward the voice. She saw an old man with a long, white beard and knew this had to be God. Tears began to cloud her vision. When they cleared, the young boy was standing where the old man had been. The boy took her hand, helped Janice to her feet, and said, "Come, let's walk—we must talk."

Janice looked at him and knew in her heart that the boy was the old man. A sudden calm came over her and she asked, "You are God, aren't you?"

The boy looked thoughtfully and replied, "Yes and no."

Memory of the moment when the bullet struck, still hurt in her mind. The perplexed girl asked, "You brought me back from death. If you're not God, then who are you?"

He sighed and impatiently said, "I am Lucifer. I am not the god to whom you eagerly pray."

Janice jumped back in fear, "My God, what have I done to bring down this evil on me?"

Lucifer laughed and replied, "Evil am I? Didn't I just save your life?"

The fearful girl screamed, "This is some devil trick. I

forsake you, Lucifer. Return to Hell where you belong."

Lucifer smiled amusingly and asked, "Why should I return to somewhere I am not from?"

The terrified girl turned and ran. Her breath was coming in sharp pants as she strained to run faster than her body was capable. Not watching where she was running, she hit someone and they both tumbled to the ground. It was an elderly man, to whom she immediately apologized through waning tears. "I'm sorry, sir. I was just so frightened... there is... this man," Janice said while looking in the direction from where she had just come.

The elderly man said with a voice that didn't match his, but that of Lucifer, "Don't be afraid of me, there is nothing to fear." The tormented girl ran, propelled by terror.

Her breaths were coming in gasps as she arrived home, ran to her room where she slammed the door closed, and twisted the lock closed. She collapsed before her homemade shrine and began fearfully praying. The telephone rang, interrupting her prayer. She hesitantly answered. Before she could speak, a familiar voice pleaded, "I have to speak with you. I beg you for your help. Your parents' soul could depend on you."

Janice slammed the phone down on the table and trembled with fear. She wondered what she had done to deserve the wrath of the devil. The phone rang again, but she ignored it, and in an effort to stop the calls, jerked the cord from the wall. The phone continued to ring. Giving in to a power that she knew was greater than her own, she answered and Lucifer said, "Meet me at the old abandoned bridge. Janice gasped at the mention of the bridge. This was the place she went to when troubled. No one on the planet knew she went to that spot. Her mind tried to write it off as a coincidence, but knew it was much more.

The blood stained dress lay crumpled in the trash. She had partially ripped the dress off as if shedding the dress might carry with it the terror of the moment when the bullet ripped into her chest. Janice pulled out the jeans she rarely wore and a loose fitting shirt. The preacher taught that a lady does not wear pants. She walked past the mirror and stopped to look at the spot of dried blood that still clung to her chest. She pulled the neck of the shirt down and felt the spot where the bullet had entered her chest and saw no sign of a scar. The religious girl wondered why Lucifer would save her life. "Would a man of evil truly save her?" She asked herself, trying to rationalize the events that had happened in the park. She decided to leave the spot of dried blood on her chest as a reminder.

Water made a bubbling sound as it ran under the old, rusting, steel truss frame of the bridge. A path led to the old bridge, the only remaining sign that a road had ever ran to the bridge. Sitting on the bridge, was the boy she had met in the park—the boy who was also Lucifer. With gathered courage, she walked to where he sat with his legs dangling over the side.

"Sit down," the boy said, as a hand waved to indicate a

place beside him. She sat next to him. His boyish face made it easy to momentarily forget that he was Satan.

"Why do you torment me, Devil?" she pointedly questioned.

His smile was warm and inviting. "I am not here to torment you, my friend. I am here to offer you the truth, to give you knowledge beyond others."

She trembled and shakily asked, "As you gave knowledge to Eve?"

"Ha ha ha no, not as that serpent of yours did." He replied.

"Why do you call it, my serpent?" She asked.

"The tale of the serpent is not of my making, it's of yours. I don't mean you, but your people, our people, of course. That's just one of many fanciful tales you humans created," he said, slightly amused.

The girl looked at him with more than a little confusion. Lucifer took advantage of the silence and asked, "That book you faithfully read—how would you react if it were mostly false?"

"It's not fake, it's the word of God," she defensively replied.

The boy shimmered and became a ghost of the old man she had seen earlier in the day, and then he was once more the young boy. He calmly said, "You are correct, in part. Some of it is the word of God and some of it is a fabrication created by man and the evil that exists in the universe. Remember the text in the Bible that tells how Satan is the ultimate liar?

"Yes"

"He is truly that, and he uses many names, but there is one, less known, mentioned in the in the Bible, and that name is, Iam," Lucifer said.

She looked at the boy and tried to see the evil in him as she had been taught, but it wasn't there. As her beliefs were being torn apart, she asked, "If all this is true, then why tell me? You should be talking to the pope or some other religious authority."

He shook his head in dismay and replied, "I have done that in the past and was crucified for my troubles. In other times, I have been called a heretic and burned at the stake."

Reality crashed down on the girl with the force of a hammer. His words made sense. The things he said covered many of the questions she had often asked herself, but never dared speak. Janice said, "I'm beginning to understand what you're saying, but what I don't understand, is why are you telling this to me?"

He smiled warmly and replied, "I am planting a seed that could someday reap the flower of truth."

She looked at the boy with puzzlement and asked, "If you're really God, why not just make everyone know the truth?"

The boy heartily laughed and replied, "I am Lucifer. I have never said I am God. There is no one with the name, God."

The bewildered girl said, "I don't understand."

His hand comfortingly touched hers and he said, "There is

11

no all empowering god. If there was a God as you worship, then he or she could make everyone a believer, as well as remove all evil. Oh yes, there is the freewill clause to explain this, my dear. I could go on for the next century explaining things to you, but there is no time for that. If you have questions, I'll just answer them."

She stared blankly at him as the boy was no more and had transformed into the image of the old man. The old man sat with her on the bridge and waited for her questions. "What is it you want me to do with this knowledge?" She asked.

"Why, nothing, if that is your wish, my friend. Do nothing." he said flatly.

Bewilderment had passed and pure shock had set upon the girl. She stared at the old man and wondered what she would do with the knowledge that she had been given, if it was all true. Janice asked, "Then why tell me if I am to do nothing?"

A smile that contained amusement and warmth spread across his face. He said, "I never said you were to do nothing. I only said that you are to do nothing if that is your wish. No matter what you do, I warn you to beware of my brother, Iam. He exists only for worship and will do whatever it takes to have people pray to him. Look at the wars that are fought in his name. He delights in this, as he would delight in your death in his name. The biggest help I can give you is that the Bible has been manipulated for his cause."

Her head ached from the jumble of thoughts that ripped apart almost everything she believed. The religion she had devoted her entire life to was unraveling. In fact, it was nearly the reverse of the truth, it was becoming an unspeakable lie. Janice turned to speak and Lucifer was gone.

She hurriedly made her way home as the sun was setting low in the sky. The last thing she wanted was to be alone in the forest at night. The house seemed no different from that morning and that brought some sanity back to her mind. The smell of her mom's roast beef permeated the air. A soft voice called out, "Janice, is that you?'

"Yes, mom," she sullenly replied.

"You shouldn't be out so late, it's nearly dark. Come and eat," her mother said with slight worry.

Janice went to the dining room and her mother gasped and angrily shouted, "Those demon pants! What in God's name are you doing wearing those? They are so tight and revealing. I thought I told you to throw those jeans away."

The events of the day made the sin of wearing jeans have little consequence and she casually replied, "I'll get rid of them, tomorrow."

When they were all seated, her mother asked Janice to say the blessing, letting the matter of the jeans drop, for the moment. She opened her mouth to begin, but the words caught in her throat. For some reason the simple act of praying didn't seem the right thing to do, anymore. Janice said, "My throat is a little scratchy, please pray for us, mother." As her mother blessed the food, she watched her dad ignore it, as usual, and began to eat. Most nights this caused an argument, but, thankfully, this night her mother

13

ignored her husband's assault on her religion.

Janice watched her parents as her fork wandered aimlessly around the plate. Her father, Martin, was a supervisor at the factory. He made a good living. He was nearly the perfect dad, other than his lack of beliefs. She studied the black curly hair that tipped his ears and thought how his kind smile made him the type of man she wanted to, someday, marry. Janice nearly laughed aloud as she realized that all along, he might have been the only one right about God.

Her mother, Delores, seemed to love Martin, but she couldn't get over his lack of faith. Delores would have had Janice at church praying all night if she knew about the events that had transpired that day.

Janice watched her mother eat. Most thought Delores had a pretty face. Janice looked much like Delores except for her mother's darker, blonde hair.

"Are you going to eat or just stir that food until it's worn out? "Martin jokingly asked.

"Are you alright, Janice, dear?" Her mother asked.

"I'm fine, mother, I'm just not hungry. May I be excused and go to bed early?" She asked, and then added," I have a big exam at school, tomorrow."

This had been the first lie she had ever purposely told to her parents and it made her gut wrench. It hurt, but she felt there was no choice without being asked questions, for which there were no answers that she could give without being punished for blasphemy.

In her room, she stripped off her clothes. Janice looked at the jeans she had promised to throw away and then at the trashcan. She decided to keep the jeans and dropped them in the dirty clothes hamper. Janice found her favorite white, linen gown. Without thinking, she knelt before her makeshift shrine and the day's events flooded her mind. The girl knew that after this day, she would never be able to pray to that god in the same way she had most of her life. She said a short prayer and then disassembled the altar and placed the assembly of crosses and candles in the closet. .

Janice threw herself on the bed, looked at the opposite wall, and stared at the emptiness that had been her alter. Regret began to fill her mind. What she had seen today could have been just a trick of the devil. The girl thought about slipping out of the house and going to church where her theologically trained mind might find answers to all the questions bombarding her mind. There were questions she hadn't asked Lucifer that day—questions to which she desperately needed answers.

The phone rang and she crawled along the bed to retrieve it from the floor where it had fallen earlier in the day when she slammed it down, and answered, "Hello?"

"So, you have questions?" The familiar voice of the old man asked.

Not near as surprised as she should have been, the girl replied, "Yes. I need to know about heaven and hell."

"My child, you already know about hell, it's as described in the Bible."

"Hell fire and brimstone?" She asked in confusion.

The older, wise voice on the phone laughed and replied, "No. No my child. It's kneeling before Iam for eternity."

The phone crashed to the hardwood floor when her hand lost its will to hold the device. Her mind somehow saw the obvious and wondered how she could have been so deceived. Yet parts of her mind screamed that he could be lying. She reclaimed the phone and noticed for the first time that the cord was still not plugged into the outlet. "Still there?" She asked.

"Yes," he replied.

"Tell me about... err Heaven or wherever it is you come from," she curiously asked.

Lucifer hesitantly said, "It's not much different from here, only you remember all there is that you are not allowed to know on Earth. I shouldn't tell you much, but I can say it's a nice place with no violence."

The phone went quiet and a dial tone buzzed in her ear. She dangled the plug in the air and cried for the first time since all this had begun. All that she had known was a lie. In all her years, God had never talked to her directly and now she had seen and talked to the one that she has been taught to hate—the one she had been taught that was the king of deceit. Something in her heart begged that her mind believe him, but her teachings said this was a trick of the devil.

That night she slept fitfully. Her dreams were of angels chasing her through a maze of burning pylons. A voice boomed in her head, "They are all liars, trust only your God—

16

keep the faith. I am thy God, thy only God. Forsake me and burn in hell for all of eternity."

One of the angel's faces changed to that of her mother and said, "I never thought I would see the day that my daughter would turn away from God. You have sold your soul to the devil for a pair of tight jeans." Her mother, the angel, charged at the daughter, grabbed her throat, and began denying her the life giving air that she needed to live. Her mother said, "I would rather see you dead than to see you defy my god."

Sweat soaked the bed as she awakened from a night of tossing and turning. She rolled from the bed, dropped to her knees, and began to fervently pray. Janice kept asking God for forgiveness until her mind cleared enough to remember the previous day's events. Janice looked to where the shrine had sat and felt withdrawal from the emptiness. The girl pulled herself onto the bed and cried until she gathered enough strength to shower before breakfast.

Breakfast was no different from that of any other day. Her mother and father sat eating while reading the morning paper. With the horrid dreams of the previous night still fresh in Janice's mind, she felt nauseated from looking at the food. Not having eaten the night before, hunger caused her body to override her mind and she ate everything on the plate, and then asked for more.

The next three days were a blur to the girl. She replayed the events of that Sunday over and over in her mind. With each replay, she always came to the same conclusion, the church had to be wrong. No one she knew had ever seen real definitive miracles. Lucifer bringing life back into her dead body was surely a miracle. There was only one other explanation, she had gone insane. It would take some time before Janice would totally discount the latter.

One morning, they all sat quietly at the table eating, each doing their typical ritual. Breaking the silence, her mother said, "We need to leave early this evening for midweek service, so be sure to be ready."

The fork dropped to the plate with a twang as Janice stopped eating and looked at her mother. Janice hesitantly said, "I'm not feeling well. I think I'll stay home, tonight."

Delores leaned over, pressed the back of her hand to Janice's forehead, and asked, "What's wrong with you, child? Should I take you to the doctor? You don't feel feverish, to me"

"Oh no, mother, I'm just worn out from school. This semester has been really tough," she said in hopes of easing her mother's worries. This time the lie came easier than before.

"If that's all, then going to church will make you feel better. You know how uplifting church is for you," Delores piously said.

That evening after her shower, she sifted through clothes searching for something to wear for church. Her favorite spring dress lay bloodied in the trash. Her hands shook as she held the first dress that, somehow, found its way into her hand. The girl absentmindedly put it on, unaware of its color or description.

Janice and her mother sat on the first row, the seat of choice if there was room when they arrived at the church. The preacher seemed to be stuck on the theme of Hell. The girl's hands fidgeted with a small bow on the light blue dress. She Suddenly heard the preacher say her name. He said, "Janice Carter, you will burn in Hell's fires for consorting with the devil."

She jerked to attention and her mind screamed, "How could he have known?" Her mind focused on the minister and he was speaking normally and not to her as she had imagined. Janice wrote it off as weariness from the tormenting dreams she had been having. She tried to shake them from her mind and concentrate on the minister, but to no avail. This was the first time in her life that she was in a hurry to leave church. Something was terribly wrong in the one place that had always brought her comfort.

The sermon finally ended and people began filing out the door. The line moved slowly as the minister shook hands and greeted each person, sometimes holding a hand for an extended time to talk. Her mother was in the lead and the minister shook her hand and thanked her for all her work in the church, and for helping with the upcoming spring fair. Janice offered her hand to the minister and he said as his hand recoiled from the girl's, "You demon child, be gone with you! Never come into my house again or I will bring my wrath down on you and your family. I'll cast you into the fires with your new friend, Lucifer. "

Janice blinked her eyes and the preacher was, now, pumping her hand and saying nice things about her as he often would after any service. She then realized it hadn't been the minister talking to her, but God himself!

After making an excuse, Janice left her mother at the church, ran into the woods, and began to sob. "Could the things the voice said to her be true? What kind of fool have I been for going against everything the church taught?" She asked herself.

The gentle voice of Lucifer asked in her mind, "Have you seen the anger from me that you just saw Iam display?"

The bewildered girl looked around for the source of the voice and said, "You're lying to me. You are being nice to trick me."

The disembodied voice of Lucifer drifted in the air as he dejectedly sighed and said, "Then I will go and leave you be. Go back to your church and whatever fate it brings you."

"I have one question," she quietly said

"Yes?" He asked. There was an anxious tone to his voice.

"Why me?" She asked.

The voice was silent for several moments and it finally said, "That is one of the hardest questions you could have asked. Also, it is one to which I can't give you all the answers." After some hesitation he continued, "Some believe that mankind has a bit of god within them, which is true. Every few hundred years, some are born that have a bit more of us than usual. You have heard about some of them in your history books. You might recall Joan of Arc."

Janice interrupted, "Didn't she fight for God?"

Lucifer said, chagrined, "She did fight for Iam. I never said all were persuaded to my side. Thousands died because she fought for Iam and some mortal king. Iam's way is death and destruction, all the while pretending to be good and blaming the ills of the universe on me."

She thoughtfully asked, "What can I do that you or anyone else could never do?"

The wind began to pick up as if a storm was rising, and he replied, "You may be able to do no more than to spread the truth. One soul that you save is worth our efforts. Child, I don't think you wish to spend eternity on your knees before an ungrateful god. I don't think you would want to see anyone else spend eternity that way, especially those close to you."

Janice turned around as she looked upward, her eyes searching for substance to the voice she heard in her head, and said, "Today, God... err... Iam spoke to me in church. In the past I thought I had heard him speak to me, but nothing like this. He threatened me and my family."

Lucifer sadly said, "I am aware that he spoke. I can tell you that your family and friends are in danger, but he cannot hurt you as long as you are defiant of him. Only if you give into his control can he truly bring harm to you."

Anger rose in her voice and she asked, "How can I protect my family from God?" She began to cry.

The older form of Lucifer was suddenly standing next to her with a consoling arm around her shoulders. She leaned into him and cried for several minutes. This is when she knew what must done. Something deep inside had given her the correct answers, "I'm going home," she suddenly blurted, but Lucifer was already gone before she had spoken.

Janice had been in the forest longer than she thought. Darkness was quickly falling and the wind hinted that a storm was closing. The wind began to pick up debris and tossed it in the air. Lightning cracked closer than she liked. The dress she had worn to church threatened to lift and expose more than modesty allowed. Somewhere in the wind, Janice thought she heard laughter as lightning struck a tree only feet away. Janice stumbled, fell, and scraped her knees on the ground.

Tears in her eyes mixed with the beating rain as she began running. Lightning struck closer and trees fell, missing her by mere inches. It had become obvious to the frightened girl that this storm and the accuracy of the lightning was no accident. It had become clear to her that death would be imminent if she continued. Lightning was circling her, closing in to find its intended target. She did the unexpected, stopped, looked defiantly at the sky, and shouted, "Go away, I hate you. I won't fear you."

The rain suddenly stopped, the sky cleared, and a sliver of moon appeared in the night sky. The amazed girl stood staring in disbelief. Even her dress that had been rain soaked was completely dry. A familiar warmth surrounded her and she knew immediately that it was Lucifer somewhere near.

On her return home, Janice's mother called to her as she closed the front door and said, "Dear, come sit on the couch with me—we need to talk. I've noticed the last couple of days that you have been acting strange, so I prayed on it and God told me you are troubled."

The girl cringed, not knowing what to expect with the lightning fresh in her mind. She hesitantly asked, "What did he tell you?"

Delores began to sob. She said, "He told me you had stopped believing in him and was now a devil worshiper. He says you have to be cleansed. I am to take you to a church that can remove the demon from your soul."

The girl pleaded, "Mother, I have to tell you everything that's happened. I hope you'll believe me." She retold the events since meeting Lucifer in the park. When she finished, her mother dropped to her knees and fervently pray to save Janice's soul. In the next moment, her mother had drawn a knife and was lunging for the girl. Janice was struggling with her mother when Martin entered the room after hearing raised voices, and asked, "What's going on in here?"

When his eyes caught sight of his wife and daughter on the floor, he lunged for his wife, pulled her from his daughter, and angrily shouted, "What in God's name are you doing, Delores?"

His wife replied, feigning innocence, "Thank God, you arrived just in time, Martin. She tried to kill me when I tried talking to her about her strange behavior the last couple of days."

Janice froze in shock at her mother's accusation. She quickly recovered and said, "She's lying, dad. She's the one that tried to kill me."

"Calm down, the both of you. Let's the three of us sit down and talk about this—with no knives," he sternly said.

Janice once again recounted the events of the past few days and when she finished, the room was swallowed by silence. Martin said to his wife, "What was it that you said to Janice that made her attack you?" Janice started to protest his phrasing of the question, but he raised a hand and pointed a finger to silence his distraught daughter. She stopped talking and sat quietly.

Delores reassuringly said, "I told her how our minister suggested a church where there's an expert in troubled children, and that's when she attacked me."

The girl's father wasn't sure about Janice suddenly becoming a troubled child, but he was compelled to listen to his wife. He did agree that Janice had been acting differently the past few days. His first thought was that she might be taking drugs, but knew that was improbable.

Her father sat between them, raked his large hand through his black hair, and finally asked, "When can we see this place that was suggested?"

Delores replied, "The minister thought it best to take her tonight."

"Hold on, now. We aren't taking her anywhere, just yet.

We will go to this place and see what it's all about." Martin emphatically said.

Janice was, at least, thankful that her father was being cautious and going slowly. Somehow, the girl would have to get him alone and try convincing him that she was telling the truth. The girl was coming to realize that she couldn't trust her mother, and that hurt deep within her soul. The sudden realization that this was about the truth, terrified Janice. "If she couldn't convince her parents, how could she convince anyone else?" She asked herself.

The drive to the church would take the better part of an hour as it was located in the next city, about forty miles away. Trees lining the side of the highway streamed by as her mind flashed back to the woods and the storm earlier that day. Janice thought of escaping when they reached the church, but where could she go? The earlier events in the forest had been terrifying and to face that or something similar this far from home, terrified her even more than what might await in the church.

She had no close friends that might give her a place to hide. All her spare time had been given to the church. The girl finally surrendered her fate into the hands of her parents.

Cars passed on either side as they eased their way into the large city. During the night, tall buildings always reminded her of some Gothic city in a world different from her own. She imagined buildings with tall crooked spires that reached into the sky as far as the eye could see, covered with gargoyles and demon statues.

Tires made a crunching sound on gravel as the car came to a stop in front of the church. Looking at the structure in the darkness made Janice realize that calling this place a church was a far-fetched supposition.

Exiting the car, she looked up and screamed in horror. This was what she had imagined the other buildings to be. What she saw was no church, but some medieval castle. She grabbed her father's arm, and with panic in her voice, shouted, "Dad, can't you see what this is?"

He looked at his daughter with bewilderment and replied, "Of course, dear, it's one of the older churches in the city. A beautiful piece of historical architecture, if I must say so, myself."

The structure Janice saw was nothing like what her father described. This building could have been created only in the bowels of Hell. The towering spires tore into dark clouds above. There were no lights coming from the church, or there were no windows, she wasn't sure which. Dead vines snaked their way up the structure's side. Growling and screaming sounds that sent shivers up her spine came from within the building.

The door of the dark, foreboding building opened and bright light flowed out of the inky darkness of the church, causing Janice to scrunch her eyes. Once her eyes adjusted to the light, the building was no different from any early, eighteenth century cathedral. The sky reaching spires transformed to typical parapets. A priest greeted them and graciously invited them inside. The interior of the church was no different than others around the world. Golden, religious artifacts filled the huge room with vaulted ceilings. Janice was awed by the glare of the gold. At one time in her life, she might have knelt and prayed from inspiration, but now such symbols only made her shiver with fright.

A nun entered the room and the priest nodded to the woman. She approached Janice, took her hand, led her to an adjacent room, and closed the door. The priest explained, "I would like to talk with the two of you alone. She will be safe with Sister Agnes."

Images of Mary and other holy symbolic paintings covered the walls of the small office. Even at Janice's age, she knew that many of the paintings were famous and priceless. Why the church held such priceless treasures while begging for money had never occurred to her until this moment. A golden, antique clock rang eleven times to announce the time. Through the door, she could hear the voices of her parents and that of the priest who had greeted them. The voices soon faded and she heard a car drive away.

The priest entered, looked angrily at the frightened girl, and said, "So, you're the demon bitch we have been hearing so much about. We're going to put you where you will never cause anymore trouble."

"I've not caused any trouble," she truthfully pleaded.

"The day you spoke to Lucifer, you became trouble. No one can know the truth—any that do, must die," the priest angrily growled.

To hear a priest talk like this was as shocking as any of the events since meeting Lucifer. The nun roughly grabbed her arm and said, "Come with me, we have places for creatures like you."

Janice tried to jerk away, but the nun was stronger than she appeared. The panicky girl shouted to the priest, "Let me go—I want to see my parents."

The priest laughed wickedly and said, "Your parents have gone and left you in the safe hands of the sister and myself."

The nun, in her long, dark, foreboding habit, led the girl out of the office and into a narrow passageway. They slowly descended spiraling stairs. The farther they traveled, the older the church looked, with fewer adornments littering its walls. They came to an iron door that was barely wide enough for the nun to fit through. She pushed the door and it creaked as if it hadn't been opened in years. Janice was led through and into an area with more stairs..

They descended the downward spiraling stone stairs that looked darker and older than the ones they had just traversed. To Janice, this passage looked more fitting for the medieval castle that she had first seen upon arriving. The farther they traveled, the air became thickened with mold and dampness. At this point, Janice was sure she should go no farther. She tore loose from the tight grip of the nun and climbed the stairs in a run. Just as she reached the door, it slammed shut by unseen hands.

A cold hand grabbed the back of her neck and the nun

said, "You are wasting your time trying to escape. God himself protects these halls. "

Resigned to her fate, Janice followed the nun to the end of the stairs where she stared off into darkness. A torch was lit by means the girl couldn't detect. The stone walls along the corridor were checkered with steel doors etched with patterns of rust. They walked down the corridor where inhuman sounds of torment came from behind the doors. The nun stopped at one of the steel doors and pushed it open. The nun's spindly hands grasped the collar of the light blue dress, flung the girl into the darkness that laid beyond the doorway, and said, "Enjoy your eternity in Hell, little girl."

The door slammed shut with an ear-shattering ring. All light disappeared from the girl's immediate world. Janice laid in a heap in the middle of the darkened cell. Tears welled in her eyes. All hope evaporated with the extinguishing of the light and she cried until sleep briefly spared her from the terror.

Her eyes eventually opened and she was forced to confront the darkness of the room. Her fingers balled into a fist and rubbed her reddened eyes. A tear welled as she remembered the dark horror into which she had been cast. Finding hidden strength, she sat up. A scratching sound in the distance was all she could hear. The imprisoned girl hoped the sound came from only a rat, even though she feared rodents. In this place, a rat might be the better alternative to what could be hiding in the darkness.

Somehow finding strength for her legs, she tried to stand,

but her head hit something solid, knocking her to her knees. Dainty fingers more suitable for knitting, reached up and touched the rough stone ceiling of the cell. Getting on her hands and knees, she crawled, feeling her way. The wall was only a short distance away. After careful study, the captive knew the cell was only a few feet across. It could be better described as a tomb than a cell. Janice hoped her time in the cell would be only hours or days, but she was sure it would be much longer than her mind was willing to admit.

A voice whispered to her mind, "Cast out thy demon and come unto thee for forgiveness."

Scared and weak, Janice replied, "I'll fight you for eternity."

The Almighty's laughter shook the foundations of the church. Those far above in the church were unaware of the tremor's origin and thought them to be a moderate earthquake. The booming laughter faded to silence, and the voice that came next was that of mild amusement. It said, "You still have no idea why Lucifer chose you."

"No," she replied

"Do you want me to tell you?" Iam asked.

She hesitated, but finally replied, "No."

God roared with laughter and said, "You hesitated too long, my child. You have given away your desires. The reason that he chose you is because you see the world for what it is. You saw upon arrival that the church was not as others would see it." He was silent for a moment and then continued, "That is why you can never leave this room. In joining with Lucifer, you have created your own Hell. In here you can never die—you are here for eternity. You will find eternal starvation and darkness your only allies."

She wept.

Day and night became one as she sat and cried. Her belly ached from hunger. She called for Lucifer, but he never came. The tortured girl was thinking that she had made a vast error. The god to whom she had spoken was not a benevolent god. Yet she often wondered if his wrath was upon her because she had forsaken the deity. As time went on, she became sure that was the case and began calling for God, but there was no answer. In the darkness, there was nothing to do other than to think.

God's silence made her come to accept that she was there only because of who she was, or what abilities she possessed. Janice would curse God, Iam, and Lucifer to pass the time.

Pangs of hunger and thirst racked her body. She lay on the cold stone floor in a fetal position clutching her stomach. When the pain occasionally eased, she found too much time to think. Her mind occupied itself with the memories it contained. The memories started with times she had never before remembered and reeled on like a movie to the present. Each time Janice replayed the memories, she began to wonder if they had ever existed or if they were something her mind had contrived in the insanity that had become her life.

Time became an outdated phenomenon as she laid, and sometimes crawled, in the darkness. Long ago a smell had entered the tomb that was her prison and she knew that smell was her own odor. The girl came to know each crack of the cell as she searched with her fingers for an exit. Each time she found a new crack, hope would rise that she had found a hidden exit. Each time this happened the disappointment would tear her apart.

Hope of escape had long passed as time lost all meaning. She moved around only to relieve her aching joints and to try and forget the abominable hunger that raged within the pit of her stomach. The tormented girl came to understand how those stranded in remote regions came to eat one another. The thought of cannibalism made her sick, but she understood the driving hunger that led some to such a ghastly act.

Loneliness and despair had become constant companions. Janice might have given up and accepted her fate, but she knew this was no jail term—her incarceration was for eternity. Her mind searched, in what had been in her world, day and night, for a solution.

Janice suddenly sat up. Something God had said began to take hold in her mind. Neurons holding the information twisted and manipulated it to find a meaning that hadn't occurred to the captive until this moment. She had an epiphany. Iam had unwittingly given her the means for escape.

With legs crossed, she sat in the middle of the cell and closed her eyes to the darkness. Slowly and repeatedly she whispered, "I will see only the truth. I will see only the truth."

Nothing happened at first and she was tempted to give into despair, but Janice knew she had an eternity to make it work.

How long she sat and said those words, she wasn't sure, but suddenly there was a burst of light on the other side of her eyelids. She slowly opened them and winced from the brightness. Janice was sitting on the sidewalk under a street lamp. The weary girl stood on wobbly legs, looked around, and realized her home was only a block away. Unsure of what would happen when she arrived, Janice had no alternative other than to go home.

As she approached the door and stepped into the bright light of the porch, she noticed her dress was tattered and rotten with age. It would have taken years for her dress to reach such a state of disrepair. The unlocked door opened and her mother said, "It's about time you got home, we were beginning to worry about you. Hurry to the table, quickly, before supper gets cold."

Janice wasn't sure what she had eaten, but she devoured everything in sight in an effort to quench the raging hunger that held her in its vice-like grip. It was only after she had satisfied the animal-like hunger did she realize that her parents hadn't noticed the rotten dress that threaten to fall away at any moment.

With a full belly, her body settled into the hot bath and slept in comfort for the first time in a period she couldn't define. Dreams caught her as she slept in the warm water, and a haunting god chased her through a maze. At each turn, he stood mocking the frightened little girl. The dream wakened the weary girl and she climbed into bed without drying off or putting on a nightgown, where she slept peacefully for the first time in, possibly, years.

A bird chirped loudly outside her window that morning as she woke. Janice stretched her lithe frame under the soft quilt and her eyes popped open in sudden awareness. Her mind fought to accept the reality that she was once again home. Janice closed her eyes and opened them slowly. She was still in her bedroom. A bright smile crept across her face at the realization that she was truly home again—truly free.

Feeling a new-found power, she dressed in preparation for a dashed to the kitchen. Her stomach still ached for food. As she opened the door of her bedroom, the girl stopped in thought. Her parents didn't seem to be aware of what had happened. This meant that Iam had manipulated them and, possibly, time itself. The confused girl wondered if she could trust them—or anyone for that matter. Janice immediately knew the answer to her own question. She couldn't trust them with the knowledge that the world wasn't as it appeared. Janice also knew that no one would believe such an insane tale.

The Nuns retreated to a corner as Father Daemon ranted, "How did she escape? Which one of you let her out? When I find out, I'll have you in a Siberian monastery."

"Father." the nun said, "No one let her out. We went to feed the guests and she was gone." The nuns saw only typical guest rooms when they visited the dungeons. None noticed that they never took meals to Janice as they did the others."

"Then who?" He raved, causing the nuns to tremble.

One of the nuns stepped forward and demurely said, "I saw her leave, Father."

"Oh?" He asked with intent interest.

Choosing her words carefully, knowing it was going to come out wrong no matter what, she hesitated and said, "I was reviewing the security tape and she was sitting on the floor with her legs crossed... and then disappeared. I swear father—I'm not lying. She just wasn't there anymore."

Father Daemon felt the energy leave his body. Anger was replaced with fear and worry. Something unholy had happened in his church that night and he was going to find out what it had been.

The next morning, Father Daemon drove the forty minutes to Janice's house. He parked across the street and sat staring at the house. It seemed normal to the priest. He wondered how the events of the night before could have transpired.

He sat hunched in the car in hopes of not being noticed and tried to decide if he should confront the child. His first thought was to rush into the house and demand an answer. Unable to find a suitable plan, he decided to knock on the door and test the waters.

He opened the car door, but his body refused to leave the safety of the car. The priest sat for a moment with his fingers turning white as he tightly gripped the steering wheel of the old Dodge. The time had come for him to face his fears. He exited the car and his weak knees, somehow, managed to carry him up the sidewalk to the house. After finally reaching the door, he knocked once. It took only a short time before Martin opened the door. Father Daemon held out his hand in greeting and said, "It's good to see you again, Mr. Carter." Martin looked bewilderingly at the balding priest and asked, "Pardon?"

Confident and cordially, he replied, "Last week at the church, you brought your daughter to us."

"Is this some kind of joke?" Martin incredulously asked.

The Priest was sure the man was the one who had brought the girl to his church. He thought to quickly escape and asked, "Is this 2251 Maple?"

With agitation growing, Martin replied, "No. This is 2215 Credence Drive."

The Priest begged the man's pardon and nearly broke into a run getting back to his car. Inside the protection of his car, he decided to drive a short distance down the street and wait for the girl who apparently held all the answers.

As Martin closed the door, Delores asked, "Who was at the door?"

"Some weird priest. I think he had the wrong house," he replied.

Delores responded, "I never trusted those Catholics all that much, myself."

Crouched at the top of the stairs, Janice watched the confrontation at the door. The priest had a demeanor different from the night she had arrived at the church. This priest had seemed as confused about the situation as her parents, yet he had come. That meant he had some memory of the events that night. That meant he was dangerous—he was the enemy.

When her parents were out of sight, she sneaked down the stairs and peeked out the window beside the door. The old Dodge was gone. Janice desperately needed to escape the confines of the house and get in the open air. She had spent, what seemed an eternity, in darkness. Now, she had to have the fresh air of open spaces even if it meant risking the chance that the priest might still be near.

The cool air felt good on her face as she stepped off the porch onto the walkway. The day was nice so she dared to take a walk and clear her mind from the trappings of her torture. She may not have shown it outwardly, but the torment of being locked in that hole for months or years was hell, one she didn't wish to ever experience again. Janice swore she would die before ever allowing herself to once again be held captive.

Her mind jumped back to the present as something caught her arm. The priest stared at her with cold eyes as his hand tightly gripped her arm just above the elbow. He reluctantly relaxed his grip and asked, "Have we met before?"

Janice jerked free and rubbed her arm where the priest had grabbed. Taking a step back, she replied, "This some kind of joke?"

"No joke, I assure you," replied the priest.

Anger rose and threatened to explode in violence against the bewildered priest. She said, "You know damn well we've met."

Not sure how to proceed since she obviously remembered what he perceived to be the previous week, he asked, "Do your parents remember that night at the church?"

"No," she curtly replied.

His stubby fingers rubbed his short manicured beard and he asked, "How did you escape your room?"

Her body tensed in anticipation of trouble and she shouted, "Room? You dare call that hell a ROOM?"

A puzzled look framed the face of the aging man and he replied, "I don't understand. I had Sister Agnes put you in one of the nicest rooms in the church."

Anger overrode caution as Janice leaned in close and tersely said, "Why don't you go spend a few years in that room."

Even more confused, he asked, "I don't understand. What do you mean—by years?"

"Go ask that fucking god of yours how long I was down there," she spat. A moment of guilt passed through the girl for speaking in such a manner about the god to whom she had so often prayed. That moment passed and she added, "Time had no meaning in that dungeon. I may have been there for months or years, I can't say for sure. Let me show you my tattered dress and you tell me how long I was down there."

Father Daemon slightly stuttered and asked, "Can we go somewhere and talk. The more you say the more confused I'm getting."

Not wanting to be alone with the priest, Janice suggested they walk to the nearby park. This time of year, with the weather turning warm, the park would be full of people.

Several people shuffled by as the odd pair sat on a park bench. The warm air made it the perfect day for sitting in the park and chatting, while this conversation could only make the day darker.

Too many thoughts tried to form into one question. Finally, one came to the priest's mind and he asked, "Tell me about this room. You said it was more like a dungeon."

She replied, "I didn't say it was like a dungeon. I said it was a dungeon." Janice saw the continued confusion in the man's eyes and told her story. She began with the long downward stone stairs to the dungeon and the torment in which she had been held. Rage spilled from her lips as she described the endless starvation. The enraged girl told of the rotten, tattered dress that lay in the waste basket in her room.

"This is impossible!" The priest exclaimed. He added, "You are either mad or this is the work of the devil."

Laughter drifted through the park. Anyone near might have thought the girl mad, and maybe she was by psychiatric standards. Janice said, "The so-called devil is the one that saved me from the hell your god created for me."

"I will not listen to anymore of this blasphemy," he said as he rose from the park bench.

A calm she had not felt in the longest time passed over Janice. She smiled and said. "When you get back to the safety of your church, think of how I escaped your lair, whether it's a dungeon or the room that you saw."

Blood rushed from his face to form a pale canvas that had been forced to face the terror of truth. "May God save us all," he said while making the sign of the cross.

The priest stood and turned to walk away. Janice reached out, grabbed his arm, spun him back toward her, and said, "May your god spare you the pain he so easily gave me."

He said, "God save you child."

Chagrined, the girl stood and said, "I'd rather sit in hell than watch your god's form of saving." She turned and walked home with a glimmer of the earlier peace still enveloping her soul.

That night on the news a blonde reporter stood in the foreground of flashing lights and shouting firemen. In the distance, flames and rubble filled the small screen of the television. The reporter told of Islamic terrorists and a car filled with explosives. She told of a letter found in the suicide attacker's apartment describing his fight against Americans and Christianity. The reporter went on to read the names of all those that had been killed in the explosion. Father Daemon's had been in the list.

After turning off the television, Janice collapsed on the bed and knew the untold truth of what she had just seen on television. That day she had planted Lucifer's seed in the priest and the explosion was Iam's retribution for the priest's moment of doubt. His words had not hidden what she had seen in his eyes. The priest had begun to believe the truth. That night he paid the price for that small amount of truth.

Even though the priest had locked her in that hell, she wept for him. Janice knew that he was only a pawn for something of unimaginable horror—the same something that sought to destroy the girl who could see past the heavenly deception.

Chapter 2

School had become easier these days. Janice breezed through tests with an ease that she never had in the past. It was obvious to everyone that she was much older than she looked. Her body might not have aged while she was in the dungeon, but her mind and soul had aged normally.

She was about to close her locker and walk away when a familiar voice said, "Hi. I never knew we were locker neighbors."

She knew the voice belonged to the school's star athlete. He dated only the most beautiful, popular cheerleaders. The two of them had been locker neighbors for two years and he had never before spoken to Janice. The world had changed around her so much that Janice looked for the worst to happen in every situation. She couldn't afford to be caught off guard. "Hi," she guardedly replied.

"My name is Pete," he cheerily said.

"I know. Everyone in the school knows your name," she dully replied.

He closed his locker, turned to face her, and said, "You seem angry with me."

"I'm not angry with you," she monotonically said.

Pete Davies was well aware of his six feet, slim, athletic body and knew how to use it to his advantage. His face was soft for someone of his statue. This face made most of the girls in school dream of, someday, dating him. That most had included Janice.

He directly asked, "You're different, somehow. Would you like to go with me for a burger after school?"

She closed her locker and said, "I thought you were dating Donna Price."

"We broke up yesterday," he truthfully replied.

"Don't you have baseball practice after school?" She asked.

Determined not to take anything other than yes for an answer, he replied, "We never practice on Fridays."

Flattery overcame her wariness and she said with more excitement than she had meant to show, "I'd be happy to go with you."

People crowded into the popular after school eatery. Kids whispered scandalously to one another as they entered and noticed the unlikely couple. Janice noticed the whispers and giggles from her peers, but ignored them. The happy girl wasn't going to allow anything to destroy such a wonderful day. Janice nibbled at her fries as they talked about school.

This was the first time she had relaxed and actually enjoyed herself since her return to the normal world. Janice was determined to soak the moment for all it was worth. She was also aware that this would likely be the last date she would have for a long time. Boys had never been overly attracted to her, but in hindsight, she could see how her faith might have played a role in her status as an outcast. Her heart held out hope that Pete might ask her out again, but her brain said otherwise. Laughing at some witty thing he said, she decided to let despair take a back seat and enjoy the moment.

The next three weeks were as close to heaven as she could ever hope to find on Earth. Something magical had developed between the two. They became a constant couple. Dating a star athlete gained Janice acceptance in the, so-called, in-group. Janice's devotion to Christianity had ostracized her from most of the kids at school. With that behind her, she was able to make new friends, and not only because she was dating one of the most popular guys in school.

Never before had she kissed a boy until the night of their second date. As any gentleman would do, he had not made any advances that might have seemed too forward. They were standing at her front door when they kissed. There wasn't the shy embarrassment so often represented in books and movies. It was natural and spontaneous. It was miraculous how all her apprehensions and wariness melted away in one kiss. That kiss left no doubt in either of their minds that they were in love.

It was the second week of dating as they sat in his truck outside Sam's Shakes where they had gone on their first date that true magic happened. She sat next to him in his truck, his arm wrapped lovingly and protectively around her, when he turned to look at her with eyes she had not before seen. It was a look that stole her body. His words took her soul, "I love you."

"Oh God, I love you, too," she said before they collapsed into a passionate kiss.

Janice gave Pete all her love, but she would not give him her body. Chastity was still one of the things in which she still believed, even without the Bible's teachings. With the world as it was, there was no way she could risk bringing a child into such chaos. After what had happened to her, even falling in love was a risk. Pete had sought her heart and she would give it willingly. Something deep within told her that she would never regret giving into that love. She hoped that voice from within was right. Janice also hoped that he would never regret falling in love with the girl whose existence he only recently recognized.

Reality forced Janice back to important matters and she broke the kiss while pulling his arm tighter around her shoulders. She said, "I need to talk to you about something. There is something about me that you have to know."

Pete's heart nearly stopped from the despair in her words. He said, "I'll love you no matter what you tell me. I'm not sure I want to hear anything that could come between us."

Even though he did want to hear what she had to say—he wanted to share everything with her, even the bad.

Janice pulled slightly back and said, "You will have to love me despite what I tell you."

The boy bit his lip and nodded as he prepared himself for what he thought could be the worst.

By the time Janice finished telling Pete about the things that had happened, the parking lot of the eatery was nearly empty.

The boy she loved sat speechless for several moments after she stopped talking and finally said, "My God, this can't be true, I've never been a religious person, and lately considered myself an atheist. Now you tell me this."

Janice broke out in tears, trembled, and said, "Oh, please tell me you still love me. I know that I'm some sort of aberration. Until we met, I wasn't sure how I was going to face life after that torture. You gave me the strength to go on."

"Of course," he said, "I still love you. It's going to take some time for me to fully absorb this, but my love for you is the same as it was yesterday." He paused and added, "It's my beliefs that are shaken. Everything I've been so sure of has been wiped out in the past hour."

The next few weeks were amazing. Janice had been able to teach Pete to see glimpses of reality. They would drive by churches and sometime sit for hours before Pete could see only a fraction of what she saw, but never anything definitive.

When Janice looked at the simplest of churches, like the small, wood frame building at which they sat parked, she didn't see the typical cross on a steeple. Janice saw a black stone building with archaic carvings covering its surface. The spire held no cross, but continued upward into the clouds. Flowers that had been planted around the church by the Ladies Club, were all dead and rotting.

Pete said, a little agitated, "I thought I almost saw something. Do you see the graveyard?"

In an effort to be patient, Janice replied, "Yes, I can see it, but it's no different in the altered reality. Look at the flowers and see if they are different."

"The Lilies are pretty even if they are blooming a little early," he said.

A small smile lit her face and she said, "You see some of the truth, but just a small fraction. The Lilies should be weeks away from blooming—it's not been that warm at night. There is much more. Relax and empty your mind."

He focused on the Lilies, not letting his attention stray. Pete did this for an hour and was about to give up and apologize to Janice when he saw the bright blooming Lilies fade to a crumpled dead mass, "My God, the Lilies are dead. They were so pretty and now they are—just dead," he said with a look of astonishment. This moment of true sight validated everything she had told him.

Her smile brightened as she squeezed his hand and said, "That is the truth. Blink your eyes and bring back the altered state."

He did and the blooming Lilies returned. Before the day was out, he could easily see the Lilies in either state. The flowers were all he could see, but for this day, it was enough for the both of them. That night they celebrated his fantastic accomplishment at Sam's Shakes.

After the usual good night kiss at the door, her mother started as soon as she entered the house. "You've been out with that boy again. He is going to ruin your life. The ladies at church say he and his family never go to church. They are heathens."

Janice had met Pete's father a couple of times and found him to be a nice man who treated her well. Pete's mother had died when he was young, some sort of accident his father never cared to discuss.

In despair, the girl did the only thing that would quiet her mother and said, "I'll have him come to church with us this coming Sunday morning." This had the desired effect. Her mother was so pleased that Janice was going to church with her that she forgot about Pete.

In her room, the desperation of the act began to settle into realism. Janice hadn't been in a church since her escape from that hell in the dark prison. The thought of entering another church wasn't something to which she looked forward.

Janice slid a box from under the bed that contained the tattered dress she had retrieved from the wastebasket and placed in a plastic bag. She pulled it out of the bag and held the remains close to her face. The molding, rotting smell

48

reminded her of those haunting months in Hell, a memory she needed to hold near for her own protection. The girl feared that if she forgot the torment, she might make a mistake that could place her somewhere even worse. She feared the next time, escape might not be possible. The thought of eternity in that prison made her tremble. Despite that fear, she would never concede and give into Iam's deception.

That Sunday, even her father and Pete acquiesced and went to church with Janice. Pete looked handsome in his tie and slacks. His usually misaligned, dark blonde hair was neat, or as neat as nature would allow. In back, the cute cowlick stood at attention as a reminder to everyone of his hair's true, unruly nature.

Outside the church, Pete squeezed her hand in an effort to give the terrified girl some comfort. He knew what it took for her to enter the church. The boy tried to use some of his new-found abilities to scan the church's exterior, but saw nothing abnormal.

Janice fought to hide the true state of the church from her mind. She knew what it looked like in reality and didn't care to see it this morning. If she allowed herself to see the church's true nature, it would have been impossible for her to enter.

Her father noticed her trepidations and gave his daughter a reassuring look. Having Pete and her father with her is the only thing that made it possible for Janice to take the steps that carried the nervous girl into the church. The church she had attended all her life was once a sanctuary, now it terrified her beyond imagination.

"Pete?" Janice asked.

"Yes?" He replied

"I'm so scared." she confessed.

He gave her hand, that was sweaty with apprehension, a little squeeze and said, "So am I." This caused the both of them to smile a little.

Janice heard little of the sermon to which the congregation sat intently listening. While the others heard about the four horsemen of the apocalypse, her ears were bombarded with, "Slut, whore, demon girl." Throughout the sermon she clung to Pete's arm and trembled.

Pete intently listened to the sermon. He hadn't been in a church since he was nine years old and never quite understood what the preacher was saying. This time he listened with a mindset to hear only the truth. The preacher talked about murder. He told some story about how a man had caught his wife in bed with another man and killed the two of them. The preacher said it was a sin to murder, but so was adultery. The church became unnaturally quiet. The preacher looked at Pete and said, "Your whore beside you will cheat on you and you will kill her just as your father killed your mother. You will never know her as a man knows a woman. She will marry another."

Pete stood and shouted, "No!" He pulled Janice from her seat and they ran out of the church. Once safely outside,

Janice looked at him and knew he had slipped past the church's altered reality. What she wasn't sure of, was what he had seen. Whatever it had been, she knew it was terrorizing his soul.

While sitting on a bench under a nearby tree, Pete told her what he had heard the preacher say. He said, "I know you would never cheat on me. It's what he said about my father and mother that scared me so much. I have always felt there was some mystery to my mother's death. My father has never really talked about it." He wiped a tear from his eye and asked, "That preacher said my father killed my mother. Do you think that's possible?"

She replied, "That's impossible. Iam was just trying to trick you—to scare you."

"You're probably right," he said in an effort to believe the words had been only lies.

Janice leaned into his arm and shoulder, consoled him, and said, "I'm so sorry that I brought you into this. I should have never told you the truth about me and brought you to a church that you hated even before you met me."

Pete kissed her tenderly on the lips and said, "I don't regret anything about you. If the knowledge that my father killed my mother is something I must have to be with you, then I willingly accept it."

"It can't be true," she said, "Iam lies constantly. He takes truths and twists them to his own purposes."

"There is only one way to find out, and that's to go and see my father," Pete said with conviction.

51

The others filed out of the church and Delores looked around for the two teens. She saw them under the tree and waved for them to come. As they slid into the car, Delores asked, "Are you alright, Pete? You looked pale as you rushed out of the church."

The boy stammered and replied with the first thing that came to mind, "I guess it was the heat—I was feeling... err... sick."

"Yes, it was stifling in there. I do hope they get the air conditioner repaired by Wednesday's prayer service," she said as her mind drifted back to the sermon about the four horsemen.

They stopped at Janice's house long enough for her to change clothes. She was happy to once again to be wearing the jeans her mother had declared taboo. She liked how they accentuated her youthful body, as well as allowing her less chance of an immodest moment when the wind blew.

Pete hated having Janice in the middle of this sordid moment, but he needed her close. He needed her support in case the answers to his questions were as devastating as that moment in the church. On the ride to Pete's house, Janice asked, "How are you going to bring up the subject?"

"I'm going to ask him directly. This is too serious not to," he replied in a tone that hid his true nervousness.

The house was smaller than the one in which Janice lived. It was a modest single level, covered with white vinyl siding. Frank Davies wasn't a wealthy man, but worked hard at the glass factory and provided a good life for Pete. He rarely dated, and never brought women around Pete. The inside of the house was clean, but cluttered by sports memorabilia, mostly Pete's trophies and framed articles of his accomplishments. Janice's conclusion was that she liked her boyfriend's home. It was also obvious that Frank loved Pete very much.

"Dad? You home?" Pete asked as he entered the house.

"In the kitchen," his father replied

Frank had just arrived home and was preparing a meal of fried chicken and mashed potatoes for two. He always prepared for two, even if Pete didn't come home for dinner. Pete would often eat his portion as a late night snack. "Smells good, dad," said the appreciative son.

Frank turned and said, "Yeah, it does." He then noticed Janice and added, "I'd better put on more chicken."

Janice politely said, "No thank you, Mr. Davies. I won't be staying for dinner, Mom is expecting me at home for dinner."

Frank smiled invitingly and said, "It's no problem, really. I have plenty of chicken in the fridge. You're always welcome, here."

Janice felt sad about the subject they were about to broach. She knew his dinner was going to turn into sadness no matter what answers he provided. The question alone could cause enough pain to destroy a family.

"Dad," Pete falteringly said.

The tone set off every parenting alarm. Frank knew

something was wrong and asked, "Something wrong, son?"

Tension filled the room as Frank turned off the chicken and said, "Let's sit and talk."

The three sat at the kitchen table. Frank's finger traced the carving of a car in the table that Pete, as a kid, had used his new pocketknife to produce. It could have been sanded away, but it was left as a memory that all homes hold of children growing up in them. He had been sentenced to his room for a week because of that misdeed.

The silence became almost deafening when, finally, Pete said, "I need to know about mom."

Frank's finger stopped its unconscious movement on the carving as he looked up nervously and asked, "What do you need to know, son?"

"How did mother die?" Pete asked with a stern look that scared the father.

It was obvious that the question had an ominous impact. The chagrined man lowered his head and shrank visibly in his chair. He had been asked the one question he never wanted to hear from his son, yet he had known it would be the one his son would ask. Frank paused for the longest time and said, "You sure you want the answer to this?"

His son quietly nodded. He wasn't sure he could have said yes if it hadn't been for Janice at his side. Her delicate hand held his, offering confidence and the desire for truth. It was time for Pete to know the truth and not see only the altered reality that his father had presented for so many years.

"I should have told you this a long time ago, but I wanted

to spare you the pain, as well as my embarrassment," he warned. With no fanfare and no excuses, Frank said, "I loved your mother more than any person on this planet. We dated and married after only a short few months. Was either of us ready for the commitment? I'm not sure. We were at the prom when Patti told me she was pregnant with you. It was then that I asked her to marry me. We spent graduation night on our honeymoon. It was truly a love affair. No two people could have been happier."

He paused, took a drink of tea, looked guiltily at his son, and continued, "When you were born, I felt left out of her life. I loved her so much, but she adored you so much more. I began to drink and feel sorry for myself. Your mother quickly tired of my drinking. When you got older, she began to spend more and more time away from home. Patti told me that she was working with a charitable organization, which was true. I had no idea that she was having an affair, until that night."

Despair filled the man as tears came to his eyes. The words choked in his throat, but he somehow managed to continue, "A policeman came to the house to tell me she was dead—a car accident, he had said. She and her lover had been out drinking and were on the way to a motel. He swerved into the opposite lane and hit a car head on. There were no survivors."

Pete released Janice's hand and sat up straight, "You didn't kill her?"

Despair was replaced by shock. "Oh God no, I loved her too much, son. I never even blamed her for what she did. I took all the blame because I deserved it." He looked down at the carving and said, "In a sense, I guess I did kill her. If it hadn't been for me, she might have been at home that night. The woman in the other car might still be alive as well."

Pete looked at Janice. She knew his question before he asked, She said, "As Lucifer said, he is the master of deception. He took a half truth and twisted it to his own means."

"Dad?" The son asked.

"Yes," the subdued father said.

"How come you never told me the truth about my mother?" The distraught son asked.

Through tears, his father replied, "I was too ashamed of what I did."

Pete went to his father, put an arm around him, and said, "Dad, you didn't do anythinhg wrong. No matter what you were like, she had no right to be in the car that night. I'll never blame you."

The father and son hugged because of truth. The past no longer placed a boundary between them, but gave them a strong future. When the moment had passed, Frank looked to his son and asked, "Why did you ask if I harmed your mother?"

Pete looked to Janice for the answer. It was she who said, "Truth is our only weapon. Without it, we fail miserably."

Frank looked at the girl oddly. He knew what she meant, but wondered why she would say it in such a way. He looked at Janice and Pete disconcertingly and asked, "Care to explain what you mean by that?"

The boy nervously said to his father, "Janice has something to tell you. It will sound wild and fanciful, but I swear to you on all that I hold dear, it's the truth." Frank knew that whatever he was about to hear was the truth, at least what his son believed it to be the truth..

Janice knew there was a chance of being ridiculed, but she told everything that had happened, up until church service that morning. Pete told his father about the day they had spent exploring reality and how he had seen the withered flower. He then told of the sermon that morning and the words he had heard about his mother.

Frank looked at the girl, and then to his son in disbelief. Something inside told him that he had just heard the truth. The question that he asked shocked them both, "Can I see that dress?" The two had expected a multitude of questions, but never suspected he would ask just that one. In hindsight, it was the obvious question to ask.

Janice looked to her boyfriend, then to Frank, and stuttered, "I... guess so. Why?"

A perplexed look crossed his face and he said, "I'm not really sure. Maybe I need something solid to grasp onto."

This brought a smile to her face, and Janice knew she had found another ally. The girl knew there was no time to waste gloating over small successes, stood, and said, "Let's go see the dress."

Pete and his father looked at each other and asked nearly

simultaneously, "Now?"

She laughed and replied, "Now. I've found that time is too precious to waste." She looked at the chicken sitting in the cooling frying pan and added, "Not even for your delicious chicken."

Frank laughed and said, "I can see you have never eaten my cooking."

Pete said to Janice, "Don't let him fool you, he's a great cook." The father and son smiled at each other.

They followed Janice into her house. Martin was sitting on the couch and looked up questioningly at the intrusion. She wasn't going to stop, hoping to avoid questions, until her father asked, "What's going on, here?"

Janice hesitated and said, "I want to show them something in my room."

Martin stood and asked, "Who is this man?"

Frank stepped forward, offered his hand, and said, "I'm Frank Davies, Pete's father. I apologize for the abrupt intrusion. "

The father shook the man's hand, turned to his daughter, and asked. "What's in your room that they would be so eager to see?"

Janice felt so stupid for not anticipating questions from her father. The only thing that came to mind was the truth. She shrugged and thought, "Why not?" Her father could be one more ally, but again, sadly, she knew her mother could be her worst enemy.

Janice's father looked at her as if she had gone mad after finishing her unbelievable tale. Martin shouted at Pete and his father, "What kind of nonsense are you putting in my daughter's head?"

Janice answered, "They have nothing to do with it." She was beginning to regret telling anyone.

"Mr. Carter, I'm as skeptical as you are about this. I agreed to come look at the dress your daughter said she was wearing," Frank said in an effort to calm Martin.

The confused father tried to make sense of what was happening and said, "I was there at the church that night. It was no medieval castle—it was just a church. "

Janice stared at her father in surprise. Martin suddenly went pale, looked at his daughter, and said "My God, I left you at the church that night. I had forgotten all that until this moment. This is impossible." He paused and added, "Let's have a look at this dress." Martin was as shocked as Janice by the unexpected memory.

Her smile was brighter than it had been all day as she led them up the stairs and into her room. She pulled the plastic bag from under the bed and her eyes caught Pete's. The realization that the boy she loves was in her bedroom caused a momentary blush.

Janice carefully pulled the rotting dress from the bag and laid it on the bed as she looked around at the expressionless faces. Martin touched the material with the tips of his fingers and jerked them away as if he had touched something horrible. He put an arm around his daughter and said, "I know this dress, it's your favorite church dress. How could it..." His voice trailed off as he faced the reality of its meaning.

He asked as he sat on the bed holding his daughter's hand, "That night we took you to the church, you weren't attacking your mother as she said? She was attacking you?"

"Yes," she replied, reliving the sad memory of that night. The girl had never seen such sadness in her father's eyes as she gave details about the confrontation with her mother. "It happened just like that. Don't blame her. She wasn't in control of herself. Iam makes people do things they would never do otherwise, especially those that believe in him like mother," she explained.

"Iam?" Frank quizzically asked.

"God," she replied. She thought for a moment and added, "or one of the gods. I'm no longer sure who is whom, anymore."

Martin was close to tears when he thought back over the last few weeks. His face began to glow with enlightenment and anger. He said, "This explains a lot, like your suddenly not wanting to attend church. I should have known something was wrong—I'm so sorry, honey."

Janice hugged her father tightly and said, "It's not your fault. Iam had a veil over your eyes and you saw only what he wanted you to know. Only the truth can lift that veil."

"Honey, why didn't you explain all this to me?" Janice's father asked.

She released her father from the hug and replied, "You

were in his thrall. There was nothing I could tell you that you would have heard. You believed in him just enough that he could control you." She chagrined and added, "I was scared you wouldn't believe me."

Her father said, "I'd like to think I would have believed you, but in all honesty, I know I wouldn't have. It's hard to believe even while looking at that dress with the memory of taking you to—that place."

Pete asked, "What made you keep the dress?"

She smiled and answered, "So that I never forget that hell. So that I'll always remember that I had beaten him on his own ground. Now I find a reason that I had never thought of until today, proof of his lies and brutality."

Silence hung over the room while they watched the girl and wondered how she had endured such torment. She was truly someone to admire. Janice had been greatly elevated in their eyes. Pete thought he couldn't have loved her more, but, at this moment, he did.

Frank changed the mood in the room by asking, "What do we do now?"

Pete said, "Janice has been trying to teach me to see reality." He went on to explain to Martin how that day they sat outside the church and how he saw the wilted Lilies.

Changing the subject in hopes of cutting through the tension in the room, Martin said, "First things first. I want to get to know the boy my daughter is in love with, and his father. Dinner is in the oven and Delores won't be home until late." The mention of his wife brought his mood to where it had been moments before. "Do we tell her?" Martin asked his daughter.

"Dad, I love mom, but we can't trust her. She would never go against the church and its teachings," she solemnly replied.

"I agree," he said.

The sounds of metal clanging against porcelain echoed through the dining room. Only the constant chatter replaced this sound. Laughter harmonized with other sounds to form a symphony of happiness. All the worries and fears were pushed to the side, at least for the night. Janice was delighted to have Pete and their families together for the first time, even under the circumstances that had brought them to her home.

Lost in the enjoyment of fellowship and hunger, no one heard the front door open. A voice filled with pleasant surprise asked, "What's all this?"

Martin jumped to his feet and began the introductions. Delores cordially greeted Frank, but leered at his son as they shook hands over the dinner table. Pete could have sworn he heard a voice when he touched Delores' hand. The voice had filled his head with certain clarity, "So, you're the bastard that's raping my daughter."

Delores joined the dinner, but the crowd of new friends became more subdued as they finished the meal. The rest of dinner was filled with silent, knowing looks. Martin was aware that his wife was being treated like the enemy. He should have resented that, but knew deep inside she might be a great threat to them all.

Chapter 3

Hands groped at Janice, tugging and trying to pull her to the ground. As far as she could see there were kneeling worshipers. She nearly fell over someone as she looked into the eyes of a woman and saw something vaguely familiar. The eyes were as vacant as an abandoned, decaying building. The woman's mind had only one purpose, to worship. In a voice strained from an eternity of silence, she hoarsely said, "Worship the king. On your knees harlot, and worship the king."

Janice jerk away from the woman and tried to run, but to no avail. People were jammed together like cattle in a slaughter pen—only these cattle would never die. They had an eternity to do nothing except worship their god.

A man drifted over the crowd and smiled at the frightened young girl. Janice's hands trembled as she pushed a golden lock of hair from her face so that she could better see the man. His hair was long and white as a winter's snow. His beard, over a foot long, matched his hair in its absence of color. His white robe added to the overall look of a pure and holy man. He placed an old wrinkled hand on her shoulder and meekly said, "I forgive you for your sins and transgressions. Kneel with your brethren and bask in the glory of God. You have been a believer all your life and then Lucifer used his lies and deceit to take you. Lucifer, not I, is the ultimate liar. Look around you and experience Heaven in all its glory."

The scene changed and Janice stood beside the most beautiful lake she had ever seen. Its surface looked as if it was speckled with small diamonds as water formed small peaks in the lazy breeze that blew gently over the lake. Growing in the rock filled brook that fed the lake were Rocky Shoals Spider Lilies, one of the rarer flowers on Earth. She recognized the place. Janice and her family had gone there when she was a small child.

On the other side of the lake was a small cabin. Her family had stayed in the same one. Laughter drifted across the water. It was the laughter of melancholy happiness. She knew the laugh, it was the laughter of her parents as she remembered from that time of her life.

The girl thought how she would love to spend eternity here. The deity, knowing her thoughts, said, "You can, dear. You can stay here with your parents for eternity."

Finishing his sentence, she asked, "And kneel in the mass of lost souls I saw earlier?"

"No, no my child. They worship because that's what they

choose. Your place is here, if you like. You can do or be anything you desire," he honestly said.

Janice listened intently and the memory of that dark prison brought her back to something she knew as fact, "Why did you lock me in that hell?" She asked, not as angrily as she had intended.

The deity laughed heartily and asked, "You think it was I that locked you in that prison? You might want to ask your friend Lucifer about that."

Seething anger rose and she asked, "Was it not one of your churches that put me in that hell?"

A sad sigh came from the old man, "Sadly, all churches are not mine. Lucifer has more control over some than I do."

The smell of bacon and eggs invaded her senses as she opened her eyes to see that she was in the safe confines of her bedroom. The dream, if that's what it had been, was fresh in her mind. Janice knew the dream was based more in reality than in her mind.

She climbed out of bed and stretched. Something caught the corner of her eye. On the edge of the bed, laid a Spider Lily. The girl scooped it up in her palm and sniffed. The fragrance was that of a freshly picked flower. The Spider Lily didn't grow within nine hundred miles from where she lived, and it was illegal to pick one, yet she held one in her palm.

Breakfast left an empty feeling in her stomach. The dream had played on Janice's already fragile state. The only thing she could think of was getting to Pete's house. When she had eaten all she could hold, which was little, Janice lifted the plate to put it in the sink as usual. Underneath the plate laid a pamphlet. It was one she was familiar with, having handed so many out herself. Her fingers lightly touch the wording on the front of the pamphlet: "Don't risk your soul…" They used them to invite people to church. Janice left it laying on the table as she rushed out of the house.

Pete was sitting on the porch when she arrived at his house. His smile was bright and wide at seeing Janice, that is, until she came closer. His smile faded to a grimaced at seeing the worried expression molding her face.

They sat on the porch swing as she told him about the dream and the Spider Lily in her bed that morning when she had awakened. After listening intently, he asked, "The Lily proves it wasn't just a dream, doesn't it?"

"Yeah," she replied

"What do you think? Who is telling the truth?" He asked in confusion.

Since her escape from Hell, Janice had formed a hard shell to protect her from the pain and memories, but that hard shell began to cracked and she cried. She had no answer for him. Pete said nothing as he held her, comforting the girl he loved. No matter which side she chose, he would stay at her side. This was the only thing of which he could be sure. He also knew that she would, somehow, choose the correct side.

Nearly thirty minutes later, her sobs began to slow and he kissed the tears away from her cheek. This brought a small smile to her face. The distraught girl used the hem of his t-shirt to dab at the remaining tears.

She sat up so suddenly it made Pete jump. She said with new-found confidence, "Let's go for a ride."

"Okay, but where are we going?" He asked with bewilderment.

Already walking to his truck, she replied, "Anywhere, everywhere. I need to look at things."

The puzzled boy asked, "You have something on your mind—care to share it with me?"

"The old man in the dream said something that I can verify on my own. I can know if he is telling the truth," she said in a hopeful tone.

Intrigued by her sudden confidence, he asked, "How will you know?"

Janice laughed at how she had accidentally made him pull the information in small bits. She satisfyingly said, "Iam/God, or whomever it was, told me that Lucifer controlled some churches and God the rest. If what he told me is true, then I should be able to see the difference. Good churches should look normal."

A look of enlightenment came over his face and he said, "Then let's go seek the truth."

The couple rode by every church in every nearby town. Janice saw the same no matter where they went—The same medieval, terrifying look she had seen before. Nothing had changed. The girl was becoming sure that the old man had lied and all the churches were controlled by the same evil.

Ahead, she saw a church, and she said in wild excitement, "Look—that church, it looks normal."

Pete turned into the overgrown drive. The girl sat staring at the white frame church for several minutes and asked, expecting no answer, "Why does it look normal?" Although in mild disrepair, the church looked as normal as any other structure.

All the churches had looked normal to Pete. He mustered a reply, "Dunno."

They exited the truck and walked around the normal looking church. Janice stood on tiptoes and tried to peer through one of the stain-glass windows. Pete wandered away, around the corner of the church, and checked the back entrance. He found it unlocked. Not so loud as for anyone inside to hear, he called out, "Janice, back here."

Still thinking he was standing behind her, she turned and was startled to find him missing. Janice carefully worked her way around the corner of the wood framed building to the back of the church. She was relieved to see Pete standing there as handsome as ever. The sight of him almost never failed to evoke a smile. He tensely said, "This door is unlocked—we can get in here." The couple joined hands as she followed him into the church.

It was obvious the church hadn't seen a congregation for some time. In one of the ornate brass, wall-mounted candle-holders, sat a bird's nest. A vandal's rock had broken one of the top panes in one of the stained glass windows, offering an inviting refuge to any bird looking for a safe home. Cobwebs painted every corner of the large room. The once red carpet had faded to burnt-orange. The pine floor hidden beneath the carpet creaked with fatigue as they walked carefully around the room. The pews had been removed. Indentations in the carpet forever marked their positions.

The pulpit laid on its side, looking as dead as the church. The pair eased their way down the hall beside the choir section. The doors lining the hallway were still labeled for their respective purposes. The first few were Sunday school rooms. Crude drawings, obviously done by children, were still pinned to the walls. Janice remembered her youth in a room, not unlike this one. A small smile formed as she wondered if her drawing of the boogieman was still on the wall of her former church. Thinking back, Janice wondered if that drawing wasn't from the subconscious sight that now allowed her to see churches in their unaltered state.

A sound farther down the hall startled them. Pete automatically reached protectively for Janice who clung protectively to his arm as she stood behind her protector. Pete turned and held an index finger to his lips as to indicate quiet, but she needed no warning.

When they reached the room from which the sound had come, Pete peeked around the corner and saw a homeless man sitting on the floor with a bottle of cheap, fortified wine in his hands. The filthy derelict said, "Don't just stand there, come on in. I don't get a lot of visitors."

Janice felt the threat ease, so she stepped from behind Pete and said, "Hi."

A voice, hoarse from too many years of drink, laughed and said, "My, my, ain't you a pretty little thang."

The girl blushed slightly and asked, "Do you live here?"

"It sure looks that way. I sort of like it here. Quiet, if you get my meaning," he knowingly laughed.

Pete asked, "I'm not sure we get your meaning."

His tone became serious and he said, "I bet the girly knows what I mean."

Pete spat in an effort to defend his girlfriend, "You drunk old man, you don't know what you're saying."

The man sat up a little straighter, leaned sightly forward, and said with clarity, "Boy, you be right, I am drunk, but you better damn well believe I know what I'm talking about."

In an effort to diffuse the situation by changing the topic, Janice asked, "Do you know what happened here, why the church closed?"

"Of course I do," said the derelict man.

They waited for the man to continue, but he offered nothing more. Pete urged the man forward and asked, "Why did they leave?"

He laughed once more as spittle spilled from his mouth, running over the black stubble of his beard. He tersely said, "I ran the bastards off."

Pete and Janice stared at the man incredulously. The tattered shell of a man looked Janice dead in the eyes and said, "The girly knows why. I'll tell her the story if she wants to hear it."

"Of course I do," she said.

He pointed a dirty finger at two chairs and said, "You two sit. Ya giving me a crick in my neck."

The two teens looked at each other as if seeking confirmation from the other. They sat and tensely waited for the man to begin.

"Twenty years ago I built this church," he said while waving a hand in an animated arc to to indicate the room and church, "For as long as I can remember, I wanted to be a minister, even though I had only been in church a few times. Those few times told me that I would have to build my own, because those churches were full of sin and corruption. Therefore, I worked everyday at the sawmill until I got enough money to begin building this church."

Sadness could easily be seen on the man's face. He could have been no more than fifty, yet he looked older. His hands shook as he held the bottle of wine close to his chest like a child might hold a teddy bear. His pauses were longer than they should have been, but neither rushed him to speak. He took a drink and continued, "I began to take part of my paycheck in lumber. I dug the foundation with a shovel that I bought at the hardware store. Each day after work, I toiled alone until one day there was a frame in the shape of a church. People began to stop and ask what I was doing. I would vainly tell them, 'It's a church. I'm going to be the minister.' The people were so impressed by my effort, they began to bring tools and helped."

Janice took Pete's hand and held it as they listen to the

man. The man noticed and said, "Ya'll are in love, ain't ya?"

The young couple was embarrassed at having a stranger notice their feelings for one another, much less comment. Pete hesitated a moment, as if looking for the correct answer, and decided there was only one, the truth. He replied "Yes, we are."

The drunk man smiled and said, "It shows." He became grim as he continued his story, "The day the church was finished was a great day. Everyone that helped build it came and we had a small worship service to bless the church. Then we had a feast. My life long dream had become reality. I prayed almost constantly, offering thanks. That first Sunday people brought lawn chairs to sit on because there were no pews. I preached my first sermon and the people stood at the end and praised me. They gave money that day and every service thereafter. Soon, I had shiny new hardwood pews sitting on red carpet."

Janice interrupted, "You seem to have had a successful church. This place doesn't look like it's been used in twenty years."

He took another drink and started again, "It took only three months before things began to change. The beautiful church started to turn ugly. The building was no longer the one I built with my own hands. It had turned into something ungodly, as did the people. They became as corrupt as I had seen in every other church."

Janice asked, "You saw the reality of the church you built. How come you never saw the reality of other churches?"

He shrugged and replied, "Maybe I was just blind to it. Maybe I had too much of my soul invested in this one. By the end of the second month, I chased the people out when they came for service. I denounced God to them. The next three weeks was a living hell as demons came and tried to rip me from the church, but I wouldn't hand it over to them. He opened his shirt to reveal ugly scars that appeared to have been made from claws."

The teens gasped as they saw his wounds. Janice felt his pain and tears flowed down her cheek. The man looked at Janice and said, "You have scars as well, but yours are on the inside." She could only nod in confirmation.

With the help of Pete's comforting, Janice gathered her composure and asked, "I can understand why you're unable to defeat Iam, but how do you keep him at bay?"

"I keep him out by not bending to his will," the man caustically said. He looked directly at Janice and added, "You give him another name and do not refer to him as God."

She smiled grimly, "Is Iam not his name?"

The battered man nodded and said, "By giving him a name you take away part of his advantage."

Janice became overwhelmed by the broken man, slipped to the floor, and hugged the lonely man. She no longer smelled his unkempt body. Janice could only smell his will and desire to overcome all that had been done to him by Iam. They shared a common fate that bound them together for an eternity. They both wept.

Pete interrupted the moment and asked, "Has anyone else

been by here?"

Janice sat up as the man said, "Only vandals. Even the demons stopped coming a long time ago. When I heard you in the church, I thought that you would be more vandals. Instead, in came saviors."

The couple looked at him, stunned by his view of Janice and Pete. It was Janice who incredulously said, "We're not saviors. We are scared to death and were looking for the truth," she hesitated as she searched for the right words, but there were no right ones. She added "or a weapon."

The former minister despairingly said, "I know of no weapons."

Pete desperately said, "You beat him once. There had to be some kind of weapon."

He laughed and said, "I simply won a battle. The war has gone on for thousands of years. The best weapon of this century is your girlfriend. She seems to have some kind of ability."

Janice shook her head and said, "I'm just a frightened teenager."

The man asked, "Will you please tell me your story, how you came to be here—to find me?"

She looked to Pete for support and he gave a comforting nod. Janice told everything from the first meeting with Lucifer, her death and resurrection, to the months or years in Hell.

"How could you have survived that with your sanity

intact?" asked the astonished former minister.

She looked at him with cold steady eyes and asked, "Did I survive it with my sanity intact?"

The beaten man convincingly said, "You did or else you wouldn't be here, right now."

Janice reluctantly agreed.

Compassion overcame the distrust of strangers that Janice had been taught all of her life by her mother, and said, "You must come home with me."

He shook his head and said, "This is my home, and I'm safer here."

The concerned girl pleaded, "Just for tonight, a hot shower and a home cooked meal."

This was more temptation than he could resist. He set the wine bottle down and said, "I'd almost sell my soul to God... Iam for that." The humor wasn't lost among the three, but it didn't get the laugh it might have otherwise gotten. The three somehow managed small smiles.

On the way to Janice's house they learned the former minister's name, Chandler Baptiste. In light conversation, the man turned out to be more than the caustic drunk they had first met. His personality turned out to be charming and witty.

Chandler seemed to be an unlikely ally. Yet in the end, he might be the most important or the most dangerous.

For the battered minister, this would at least be a pleasant interlude from his battles, both alcohol and demons. For the former minister, demon rum took on a new meaning. The hot soak in the bathtub gave the aging man new vigor. At least that's what he would tell the others, but he knew the new-found vigor came from Janice. He, now, had someone to share in his battle—someone who appeared to have great abilities.

Dinner was pleasant and Martin accepted Chandler with ease. Conversations avoided the unpleasant and veered to the pleasant. The man had a sense of humor that kept them chuckling. He seemed the opposite of the withered man they had found crouched on the floor hugging a bottle of cheap wine.

When dinner was over, Chandler said, "I couldn't have asked for a more delightful evening, but I must get back to the church."

Janice asked in dismay, "You're not going to stay here for the night?"

His eyes were consoling, and yet firm, as he said, "I cannot stay here. The church is the only safe place for me." No one dared argue with him on that point. Janice wanted to argue that he would be safe in her home, but she wasn't as sure of that as she would have liked.

Pete and Janice cleared the table. Once they were finished, the rested minister was standing at the door about to leave. Pete demanded, "Hold on, I'll drive you back to the church."

Janice had already packed a bag of food and supplies that

Chandler might need. The phone rang and it startled everyone. Martin answered on the second ring. Seconds later he announced, "It's for you, Pete, your father."

He smiled apologetically to the former minister and took the phone from Martin. His expression immediately transformed to that of concern. Janice moved to his side, offering support for whatever bad news the phone held. The phone beeped as he pressed the off button. He apologetically said, "I have to get home. My Dad isn't feeling well."

Janice took her boyfriend's hand with concern for him and said, "I'll go with you."

"That's okay, I can take care of him. You have enough worries of your own. I'm sure dad is okay, I just need to be sure," Pete said in an effort to ease Janice's worry, but did little for his own.

She conceded and said, "I'll take Chandler back to the church."

Pete and her father protested at the same time. Martin said, "I'll go with you."

Her pleading eyes looked appreciatively at her father and she said, "I could really use some time alone to think. I'm looking forward to the ride back, alone." She hesitated as if reading their minds and added "If something were to happen, neither of you would be of any help. I can take care of myself—honestly."

Martin looked at his daughter and knew there was no arguing with her once her mind was set. Martin came close to using his fatherly powers to demand she allow him to go, but conceded to her will. Janice ushered Pete to the door and, sounding motherly, said. "Go, now, and see to your father. I was taking care of myself long before I met you," She wasn't about to admit that it was mostly false bravado.

Pete reluctantly left to attend to his father. Janice took the keys for the family Ford and nearly forced the minister from the house. She wanted to get out of the house before her father could change his mind and insist on coming along. She said, "Let's go."

She dropped Chandler off at the church and reflected on the day's events. This had been a good day. Each ally brought hope for the truth and the end to the lies, no matter from where they came.

Leaving the bygone church, she came to a crossroads, the true kind, not the kind in life on which she seemed to lately find herself. The overly large stop sign loomed like a beacon in the night as the car's headlights made its reflective surface glow. Its meaning was danger, but its purpose was that of safety. A stop sign larger than usual indicated there had been numerous accidents at the intersection and was meant to impose extreme caution on the traveler. For the moment, she felt safe and slowly turned right onto the crossing road. Just at the end of her headlights, she saw a girl frantically waving her arms. The fine hair on Janice's arms bristled as she eased her way along side the girl.

She was slightly older than Janice with short black hair. She wore little makeup, but only enough to enhance her already attractive features. Behind her was a car and on closer inspection, the cautious Janice could see it had a flat tire. Knowing this could be a trick, she stopped beside the girl after double-checking the door locks, lowered the window only an inch, and asked, "Having trouble?"

The girl smiled brightly and said, almost too cheerfully, "You better believe it. I have a flat and no spare. Could you give me a lift to my boyfriend's garage? My boyfriend owns a towing service and he can come get my car."

In an effort to be careful and still help the girl, Janice said, "I have a cell phone—we can just give him a call."

The girl laughed while rolling her eyes and said, "He's never in the house. He practically lives in that stupid garage of his and can't afford a phone at both places."

Janice smiled at the girl and hit the door-lock release. The stranded girl hopped in and Janice noticed the tight fitting jeans the girl was wearing. Not long ago, Janice would have called the girl a sinner for wearing such tight fitting clothing. She smiled inwardly at how they weren't much tighter than her own.

The garage was only a couple of miles from where the old Camaro sat with a flat tire. The girl pointed to a garage with an aging, rusting wrecker sitting outside. There was a dim light inside the garage. The stranded girl said, "Good, he's here. The jerk is usually never around when you need him."

Janice eased the Ford into the drive and stopped. The stranger asked, "Could you wait here while I make sure he's inside?"

Something inside Janice raised an alarm. Fear pricked her skin. Her first thought was to say she couldn't wait and rush home to the safety it provided. Instead, she gave way to her kind heart and said, "Sure, I'll wait."

The girl disappeared inside the garage. Janice thought she heard shouting, but wasn't sure. A sound came from just outside the car. Janice reached for the door lock, but she was half a second too late. The car door quickly opened. The dome light of the car glared brightly, blinding her dark adjusted eyes. The door alarm buzzed angrily. A hand covered her mouth as she was dragged head first from the car. Janice attempted to scream, but the hand only clamped tighter onto her mouth. The terrified girl saw only a shadowy movement when she heard the world explode inside her head and darkness stole her consciousness.

A dim light shined weakly from a disfigured lamp as it leaned awkwardly at an angle, which cast an eerie shadow across the room. The chair in which she sat, and the lamp, were the only two objects in the room. The walls were covered with hand-drawn runes from a time long forgotten. The only one she recognized was a pentagram, known to some as a sign of the devil. Throughout history it had symbolized many religions, even Christianity, but it seemed clear what the meaning was in this case. It was a sign of the devil. Her mind screamed one word in silent rage, Lucifer.

Ropes cut into flesh as they bound her arms tightly behind the chair as she struggled. The soiled rag that covered her mouth had the taste of oil and grease. Janice wasn't sure

81

what frightened her more, the situation she was in, or the possibility that Lucifer was her betrayer.

Out of sight and from behind, she heard a female ask, "Now what do we do with her?"

The male replied, "The old man said we could kill her if we like. He only asked that we make her suffer, first."

Janice struggled against the ropes, but to no avail. Laughter rang in her ears. The helpless girl knew it was at her expense. The guy stepped from behind and asked, "You ready to begin our little party?"

Terrified eyes were wide with fear and said what her mouth couldn't. They pleaded, trying to reason with the evil man standing before her with a wicked smile. This only drew mock laughter from the grubby man twice her age.

Janice's fear aroused something in him akin to sexual urges. It made the animal inside him rage with sexual passion. She had avoided his eyes until now. The hate and anger she saw in those eyes scared her as much as what she knew he would inevitably do to his prisoner. It was at this moment that a blurred object crashed into her cheek, which crushed the bone beneath the flesh. She saw the blurry objected to be a fist as it fell away from her face.

Screams of pain impacted with the oily rag over her mouth as his fist pummeled her body. Blood began to mix with the oil embedded in the rag that covered her mouth. A torrent of pain ran the length of her body and touched every limb with its prickly finger. The mind did what it always does when faced with insurmountable pain, it shut down.

The girl welcomed the calm of unconsciousness. There was peace in this world of darkness. Haunting dreams stayed hidden behind closed doors. The only thing of which her mind could be sure, was the continuance of time. This sleep was her savior, unlike the dreams that sometimes haunted her sleep. Janice occasionally awoke to the cruel sound of the man's voice and more pain as his fist pounded her without mercy.

"Is this bitch ever going to wake up?" The man angrily asked the girl that Janice had helped. Janice's eyelids fluttered and then sprang open. The pain in her jaw had dulled to a steady throb.

"Oh good, you're awake. It's time we got back to work, pretty thang," he said as a fist slammed into Janice's head, causing her blonde hair to fill with strands of red.

He leaned down close as if inspecting the black swollen area of her jaw. His breath smelled of decaying teeth. The girl was repulsed, but she couldn't move away. A greasy hand moved to the top button of her blood speckled white blouse and lewdly said "Let's see what Santa brought me for Christmas. I love opening packages, especially when they're as pretty as you."

The girl that had led Janice to this placed rushed in from the shadows, grabbed the man by his greasy t-shirt, and angrily asked, "Bob, what the hell you doing? You don't need this Christian bitch when you have me."

He pushed her roughly away and shouted, "Get away from me. I'm just having a look before that pretty body is marred and broken."

His fingers toyed with the top button and then menacingly ripped it from the material. Each button made a small clicking sound as it fell to the concrete floor. He laughed derisively and mockingly said, "Plain cotton, this is the type of bra I would expect a church girl to wear."

Janice found it almost laughable that she chose this moment to realize that she had never upgraded her underwear to something more stylish. They had always been chosen for only comfort and usefulness. She retained much of the modesty that had been taught from growing up in church. Thought of the church made her wonder why the attacker kept calling her a church girl. "Could this man really be working for Lucifer?" She wondered. The pain and chaos only heightened the confusion. Janice could no longer be sure on whom to place her trust.

His large fist slammed into her small, pale stomach and it collapsed easily under the force and the air in her lungs rushed out explosively. She tried to inhale fresh, life-giving air, but her body failed at what should come naturally. It was as if someone had clamped her chest in a vise and held it tightly compressed. The usually pallid flesh reddened as if it had been burned. The girl fought against her rebellious body and tried to bring it to surrender. As her face deepened in color to a light blue, Janice's body relented and her lungs filled with cool, fresh air. It was only then, she felt the pain in her stomach and ribs. Janice felt the bile rise in her throat. The dinner she had enjoyed earlier with her family and friends exploded from her mouth and spilled from underneath the gag.

The man laughed at Janice's pain and humiliation, while the girl looked on anxiously. Janice could take no more and closed her eyes. There could be escape as there had been that time in the dungeon. Janice smiled knowingly that she was going home. With confidence, she closed her eyes and began silently chanting, "This is not real… this is not real."

She expected to see her bedroom when she opened her eyes, but the worst horror imaginable presented itself. She wasn't home, but still in the barren room tied to the chair. This was reality, not a dream or an attack by Iam. Janice knew at that moment, she would never see Pete again. Light faded once more as several blows rapidly battered her face and body. Janice sought escape in the refuge of unconsciousness.

That night when Chandler watched his new-found friend drive away, he felt something gnawing at his insides. This wasn't the feeling of guilt and betrayal that had been a constant companion over the years. This was something new. Inside the former church, he went to his room and found the familiar bottle, his best friend, he sometimes joked. His shaking hand lifted the bottle, but it froze. He couldn't get it to his lips no matter how hard he tried. Angrily, he tossed the bottle against the far wall. Glass exploded like shrapnel as wine ran like blood down the grimy, white wall. When he saw the wine was actually blood, his knees gave way. He collapsed to the floor, crawled to within reach of the crimson substance, and ran his fingers through the congealing fluid. He smeared the blood on the floor with his palm and in it he saw Janice. She sat, tied lifelessly in a chair. The former minister cried out in torment for his new friend, hoping that he had gone mad and what he saw wasn't real.

He blinked his eyes in hopes that he was hallucinating. The vision disappeared. The scent of wine invaded the room. Before him was a pool of spilled wine. He leapt to his feet, ran from the church, and stopped only when he had reached the highway pavement. Standing in the cool night, he wasn't sure which way to go. He began to walk into the darkness, unsure if he was going in the correct direction. The only thought in his mind was to save the girl. It was more than friendship that possessed Chandler. This was some deep-seated drive like he had never before felt.

He dived just in time for the car to miss. The car stopped a hundred feet away and turned around. Chandler looked for someway to escape the car that had nearly run him down and was coming back to finish the job. The khaki pants and shirt his new friends had given him were now stained with green from the roadside grass. With no time to react, he could only stand and accept his fate.

The car, surprisingly, rolled slowly toward him and not the high rate of speed he had expected. The headlights blinded Chandler as they bore in on him as if it were some self-guided weapon. The man was ready to stand his ground and do battle with whatever evil lurked inside the steel machine.

The car stopped and a window lowered with the electric

motor's rhythmic whine sounding louder than usual in the quiet night. A familiar voice nervously called out, "Mr. Baptiste, it's me, Pete Davies. Are you alright? I thought I had run you over."

The car's interior light came on and Chandler let out an audible sigh of relief. He breathlessly said, "Am I glad to see you."

Pete said at the same time as Chandler, "Janice." There was no need for either to say more because each knew why the other was on the road that night. Having been strangers only hours before, they physically collided with each other and fate to become allies in a fight for all things good.

They searched every road that Janice might have used to go home. Around each curve they expected to find the blue Ford in a ditch, or sitting lame with a flat tire. They searched until the sun had broken through the treetops. This brought only despair to the once hopeful rescuers.

Their search was nearing a futile end. With almost no hope left, they made one more pass of the roads and finally the one that would take them back to the church. They passed through a crossroads and rounded a curve. There it was, the blue Ford wedged dangerously down a bank

The car hadn't completely stopped when Chandler leapt from it and rushed to the Ford. In the driver's seat sat Janice. He withdrew in shock as he saw her bloodied and, seemingly, lifeless body leaning against the steering wheel. Pete screamed in rage and despair as he appeared behind Chandler. The former minister reached into the open window with little hope and placed his fingers on her neck. He shouted with reserved hope, "She's alive. Her pulse is very weak, but she is alive." Afraid to remove her from the car, they called 911 from Pete's cellphone that he had a habit of forgetting and leaving at home.

The ambulance raced away in a fury of wailing sirens. Several police were on the scene. An older man wearing a rumpled sports coat wandered around and through the car. He Eventually found his way to Pete and Chandler, who hadn't been allowed to follow the ambulance. The detective looked at a well-worn notepad and said, without looking at the pair, "You found the girl, I'm told, and her name is Janice Carter of 2215 Credence Drive?"

Pete nodded a reply.

The detective looked at the two men without blinking and said, "Her injuries couldn't have happened in the car accident. The officer on the scene told me that you are the boyfriend." He paused, looked at his notes, and continued, "You would be..." He looked questioningly up at Chandler.

Pete interrupted, "He's a friend of the family."

The rumpled cop ignored Pete and continued, "You would be Chandler Baptiste, former minister, currently employed as a drunkard. You have been arrested four times in the last three years for public drunk." The detective paused, looked over his dollar store reading glasses, and asked, "Why are you here?"

Chandler thought quickly because the truth wasn't an

option. The former minister settled on partial truth and replied, "Janice, her father, and the boy, here, have been helping me rehabilitate. I've given up the bottle," Which was the truth. Chandler knew he had more important demons to battle. He continued, "The boy became worried about Janice when she was late coming home after bringing me back to the church. The boy came to the church looking for her, so I offered to help him search."

Chandler didn't want to tell the detective how he truly came to know something was wrong, because he wouldn't believe that he had seen it in a vision. The former minister shivered when he thought of that moment when the spilled wine transformed to blood, and then the image of Janice slumped in the chair. He hoped the detective hadn't noticed him falter.

The detective couldn't help but notice the slight tremble of the minister as some thought passed through his mind. He wasn't sure if he was hiding something, or was just upset over his friend. Consulting his notes, he said, "The reason she was out was to take you home." He had not asked a question, yet it demanded an answer.

"That's correct. I told you that already." Chandler said.

He rubbed the day old growth of beard. This was an indication that the detective had rushed from the house without breakfast or time to shave, which happened often. His disgruntled attitude reinforced this presumption. Leafing back and forth through his ratty notepad, he stopped at a particular page, looked at Pete, and asked, "If she was missing all night, why hadn't you called the police?"

The chagrined boy knew he couldn't tell the truth and lied, "We thought her car had broken down. We didn't think she was in any danger."

His stubby pencil wiggled in his large hand as he wrote something in the pad. He wrote one word in capital letters, "LIE," and then Pete's name. He smiled cordially and said, "Go see to your friend." He then added with consternation, "I'll be in touch."

Detective Johnson leaned into the car to take one last quick look before the wrecker pulled it away. In the passenger's side of the car, a glint of light on metal caught his eye. Wedged in the seat was a golden cross with a broken chain. He used a latex glove-covered hand to remove the cross and slip it into a plastic baggie. If it had belonged to the girl, he thought, it wouldn't have been in the passenger's seat. He stepped back and waved to the wrecker driver as a signal to pull the car away. The detective stared at the lightly damaged car and felt an uneasiness in the pit of his stomach.

Martin sat alone in the crowded waiting room. He looked up when he heard the elevator door open. He rushed to Pete, hugged him, and said, "Thank you for bringing her home to me." He looked past the boy to Chandler and gratefully said, "Thank you, as well."

They both cried together. Pete had to force himself to say the words, but finally said, "She looked so bad sitting slumped over in the car. I'm so afraid she won't make it."

Martin held the boy at arms length, looked into his eyes, and optimistically said, "You have to believe she will. Have faith in her abilities and in whatever it is that looks after her."

Pete nodded agreement, even though he wasn't sure if anyone, or thing, truly looked after the girl he loved.

They managed to find a seat away from others in the waiting room. Martin sanguinely said, "The police have been here asking me a lot of questions. They wouldn't tell me anything, but I'm guessing this was no accident."

Pete said, "It couldn't have been an accident because her car was barely damaged."

They stopped talking as someone came to collect a magazine from the table next to where they sat. When the woman was out of hearing range, Chandler said, "Her injuries didn't come from the car accident. I would guess the car was pushed into the ditch."

"Who could have done this to her?" Asked the distraught father. He hesitantly added, "Couldn't her abilities protect her?"

"Her ability can only protect her from things not of this world. To things of this world, she is as vulnerable as you and me," the chagrined Chandler replied, and after some thought, added, "Maybe more so."

Pete sat quietly listening to them talk and tried to rationalize her accident. He asked, "Couldn't this have just been something that could have happened to anyone. Do you really think this was connected to... you know, the other things?" The hesitation said more than his words. They were facing an evil for which they had no weapon. If Janice was to die, so would the hope of mankind, possibly, forever.

The doctor approached in her white coat, surveyed the room, and asked, "Is there a Mr. or Mrs. Carter here?"

Martin hurriedly stood and said, "Yes. I'm her father. Please tell me she will be alright."

The doctor solemnly said, "Come with me, Mr. Carter."

Pete rose to follow, but the doctor looked at the boy and said, "I'd rather speak with Mr. Carter alone."

Martin pleadingly asked, "Please let him come, my daughter needs him."

The doctor relented, rather than cause undue commotion in the waiting room. Chandler remained seated and said, "I'll wait here for you."

The office was small and at the far end, sat a mahogany desk. A multitude of diplomas and awards for excellence covered the walls. Her youthful appearance was just camouflage of her true age. The expanse of education suggested a much older woman. She waved them to a small couch against the wall, just inside the door. She sat on the edge of a matching chair as the two tense men leaned forward. No one was ready to relax.

Unable to find a pleasant way to offer bad news, she abruptly said, "There is no easy way to say this. Your daughter is in serious condition. It is possible she won't live through the night. Still, I would urge you to hold out hope and pray to whatever deity your religion allows. I want to stress, there is always hope, even in this case, albeit slim."

Nerves were near the shattering point as Martin took a deep breath and asked as calmly as possible, "What happened to her? Pete, here, tells me that her wounds couldn't have happened in the car accident."

"The boy is perceptive. She was severely assaulted. I cannot imagine anyone purposely doing something like this to anyone, yet I see the results of it everyday. If she survives, I doubt she will ever lead a normal life, physically or mentally. This is why I wanted to talk to you alone, Mr. Carter." The doctor said. She glanced at Pete, hesitated as if she were visiting some past memory of her own, and added, "Your daughter was brutally raped. "

Pete wanted to cry for the girl that meant everything to him, but he sat quietly, drawing on some inner strength he didn't know he possessed. His mind began flashing pictures of some guy raping the girl he loved. The boy tried to shove them away to avoid the torment, but they kept coming. With each image, a rage rose within him, but he remained outwardly calm. Pete knew if he ever found the man, he would kill him with his bare hands. He then thought of the mental pain that Janice must have suffered. The images disappeared and the only remaining thoughts were those of the good times that had brought them to this point in time. A single tear ran down his cheek, but otherwise he remained strong—for Janice.

Quiet settled in the room as they came to terms with the brutality of the assault. The only words Martin could choke out were, "May I see my daughter?"

"Certainly, Mr. Carter, come with me," said the doctor with more empathy that she might have had in other cases.

Pete hopefully asked, "May I come as well?" She didn't reply so Pete took the silence as affirmation and followed.

They followed the doctor down a long sterile hallway and made numerous turns as if in a mythical maze. Martin heard his own footsteps echoing in his ears. He felt as if he was in some prison walking the last mile to his own execution. The hurting father was sure that if Janice died, he would surely pass with her, because without his daughter there was nothing else for which to live.

They stopped in front of a room with a massive window that looked in on a form with wires and tubes extending outward as it lay in a bed. It was then that Martin broke down and wept as he saw his daughter for the first time since the assault. He saw someone bruised and swollen to the point that she was no longer recognizable.

Martin entered the room as the doctor held Pete back with a comforting arm around his shoulder. The boy didn't argue and looked with tear-filled eyes at the girl he cared for as much, or more, as he did for his own life. He softly whispered, "I love you so much. I'll never let anyone hurt you again, even if it means my life."

Martin stood beside the bed, took her bruised hand into his, and looked through the maze of bruises and bandages to find her eyes. Her chest rhythmically rose and fell under the frosty white sheets. He could feel each beat of her heart as blood pulsed through her hand. His mind drifted back to the night before when she had been so positive. She had endured all that time in Hell and somehow, had managed to remain positive. Unsure on whom to place blame, he asked no one directly, "What more must she endure?"

Loud noises outside the room destroyed the silence and Martin turned to see Delores just as she crashed through the door. She dropped to her knees and began to fervently pray a string of rapidly spoken piousness. Martin stood and watched, unsure of how to react. He was no longer sure praying to God wasn't the correct thing to do. Desperation made the father accept anything that might help his daughter, even the prayer of his wife, despite the possibility it was the god to whom she prayed that had brought harm to Janice.

Delores switched to silent prayer, not for her daughter's life, but for the salvation of her soul. The voice of God answered her prayers and told the woman that the girl must die so that she can be sent home to Heaven. The pious woman would follow her Lord God's will, even if that meant killing the daughter, herself. This night, Delores was sure she wouldn't have to take the life of her daughter because God had seen to her destruction and put an end to her evil liaison with Satan. Deloris sat vigilantly over her daughter, but not to see her regain consciousness, but to hear the last gasping breath as she died. At that moment, she would shout in jubilation because God's will had been done.

That night Janice laid in semi-darkness, listening to the

constant, rhythmic beep of the monitors attached to her barely, living body. The horror of the things that had been done to her came in broken, shattered memories. Her mind was in worse shape than her broken and battered body. The tortured girl moaned aloud as the horror of her memories focused on the sexual assault. He had taken her as she lay dying on the floor. The girl to whom she had given help, seemed to sound as if she was cheering him on, as if it were some contest. Janice's brain began to close off the parts of the mind that contained those memories.

The stream bubbled as she sat on a rock with the old man. He smiled at her and said, "You're not looking well, today."

She replied, "I've been through a lot since we last spoke." She hesitated and added, "It hurts to talk."

The old man smiled and said, "Let me do something about that." In that moment, all the pain in her jaw was gone. She laid a hand on her abdomen and said, "You took her."

He smiled and said, "Yes. She will be safe with me. You can visit her, someday." Janice smiled.

Janice looked thoughtful, arched her brow, and said, "She needs a name. Can you call her Angela?"

The old man smiled, nodded, and said, "It's time to go back."

The girl looked at him pleadingly and begged, "Do I have to? The pain is gone while I'm here. I don't want to go back to the pain and memories."

The doctor entered the intensive care unit and looked down to see bright blue eyes staring in her direction. A quick glance at the monitor's display indicated things that couldn't be possible. Every monitor function was within normal range. Not trusting them, she place practiced fingers to the girl's neck and felt the pulse of blood as it rushed past. Watching her watch, more from habit than need, she counted and found the girl's pulse to be normal.

She leaned close and softy asked, "Janice, can you hear me?"

"Sure," she said with a clarity that shouldn't have been possible. Janice slid slightly up in the bed and said, "I'm hungry."

The doctor's knees shook and nearly buckled as she clung to the rail that was normally used to protect the patient. Unable to contain herself, she shouted, "My God."

Janice found the doctor's hand and asked, "Are you sure it was him?"

Professionalism abandoned the doctor as she looked down at her once fragile patient and wept. She had seen something that was never taught in medical school. Raised Catholic, she grew up hearing about miracles. Never did she imagine seeing one, especially when the recipient suggested, confidently, that it wasn't God that had worked the miracle.

Her hands still shook from shock as she slowly removed the bandages from the patient's face. Their looseness suggested less swelling. What she saw as the last bandages fell away made her question her own mental health. The face was still slightly bruised, but there was no sign of the shattered jaw. A quick check revealed the girl would be sore and bruised for quite a while, but there were no serious injuries.

When Janice finally got a moment alone, she unclenched her right fist. When she unfurled the fingers, a perfect, white Spider Lily lay in the palm. She was sure she heard a baby cry in the distance, but knew it didn't come from inside the hospital.

Word spread through the hospital like a plague. Strangers filed past the window to see the girl about which everyone was talking. A small religious shrine began to take form outside the room. Word spread through radio and television of the girl that had been miraculously healed by God.

In a dingy room, sat a boy and girl watching the news. When they saw the girl on television, their mood changed to that of horror. They looked at each other and wondered how she could have lived. They both knew that her living meant she would be able to identify them as her attackers. It would be only a matter of time until they were found and punished, or so they assumed.

Janice was followed by a contingent of family and strangers as she was pushed in a wheelchair to a regular room. Janice had wanted to walk, but the nurse insisted on a wheelchair. Once in the room and alone, Pete exclaimed, "I can't wait any longer, tell us what happened!"

The girl grimaced as she told, at least what she remembered, about the girl whose car had broken down, and the beatings. Her face returned to calm as she told of the dream. Pete asked, "Was it Lucifer?"

"I'm not sure, but I feel it was. Whomever it is, I have to trust him. He has something of mine that's very precious." She placed a hand on her stomach and knowingly smiled. They all watched, unsure of the cause of her sudden contentment. Whatever brought the contentment, it was accepted and welcomed. They all knew she would tell them what she had meant when the time was right. No one wanted to push the girl after all she had endured. They were too grateful to have Janice back and alive.

Chapter 4

A car traveled slowly as if looking for something until it finally stopped in front of the house at 2215 Credence. A tall woman with auburn hair exited the car and walked up the concrete walkway. Legs too long for her frame, only accentuated her beauty. The pale business suit was expensive, but not extravagant.

Pete and Janice, sitting on the porch swing, recognized the doctor as soon as she stepped from the car. Janice waved excitedly, yet wondered why she had come. Janice thought she already knew the answer to her own question. The friendly voice of the doctor asked, "How is my favorite patient, these days?"

"About as well as can be expected." Janice said as they both laughed at her mocking the classic doctor's phrase.

Pete stood and asked, "Care for some lemonade, doctor?"

She corrected, "Call me Amanda and yes, some lemonade would be nice."

Janice smiled at the boy she loved as they shared a

knowing look. He had anticipated they might want to talk alone. "Three lemonades coming up," he said cheerfully as he disappeared into the house.

The girl was sure that she knew the reason for Amanda's visit. She thought of the doctor as a friend and wanted to save her the time and trouble of asking awkward questions. Janice said, "You want to know what happened to me. You're searching for an explanation to the miracle."

Amanda said as her cheeks turned red with embarrassment, "Yes, and thank you for saving me the embarrassment of having to ask. That's only part of the reason I came, not that the miraculous healing isn't enough." The doctor handed Janice the latest edition of the local paper.

The girl looked curiously at the paper, back at the doctor, and asked "What am I suppose to be looking for? I don't see anything unusual."

Amanda's laugh was soft, befitting her features. She said, "I'm sorry for laughing, but that's just my point. There is nothing in the newspaper or on the news. Last week you were the talk of the town. Everyday you were front-page news. Suddenly, today, no one remembers a thing. When I mention your name to the hospital staff, they only look at me oddly as if confused about something. Now that I'm here, you and your boyfriend seem to remember everything and I surely remember. I was beginning to believe it had all been an hallucination."

This time it was Janice's turn to laugh. She said, "I'm sorry for laughing, but sometimes we have to or else we might lose our sanity. I think it's time to tell you my story."

Pete returned, as if on cue, with the lemonade. Janice's look turned serious and asked, "Do you think you can believe in something much more incredible than what happened at the hospital?"

The doctor looked stupefied at the girl and replied, "I don't see how anything could be more amazing than that." Amanda pulled one of the porch chairs closer and sat down. She said without prejudice, "After this past week, I think I can believe anything."

Two glasses of lemonade later, Amanda still sat on the porch with the young couple. She looked into her nearly empty glass and asked, "There is still one thing I don't quite understand. Who was responsible for your accident last week?"

A gruff voice startled them as it said, "I would like to know the answer to that, myself."

They looked around to see Detective Johnson standing on the steps. Pete whispered to Janice, "He's the detective that was investigating your… err…accident."

Amanda looked at the bedraggled detective and asked, "How long have you been standing there?"

"Long enough to double my list of questions," he assuredly said. He unexpectedly laughed and added, "It's a habit of the job—sorry."

He climbed the rest of the steps and confronted the trio on the porch. He pulled up a chair, sat down, and leaned to rest his forearms on his legs. He opened a large hairy hand and dangled a small, gold cross by a broken chain from his large fingers. He looked directly at Janice and asked, "Does this belong to you?"

The day after her ordeal in the park, she had removed her cross necklace and tossed it in the nightstand drawer in her bedroom. She unambiguously replied, "No." She hesitated and asked, "Why do you think it belongs to me?"

He dropped the necklace into the side pocket of his tweed sport jacket and replied, "I found it in your car the day of the accident." His hands moved oddly as if by habit, like they should have been holding something, and he asked, "Were either of your assailants wearing the necklace?"

Amanda caustically said, "Enough of this, she doesn't need to relive that night."

Janice placed a calming hand on the doctor's arm and said to the detective, "I never saw a cross, only satanic symbols."

He reached in his pocket and pulled out a new notepad, it felt strange in his hands. He then noticed the newspaper that Amanda had brought. He pointed to it, rubbed a face weary from too long without sleep, and asked, "Just explain that and my life will be complete." The three friends smiled at him.

Amanda looked at the detective and said, "I came here for the same reason, to find out why everyone has forgotten the past week… well, everyone, it seems, except the four of us sitting on this porch."

Pete added, "Mine and Janice's dads remember as well. "

Janice explained. "It seems that only a few have the ability to see some truth without a lot of practice. There is an added fact as to who can see." She paused, unsure of how to say what she wanted, and then asked, "Are either of you Christian?"

Alan and Amanda slightly blushed, as was habit when being asked that question. Their reply often caused people to withdraw from them as if they carried a plague. In much of the country, if you weren't Christian, you became an outcast. The newcomers to the porch normally refused to answer the question, but in this case, Amanda replied, "I'm not." The detective shook his head, indicating he also wasn't.

"Why would that make a difference?" The detective asked.

Once again, she recounted the story of the meeting with Lucifer and the events thereafter. The detective was dubious of the story, but had no alternative explanation, other than his being insane. He quizzically asked, "So, we're the only ones that remember the past week?" Unbelieving of his own words, he continued, "To the rest of the world the past week didn't exist? I went to the file room this morning and all the files for last week are gone, at least the ones pertaining to your case. Even the notebook in my own pocket. It's not as if the dates were changed, but there is an entire week missing and no one seems to notice."

Janice stood and moved to where the detective sat wringing his hands. She knelt, held his large hands in her own, and said, "Something happens to trigger this ability in us.

When this happens, we begin to see the reality of the world around us, not the altered state created by..." Unsure of how to continue, she said, "Whoever it is that controls things, here." She searched her thoughts for something more that might help her explain, and said, "Not being a Christian has some affect on the ability. I believe that once you see the truth, there is no turning back."

Detective Johnson looked questioningly at her and asked, "Is it possible that it's God that gives us this ability?"

Janice replied as her stomach knotted, "I'm not sure. I wish I knew. Lucifer, and the old man in my dreams talk a lot, but they never really tell me anything concrete. As far as I can understand, there are three entities: Iam, Lucifer and the old man in my dreams. Maybe the old man is the creator, but no god as we know it. It's all, really, conjecture at this point."

Alan curiously asked, "How many are there of us... I mean, that can see this reality thing?"

Janice replied, "As far as we know, at the moment, it's the four of us, mine and Pete's dad, and Chandler." Sadness filled her eyes and she added, "My mother is lost to the forces that control us—she is the enemy."

"The old bum that lives in the church?" The detective asked.

Janice grimaced and said, "No. Our friend that lives out in the old church."

Detective Alan Johnson apologetically said, "I've heard some of the tales the bum... uh," he sensitively corrected, "the man has been telling. Everyone at the station thought he was insane."

The doctor dourly said, "I wish we were all insane. Insanity can be treated."

Weary from the events of the past week, the detective asked Janice, "How could you endure so much and still be so positive? "

She looked at him with resolve in her eyes and said, "I didn't endure anything. I've lived only by the grace of Lucifer or some other deity. I'm not sure if some entity kept me alive for a good reason, or so that I can be punished even more. I endure because I am given no other choice. I should have died that day in the park, or at the garage."

They all stared sympathetically at the girl and could say nothing. Pete squeezed her hand, offering comfort, and after a long pause, said, "For whatever reason you survived, I'm selfishly grateful to whatever force that helped."

With a large smile, she quickly kissed him on the lips and said, "I desperately need you."

With conversation exhausted, Alan and Amanda said their goodbyes and left Credence Drive.

Glasses and dirty dishes clinked together as the busboy cleaned off tables around the couple. The restaurant was small, but maintained an elegant flair. The woman smiled at the man sitting across from her and asked, "Do you come here often?"

He blushed, which added a boyish look to his face, and

confessed, "Nope. Never been here before. I'm guilty as charged of trying to impress the doctor."

Amanda's friendly laugh set the detective at ease. She said, "Detective, this is far better than the places where I usually eat. There is a bar a block from the hospital with the best chili dogs you have ever eaten."

He laughed at her remarks. He wasn't sure if she said that to be kind, or as the truth. Either way, it made him more attracted to the woman he had met under unusual circumstances. "Call me Alan," he said in the sure voice that was his manner.

"You may call me Amanda," she pleasantly said. The woman looked at the menu, and then over it to Alan. She asked, "Would you be insulted if I asked why you asked me out tonight?"

The red tone of the blush to his cheeks was almost becoming a fixture on his face that evening. He replied, "You're an attractive woman and we have been... sort of tossed together in a mystery."

It was her time to blush. She said with a smile, "Thank you for the compliment. You're attractive in your own way." Alan rolled his eyes and laughed while she blushed. She stammered as she realized how her words had sounded and added, "I did mean that in a good way. I find you ruggedly handsome."

He smiled brightly and said, "Then I'll take it in a good way."

She looked at him curiously, laid the menu on the table,

107

and asked, "Did Alan ask me here, or was it Detective Johnson?"

He sat up straighter, looked at her, and honestly replied. "Alan asked you here, but I admit the detective is never far away. You or the kids are not part of any formal investigation."

"Tell me about the informal investigation," she earnestly inquired.

When he smiled, one corner of his mouth curled slightly upward. He asked, "Yes, what about it? What about our informal investigation?" They smiled conspiratorially at one another.

He sat drinking bourbon while searching for the right words to his question. Alan asked, "Who do you think is the evil entity?"

Unprepared for his question, she set her glass of wine on the table and confidently replied, "I saw what happened to Janice with my own eyes. I saw something incredible happen to that girl. She believes Lucifer was the one that healed her. I have no reason to doubt anything she says, no matter how insane it might sound." Taking a sip of red wine, she asked, "You were the one that found the cross in her ditched car. What might that mean?"

"Janice also said there were satanic symbols in the place where she was held," he replied, and added. "We also know that whomever the evil force is, he is a master of deception. I don't think we can take anything for granted."

She asked in despair, "What can we do to help her?"

The plastic baggy suddenly appeared from his pocket, as if on cue. In it was the greasy rag that had been used to gag Janice. It still contained the bile and blood from the girl. He asked, "Could you test this to find out if this is Janice's blood? I found it under the seat of her car."

She looked sadly at the rag and replied, "I can, but I don't think there's any need."

"Nor do I. I just want to have it on my list of tangible facts, of which there are so few in this case," he said. Alan paused and asked as the bag slipped back into his pocket and out of view, "You up for a ride, tonight?"

"Where to?" She curiously asked.

He said, "I did a little research today after I left the rest of you. In the area where the car was found, there is only one garage. I'd be willing to bet that's where Janice was held."

She cynically asked, "A week's worth of knowledge was erased to cover this up. You really think there will be physical evidence in the garage where she was held?"

He smirked and replied, "Maybe even deities make mistakes." This brought a small, uneasy laughter from them both, something they badly needed.

The rest of dinner centered on small talk. The unlikely couple found they shared several common interests. Amanda was delighted to find the detective had read Atlas Shrugged. They also had failed marriages and few worthwhile relationships in common. Their jobs occupied so much of their time that few would stay with them for long.

After leaving the restaurant, they talked about what had

happened to Janice. They simultaneously agreed to find the place where she had been held.

The moon had waned to a thin sliver in the Western sky. The detective kept referring to his new notepad as he made turns. They saw a light ahead and he slowed the car. There was a broken sign that blinked, in part, due to a failing fluorescent light. In faded letters the sign read, Joe's Garage, 24-Hour Towing.

Alan parked the car on the roadside far enough from the garage that it couldn't be easily seen. The couple walked cautiously up the road's shoulder and down the drive to the garage, keeping to the shadows when possible. There was a light in a window with heavy metal blaring from a stereo inside.

They eased their way to a window that was slightly open, which gave them a clear view inside. Leaning into the engine compartment of a car was a slim man with no shirt. Nearby on a car-seat that had been ripped from some derelict car, sat a girl with short black hair. She was smoking something that was obviously, by the smell, marijuana. The music ended and the sound was replaced by the girl's voice. She said. "Will you please hurry up? I've got to get to work."

Alan's finger motioned for the doctor to follow. They worked their way silently around back of the building. They found another open window and peered into the dark room. Alan pulled a penlight from his pocket. A beam of light sliced through the darkness to produce a narrow tunnel through the inkiness. The room appeared to be for storage. Along the walls, boxes were stacked nearly to the ceiling. The narrow beam of the flashlight steadied on one of the boxes and revealed its contents. The boxes contained car stereos, so many, they were surely stolen. This would provide the detective an opportunity to return in a professional capacity to search more thoroughly.

Alan noticed something on the floor in the center of the room. He eased the window all the way up and raised his left leg. Amanda asked in a nervous whisper, "What do you think you're doing?"

"I have to get a closer look at something. I'll explain later," he replied

The man found the doctor's gentle hand on his rear pleasing as she helped push him through the window. He fell to the concrete floor with a thud that jarred him viciously. Alan crawled to the center of the room, saw four scuff marks, and around them stains of some unknown origins. Several of the spots were obvious to his trained eye. Even in the dim light he could see they were blood. Alan froze when he heard a sound at the door. "I want you to make a delivery when you go to town," the man said to the girl.

She angrily said from a distance, "I don't have time for deliveries. I'm late for work as it is." The doorknob clicked and a sliver of light appeared along the door edge. The detective tensed and readied himself for action. Experience told him it was better to remain frozen in place, even if exposed, since it was better than risking being heard.

The girl angrily shouted, "If you have my car fixed, I'm

leaving." At the sound of the car starting, the door clicked shut. Alan wasted no time scrambling back to, and through the window. When his feet were planted firmly on the ground, he motioned for Amanda to follow. They waited out of sight at the corner of the garage as the Camaro pulled away. They ran quickly to Alan's car. Once in the car, Amanda asked, "What are we going to do?"

Alan started the engine and replied, "Right now, we're going to follow that girl. It will be easier to make her talk than the boy." Illuminated only by the dim light of the car's dash, Amanda nodded in silent agreement.

Brightly colored lights invaded their senses as they watched the Camaro pull into a fast food restaurant. The girl parked in front of a sign that read, Associate Of The Month.

They sat in the car as far away as possible while still having a good view inside the restaurant. They lost sight of her until fifteen minutes later when she reappeared in the drive-thru window wearing an orange and yellow uniform. Alan smiled at the doctor and said, "I think its time we got something to eat." Amanda didn't return the smile—she shuddered at the thought of food from this place.

The smell of hamburgers drifted through the open window of the drive-thru and invaded the car. The girl was polite as she handed them their bag of food and change. They parked, the doctor looked wryly at the detective, and asked, "You eat here often?"

He laughed and replied, "At least once a week." She rolled her eyes, unsure if he was jesting or not.

Amanda quizzically asked, "What are we going to do when she comes out?"

"I'm not sure. I won't know that until she comes out," he replied

At fifteen past midnight, the girl exited the restaurant. Alan and Amanda exited the car and walked briskly to stand between the girl and her car. Alan wasn't happy about confronting her in the open, but he didn't want to risk letting her get away. He said in a professional voice as he pulled out his badge and flashed it to the girl, "Miss, I'd like to talk to you for a moment."

Fear flashed in the girl's eyes as she looked to her car, which was impossible to reach without being caught. To her right was thick protective shrubbery bordering the restaurant. She relented, stood motionless, and waited for the detective to approach. Alan said, "I'm Detective Alan Johnson. I would like to talk to you about…"

The girl interrupted and said in a panic, "I had nothing to do with the stereos. Those are Mark's… my boyfriend's."

Amanda and Alan smiled at each other, both glad for the free information. Not wanting to show how little he knew, the detective said as he pulled the new notebook from his pocket and consulted a blank page, "I know about the stereos. We will get back to those later. I'm more interested in what may have happened at your boyfriend's garage a week ago.

The girl fully panicked and bolted. She tried to run in a wide arc around the detective to her car, but he was too quick. He caught her just as her hand touched the Camaro's door handle. The girl looked at the detective and then to Amanda. Bordering on hysterics, she said, "I can't remember. Who are you? Have you come to hurt me? Please don't kill me!"

Amanda tenderly touched the girl's arm, looked at her as a mother might, and said, "I'm a doctor. I'm not here to arrest you or to bring you harm. We just want to find out the truth of what happened at your boyfriend's garage that night."

Alan interjected, "No one is going to hurt you. We just want to know what happened. I can put you in protective custody, if you like. We have safe houses for situations like this."

The girl looked incredulously up at the detective and laughed, "You can't protect me. He was there and then he was gone. He is everywhere. No man can protect me from the devil."

Amanda placed a hand on the detective's shoulder, as much to steady herself as to offer him comfort. The two shared looks, unsure of what they had heard. The doctor asked, "You saw the devil?"

The girl hesitantly replied, "Sort of. Something was there the night I took the girl to the garage. I could tell it was evil. I still have nightmares about the things that Mark did to that girl. He has a temper, but I've never seen him like that, before."

Alan interrupted, "You helped him lure her there?"

"I was scared of what Mark might do. He was all weirded

114

out—yunno?" She said as tears began to crawl down her cheeks. She looked at the two of them and fearfully asked, "Am I going to jail?"

"Not if you tell us all you know and agree to testify about the stereos," he truthfully said. The girl wasn't aware that the detective was the only person on the force who remembered Janice's attack. With no memory of the incident, they would have thought it strange if he brought in a suspect on that case.

A hand rubbed tears from her red eyes and the girl said, "I've told you all I know—well, there is one thing more. This is what really freaks me out. Mark doesn't remember a thing about that night. That night the storage room was empty except for a lamp and a chair. I never saw anyone remove the stereos. The next day, they were all stacked exactly as they had been before this happened." She looked at Amanda and said, "You're the doctor that treated that girl. You're the one that saw her become, well, you know, instantly healed. It was huge news and now no one remembers anything about it, at least not until the two of you showed up."

Not wanting to give too much information, Amanda said, "Some people seem to see the truth while others don't."

"Are there satanic symbols on the wall of the storage room?" Alan asked.

Fear of the detective was easing and she eagerly replied, "Mark joined this group about a year ago. They used to hold meetings in the storage room. They drew a lot of strange symbols on the walls. Most I don't understand. They called themselves Satan's Sorcerers."

Large fingers pulled the cross necklace from his pocket and asked, "Does this belong to you? It was found in the car with the girl."

Her small face screwed into a twist of total confusion and replied, "Mark was wearing it that night. I've never seen him wear a cross, or anything Christian for that matter. As I just told you, Mark's a Satanist, so wearing the cross was totally out of character for him."

Small pleading eyes looked up at the detective and asked, "Can I go home? Mark gets really upset if I'm late coming home from work."

A question was forming on his lips when Amanda grasped his arm to gain his attention. Alan decided there was no need for further questions and said, "You may go." He handed her his card and added, "Call me at the station tomorrow so we can talk about the stereos."

Alan asked as he watched the girl pull away, "I don't get this. If God is behind this, why would he have this kind of control over a Satanist?"

After mulling over the question, Amanda replied, "To be a Satanist, one must have a strong belief in God, at least that's true for some forms of satanism."

Four hours after returning home, the ringing phone roused Alan from a restless sleep. He drowsily reached for the phone and knocked it to the floor. His hand groped around in the morning light until it found the fallen object. "Hello," he said in a sleep induced raspy voice. The voice on the other end spoke for only a moment. He ended the call and asked himself, "Why do people have to get killed so early in the morning?"

Directions given by the station sent him past the church where Chandler Baptiste lived. He had taken this same route that fateful morning—the morning that introduced him to the event that forever changed his life. That was the morning when he first met Janice as she was hurried away on a gurney. At that memory, a pain tore at his heart. That morning, Janice had been a stranger, but now she had become someone he loved as much as if she was his own daughter. Few people have an instant affect on Alan, but Janice was surely one of the exceptions.

A smile formed when he thought of the other person to whom he had been introduced because of that event, Amanda. The detective was quickly falling in love with the beautiful, intelligent woman. It was hard to believe that a beautiful doctor could have any feelings for him, but this was a reality he had no trouble facing. The look he sometimes saw in her eyes told him that she cared for him with great affection. Only time would tell them both if those feelings could endure a lifetime, especially the one they both, now, faced.

Alan saw the flashing lights of his coworkers' cruisers. The flesh on his arm began to tingle with advance warning. The scene set off every warning bell in his internal, professional alarm system. The scene was at the exact spot where Janice had been found. He knew that whatever awaited him held a message—a warning.

Barricade tape surrounded an area as if protecting the corpse from further harassment. Yellow warning barricade tape shifted in the morning breeze as if waving to cars that slowly crept past as people strained to see what grotesqueness lay beyond. While strangers begged for the view, the detective wanted to be anywhere else on the planet, or anywhere that would keep him from that waving barricade.

Expectations came to be realized when he stepped over the barricade and saw the small form that laid crumpled in the ditch. Her facial features had been battered beyond recognition. The orange and yellow uniform and the short black hair told him her identity. Detective Johnson had made a critical error the night before, he had allowed the girl to return home. His mistake had caused her to pay the ultimate price—her life.

The distraught detective gathered his composure, wiped away the tear that had formed in the corner of his eye, and went to work. Lying next to the girl was a golden object reflecting the morning light. He knew what it was before he was close enough to grasp it with latex covered fingers. He placed it in a protective baggy in hopes of preserving any secrets the cross might hold. The detective knew there would be no clues. The only message anyone would find at this scene would be the one already discovered, the dead girl. The corpse was the message that told him his enemy was ruthless.

He knelt beside the corpse and thought of Janice. This had been the fate meant for her that night. Only with the intervention of some force he couldn't fathom, was she still alive. For the first time in his life, he felt hopeless. Alan knew the killer's identity, but also knew man-made law could never bring him to justice.

Chapter 5

Delores bowed her head and silently prayed. This only infuriated the boy and he pushed her backwards. The attacker was aware of the trouble he could be in if she was hurt. He grabbed for Delores as she fell backward. His desperate hand caught only her blouse. The material easily ripped as the pious girl crashed to the ground. It took moments before she saw the enormity of what had happened. Her blouse had torn open to expose the plain white bra that covered her breasts, but did little for her modesty. The chorus of laughter from the group of boys was even worse.

A strong voice rose above the laughter and angrily asked, "What are you people doing?" The group, having had their fun, retreated without a fight. They were the type that only preyed on the weak, and avoided the strong. The boy took off his shirt and wrapped it protectively around the girl. He helped Delores to her feet and asked, "Are you hurt?"

His shirt covering her brought back a certain amount of

lost modesty. She shyly replied, "I think I'm okay. I was just scared—I guess."

That was the first time Delores met Martin. It was the next year before he asked her for a date. He had kept his distance because of her religious extremes. After the day of her rescue, she never let him stray far from her thoughts.

Her friends begged that she temper her beliefs if she wanted to see more of Martin. She eventually relented and her friends had been proven correct. Martin began to notice the girl he had given comfort to the previous year. Delores smiled brightly when Martin was around. Her friends began to notice the change in Delores and were happy for the girl.

A week after graduation, they were married. That's when things began to change for the worse. Delores dropped all pretenses and reverted to her true pious self. She had won her trophy and found no further need to hide her true feelings. The woman began pushing Martin to believe as she did, but to no avail. Their love remained intact, while its bonds were strained to the point of breaking.

When Janice was born, this brought the couple closer together. Martin capitulated and went to church for the baby's christening. Delores beamed from having her husband at her side in church. Until that moment, he had never gone with her to any form of church service.

No one other than Martin seemed to be disturbed by the baby's constant wailing. Janice screamed in terror as the minister performed the ceremony. The father wanted to take his daughter into his arms and rush her from the church.

Martin hated himself as he stood, watched, and listened as his daughter went through some unseen torment.

After Janice's fateful meeting with Lucifer, Delores began to sink deeper into her faith. Delores skulked around the house as if in a thrall. She continuously saw demons at every turn. She heard the family that she loved, whispering when she entered the room. God was constantly talking to her, telling her to wait and she would soon be able to free the house of the evil within. Delores had not been in Janice's room in weeks. She felt something evil inside, so she dared not enter.

The odor of fragrant herbs filled the kitchen as Delores cooked spaghetti, her family's favorite. God had told her this would be a special dinner. She had invited all of Janice and Martin's new friends. The detective and the doctor called and said they would be coming a few minutes late. They were going to go by and pick up the vagrant minister. She hated that man for what he had done to a once thriving church. He had taken a house of worship and turned it into a pit of demon wine.

Small explosions of intense heat and steam rolled out of the pot. She stirred the pasta that twisted uncontrollably inside the pot. It tumbled and screamed as if tormented by the water. Her vision shifted and she saw her family and their friends in the rolling water. Delores laughed aloud as she heard their pleas for help. She used the large, wooden spoon and swatted her husband as he boiled alive inside the pot.

The group of family and friends were seated around the table, eating, laughing, and telling jokes. Delores stood to the side with her hands knotted in the pockets of her apron. Laughter was suddenly replaced by the sound of a crashing plate as Janice knocked hers to the floor while clutching her stomach. Martin leapt to his feet, but nearly collapsed as the world spun helplessly around him. In the next second, the dinner guests were vomiting and lying on the floor. What had been a happy dinner, had turned into a death scene. Delores stood and watched calmly as her family writhed painfully on the floor. She watched as life slowly escaped from the family she had loved.

Janice looked knowingly at her mother and pleaded through unbearable pain, "Why mother... why?"

The mother looked at her daughter and replied, "I had to free you from the evil that has bound itself in you. God loves you and will take care of you, honey." The room quickly became quiet, the poison had been as potent as God had promised.

Martin walked into the kitchen, sniffed the air, and said, "This smells delicious, Delores—I'm starved."

Delores trembled as she was torn loose from the hypnotic whirl of pasta and joyously said, "I'm sure you will love it, dear. It's a special, new recipe I found."

The sound of a car outside brought Janice bolting down the stairs. She opened the front door to see Alan, Amanda, and Chandler coming up the walkway. The girl beamed at seeing her new friends again, especially on an occasion that had no looming evil. She pushed open the storm door and said, "From the smell coming from the kitchen, I would say you're just in time."

A home cooked meal was a rare treat for the three friends and they were ecstatic at the opportunity. Chandler smiled brightly and said, "I hope you have plenty, I'm starving. The can food I normally eat serves the purpose of keeping me alive, but it does little for my spirit." Alan and Amanda laughed with their friend because their diet wasn't so different.

A finger pointed to the cupboard containing the best dinnerware and Delores asked, "Would you set the table, Martin?"

He kissed his wife on the cheek from behind as he reached over her to gather the needed dinnerware. Martin left her alone in the kitchen as he went off to set the table. Delores looked around conspiratorially and pulled a vial from her apron pocket. She sniffed the contents and twisted her face at the acrid odor wafting from the bottle's contents. The liquid made a black pool in the center of the red sauce. She stirred the pool, twisting and tearing it until it disappeared into the sauce. With large mittens on her hands, she lifted the pot and poured the contents into a serving bowl.

Salad and pasta quickly followed the sauce to the waiting group of hungry people in the dining room. Martin held a chair for Delores as the wife took a seat. Chandler smiled at Delores and said, "Thank you so much for inviting me on this wonderful night. You have made me feel so welcome."

Amanda, Alan, Frank, and Pete chimed in with thanks.

The mother's smile was overly warm as she said, "Oh no, it's my pleasure, I'm sure." She stood and said reverently, "Let us thank the Lord for these blessings—let's pray." All of Delores' prayers went on longer than expected.

Chandler watched the woman pray and at times thought the prayer was more suited for a funeral than for the blessing of food. He conceded that she was a far-reaching fundamentalist and let it pass. He felt those people often found the worst in things and decided dinner would be no different. By the time she finished, the guests were squirming in their seats.

The kitchen cabinet swung open as the can of vegetable soup that had sat perilously on the edge, teetered and fell. The can hit solidly on the counter-top, but the sound went unnoticed in the adjoining dining room. A roll of paper towels was shaken from its holder by the vibrations created from the falling can. The can rolled along until it collided with the toaster, which spun and tipped over onto the stove where it connected with the burner control. The impact twisted the knob to the high position. The impact changed the trajectory of the rolling can. It rolled quickly toward the counter's edge. Just as the can neared the edge, it clipped the roll of paper towels, sending it sliding sideways. The can crashed to the floor just as the roll of paper towels came to a rest on the blazing burner.

A fork twisted with pasta paused at his mouth. His

youthful nose sniffed and caught a scent other than the spicy spaghetti. He looked at the pasta and sniffed. Pete turned and looked to his right toward the kitchen door. He saw smoke rolling from the crack along the bottom edge of the door. Pete jumped up and jarred the table hard enough for the bowl of sauce to slide near the edge of the table. For a second, it lingered precariously on the edge and suddenly crashed to the floor as Martin, who sat at the end facing the kitchen, jumped to his feet and once more jarred the table. Pete's words echoed alarmingly throughout the room. He screamed, "FIRE!"

All except Delores jumped to their feet and rushed to the kitchen. Martin was the first to reach the door. He pushed it open, only to be faced with a wall of impenetrable smoke. Through the thick acrid smoke, a bright orange glare could be seen in the direction of the stove.

Alan used his cell phone to call the fire department as Amanda began pushing people toward and out the front door. Martin had to almost carry Delores from the house. She was still sitting at the dining table staring at the sauce splattered on the floor. The mess created by the red sauce wasn't in her thoughts. Her only thought was that she had failed God.

It took only minutes for the fire department to extinguish the flames. One of the firemen turned to leave the kitchen and his foot struck something on the floor. He looked down and picked up the object. He placed the can of vegetable soup back into the slightly charred cabinet from which it had fallen.

While they all stood on the lawn, the fire chief explained to them that the damage was minor. He also explained how a stove burner had been left on and a roll of paper towels had fallen onto the flame.

They entered the house and saw the chaos they had unwittingly created. The spaghetti and sauce lay like a dead, bleeding animal spread over the hardwood floor. Janice took a hand-towel, squatted, and began cleaning the mess on the floor as the men headed for the kitchen.

No one noticed as Delores nearly knocked her daughter over to prevent Janice from cleaning the mess. The mother knew that if only one of them died, there would be an investigation and the poison would be discovered. The poison would have simulated food poisoning, so only one death would have raised suspicions. Her god had been clear with his instructions, it was to be all or none.

Delores feigned an apologetic attitude, helped her daughter up, and said, "I can take care of this, dear. I don't want you to get your clothes stained by the tomato sauce." She then proceeded to clean the floor.

They stood in the kitchen as Delores cleaned the dining room floor. The cabinets directly over the stove were charred, but easily repairable. There had been a lot of smoke damage, but that was the worst. Alan put a comforting hand on Martin's shoulder and said, "You were lucky, my friend, it could have been a lot worse."

He smiled, more from Alan thinking of him as a friend,

than from the kind comment. He thankfully said, "Yes, I think we were lucky, tonight. "

Janice and Pete sat on the porch as the others began ventilating the house and spraying deodorizers. Although the young couple had begged to help, they were banished to the porch. The boy asked Janice, "Do you think there was anything suspicious about the fire?"

She thoughtfully answered, "I don't think so. It seemed to be just an accident, but it's not like mom to leave a burner on."

He hesitantly asked, "Did Mrs. Carter seem okay to you?"

Janice looked at her best friend and replied, "She has seemed distant, lately. I thought it was just something toward me since I stopped going to church. Earlier in the evening, mom acted more normal than she has in a while, but just before the fire, her mood seemed to change. It was odd that she wasn't in the kitchen as soon as the fire was out, taking charge, and leading the cleaning. Instead, she seemed obsessed with cleaning up the spilled spaghetti sauce. When I tried to clean up the sauce, she angrily chased me away as if I had been the one to cause the spill."

"Do you know where she went?" Asked Pete.

"I think she's in her room," Janice replied.

"Shouldn't you check on her to make sure she's alright?" He asked.

The girl knowingly said, "She's probably praying. The way

she has been lately, I don't think it would be a good idea to disturb her."

The pious mother slipped away, unnoticed, to her room after dumping the spaghetti remains in the outside garbage can. No one would notice, later, as the raccoon pulled the top from the garbage can and ate a portion of the discarded sauce. No one saw as it staggered off to the nearby woods and vomited until there was nothing left except blood to rise in the bile. Before sunrise, the raccoon was dead.

Delores knelt, lit candles, and prayed to Iam for forgiveness. She had failed to do his bidding this night. For her failure, she must be punished. The pious woman could wait for Iam do the punishing, but he had standing instruction for failure.

Under her makeshift shrine, similar to the one that had been in Janice's room, was the object of her punishment. The knife felt comfortable in her hand as she took it from the shelf. Delores held the knife up to see it in the dim light of the candles. Its blade reflected the light eerily across her face. The woman had a look of purpose and determination as she held out her right palm and pressed the knife into flesh. She slid the knife and grimaced at the welcomed pain as it slashed through her hand. Delores dropped the knife to the floor, took the apron she was wearing, and wrapped it firmly around her hand to stem the flow of blood. She prayed most of the night until sleep eventually reduced her to a fallen heap on he floor. The well-used candles burned until there was no wax left to hold the remaining wick. The charred wick fell over and flickered out as it collapsed into molten wax.

Asleep on the floor, Delores' dreams took her to a distant place. She stood with Iam before a cave opening. He called out to the ones waiting inside the cave and commanded, "Ride free onto the Earth—I set you free." With that, a rider on a white horse rode from the shadows of the cave. In his hand was a bow. Iam gave to the rider a crown and said to the rider, "Go and make war on the lands."

The first rider called back into the cave, and out from the darkness came a rider on a fiery red horse. In his hand he held a sword. Iam said to the rider, "Go and take the peace and make man slay one another."

The second rider called back into the cave and from within came a man on a black horse. He brought with him the scales of famine and hunger. Iam said unto him, "Take care of the oil."

The third rider called back into the cave and from the cave came a rider on a pale horse. His name was death. Iam told him to go into the world and spread the plague.

The four horsemen stood beside each other as if they had known each other for an eternity. They looked knowingly at each other and then rode off to all four points of the compass. They did not look back at each other, but only toward their destinations and their mission.

In southern China, a young soldier received a surprising, but deserved increase in rank. All his comrades loved this man. As he received those stripes, he could have sworn there was a man on a white horse watching in the distance. The rider smiled at him and the young man knew what he was supposed to do with his new found power. The cold, deadly eyes of the rider told him how he was to form an army and conquer all of China, and then a quarter of the world.

Long before that point in time, the horseman had been called king while he rode his horse, commanding giant armies of tanks, and other mechanical might. Many times he had been visited upon the lands. All those visits had only been preparation for what lay ahead.

That night the Chinese commander began recruiting soldiers and by weeks end, he had a force of ten thousand men. Each day thereafter the number would double. His rise in power was so sudden that none in government dared question the authority of this young man.

In New York City an overwhelming majority elected a new United Nations chairman. He addressed rows of diplomats in his native Spanish, which was translated in the ear of those that intently listened. The new chairman spoke of peace, but the only thing those listening could think of, was war. While words of peace filled the room, plans of invasion filled the minds of men. Beside the Chairman was a horseman on a fiery red horse.

The rainy season had begun in the rain forest. The rider on the black horse stopped, raised his arms to the sky, and the rain stopped. It stopped, not only in this forest, but in many places around the world. In less than a week, the blazing sun wilted crops while forests began to wilt and die. Fertile fields turned to dust as rain remained locked in wispy clouds. The clouds looked down at the scorched earth as if mocking.

Curled in a fetal position on the floor, Delores smiled as she saw Iam's retribution for the evils of the world. She smiled at the deaths of a billion of evil humans. The pious woman knew her family would eventually be among those billion, but she didn't feel empathy for them, for they were, as well, sinners. When the horsemen were gone, she turned to kneel before Iam. He took her hand, pulled Delores to her feet, and kissed her on the forehead. She felt the glory of God in that kiss and in it she reveled.

That morning, Delores awakened and looked at the mangled mass of wax that had been her candles. They had burned until there was noting left to support the flame. When the flame died that night, so did the future of mankind. No one knew why Delores' mood had changed, but her family was glad to see that it had changed for the better. She whistled happily as she cooked and cleaned. She smiled cheerfully as the Earth began to die. Despite the vision, Delores had no idea what the future held for the world. She had only glimpsed the evil that had been set forth to plague the Earth.

For all of this to happen, it didn't take an alteration of reality, or a dream from a reverent woman, this was a reality that only a few would see for what it was. The events of the dream were not all new. Delores had seen events set in motion twenty years before, and some only yesterday. It had been several millennia since the Sahara had been a thriving forest instead of the sun blasted desert we see today. Her dreams only showed the culmination of those events.

The news wasn't something Delores often watched on television. This day she turned it on to see how famine was spreading through Africa. She saw how China was slowly reclaiming the lands that it had once ruled. The woman watched as a reporter with pretend sadness, talked of mutated viruses that were resisting the latest antiviral drugs and bacteria that evaded the best antibiotics. The talking head on television went on to tell how tension was high in the Middle East. There were squabbles and skirmishes around the world.

Mankind had always existed on the brink of self-destruction. With modern technology, it was only a matter of time until mankind destroyed itself. A slight push in certain areas could hasten the process. The altered state created by Iam for mankind was on a collision course with reality.

That morning, Janice wept as she looked out the window. The usually neat street was lined with crumbling shacks. Dead bodies lined the streets along with garbage that had spilled into the street after pickup service ended weeks before. Only the brave dared to venture out of their houses. This usually happened only when they brought out the dead for pickup by garbage trucks. People often lined the street begging for extra food as well-kept military trucks brought packages of dehydrated rations.

The smell of sickness and death lingered in air. Farther down the street, she watched as a man beat a woman over a slice of stale, moldy bread. The man took the bread from his beaten mother and rushed to hide in the bushes where he ravished it like an animal in the wild.

A newspaper lay on the dying lawn. It had the picture of a man wearing a silver robe. On his head sat a glowing, golden crown. He promised food and a better life for all. Janice knew this man could return the world to its altered state. She knew that the price would be high, a price that no one would pay if the costs were to be known.

The girl closed her eyes and opened them, expecting the scene to change, but it remained, horribly, the same. She did this once again and then noticed the newspaper had changed. The date was different from the one she had seen moments before. The paper's date indicated this event was weeks away. Janice had seen the future, and not an altered reality. Despair overcame the girl and she fell into a silent, restless sleep.

Lights were low and the atmosphere was romantic as the waiter took their order. The restaurant was formal and upscale. Alan had been in places like this only while doing investigations. He knew the bill would be a week's wages, but the night would be worth the expense. He looked at the woman sitting across from him. Her pale blue evening gown left her slim shoulders bare, but the shawl draped over them left only teasing glimpses.

The night before, he had trembled like a bashful teenager while gathering the nerve to ask this woman out for a real date. They had been out to dinner together in the past, but that was only as friends. He was sure their relationship had developed beyond the friends stage. He, now, wanted to be sure she felt the same way. Her blue eyes sparkled whenever he looked into them. This woman had the intelligence of a philosopher, yet she was as down to earth as an aging cop.

He had decided to ask her out just as he walked her to the door after leaving Janice's house the night of the fire. This would give them the opportunity to escape quickly if the moment proved to be too embarrassing. To his delight, she readily accepted. He tried to hide the excitement, but knew his face was betraying his feelings. She smiled at Alan and kissed him on the cheek. It was all he could do to command his knees to maintain his weight and balance. At that moment, he wanted to take Amanda into his arms and kiss her passionately. Instead, he smiled and strode excitedly to his car.

Amanda said to the detective who sat across the table, "This is a nice place. I hardly ever come to places like this."

He chuckled and said, "I've never been to a place like this."

She looked at him with concern. Not wanting to make him think she looked down on him, Amanda asked, "Would you prefer somewhere else?"

He smiled, blushed, and honestly said, "I would, but in a

lesser place you wouldn't have worn that dress and I wouldn't have seen you as you are."

Amanda waved a long, thin, bare arm at the waiter. When she had him close enough, she hurriedly canceled the order. She took Alan's hand and rushed him quickly through the maze of tables and astounded looks from patrons paying too much for a meal. Out in the street, Alan opened his mouth to apologize for whatever it was he had done. She held a finger over his mouth to quiet him and tugged his hand. She led him down the street until they came to a blinking neon sign that read, Ray's Drinks and Foods.

Everyone stared at the formally clad couple as Amanda found a booth in back and sat down. She looked sheepishly up at Alan and asked, "Well... are you going to sit down?"

Still stunned into silence, he looked at her as she said, "Now you can see me like this and you can also be comfortable. I eat here often when I'm working at the free clinic down the street."

He smiled and knew at that instant he was in love with her and hoped that some day it would be returned. He reached across the table for her hand. Her hands were on the edge of the table and he had to reach uncomfortably far to take one. Amanda extended an arm, offering her hand to him as an acknowledgment of her own feelings toward the slightly older detective.

Alan reined in his emotions and realized that a doctor would never fall for a lowly detective. Those things happened only in movies and trashy romance novels. Real life didn't work the same way. The detective did know she had become a dear and trusted friend, and something inside him knew he could settle for that, but would rather not. Having her in his life was a treasure he wanted—needed.

"A penny for your thoughts?" She asked, truly interested.

Hidden neurons played with the truth as he thought of how to reply. Alan feared that if he spoke, he would tell her how much he loved her. He sat silently and looked at her, trying to find the words that wouldn't chase her from this bar—and from his life. She squeezed his hand, as if reassuring him that she was there and wouldn't run away. He decided on the partial truth and said, "I'm thinking of how beautiful you look sitting there, and I how you might react if a poor cop asked you out again."

Her smile was radiant and warm as her eyes locked on his and said, "Let's finish this date before we plan another."

His heart stopped for what seemed an eternity. His life hung in limbo until she said, "Even though the date isn't planned, I do accept the offer for a next date—that is when you ask me." His smile could have lit the dark side of the moon.

That night they didn't speak of the evil things that had happened. They talked about themselves and their plans for the future. She found out that Alan wrote short stories in his spare time and he found that Amanda liked bowling. The couple found they both shared a love for football. They discovered a myriad of topics on which they agreed. The laughter was harmonious and joyful when it was discovered they had voted the same way in the previous election.

Neither cared they had given up caviar and wine for beer and hot chicken wings. Neither noticed as time slipped away. The couple didn't notice they were dressed differently from the other patrons.

Last call had long passed and the dim lights were slowly brightening. The hint was taken and they left, still talking ecstatically. The talk never slowed as they made their way though traffic to Amanda's house.

Light enveloped the tall, slender frame of the doctor as the interior light of the car shined on her as he opened the door. He took her hand as their eyes locked. As he helped her from the car, he noticed the long lean leg as it momentarily escaped through the slit of her pale-blue gown.

They stood at the door staring at one another like star-struck teens. The earlier enthusiastic conversation had been silenced by the moment. He didn't hesitate as he kissed her fully and confidently on her painted lips.

She reluctantly broke the kiss, lowered her eyes to the purse, and fumbled for the door key. She held them by her manicured fingers and dangled them invitingly to the detective.

He unlocked the door, fumbled for the light switch inside the darkened portal, turned on the lights, and looked at her questioningly, waiting for instructions. She took his hand and led him into her house.

Nothing in the house would make you think it was anything but a woman's. The colors were soft and fragile. The house was single story, not what you might expect from an accomplished doctor.

Amanda went to the mini bar and poured Alan a bourbon on ice. He had shown this preference after dinner in the bar. For herself, she poured a glass of red wine produced at a local winery. She handed him the bourbon, sat on the couch, and crossed her legs, this time giving him a full view of the leg he had earlier only glimpsed.

He breathed deeply and tried to contain his desire as he sat beside the teasing woman. He could feel the heat from her body as he slid in next to her on the couch. The moment he faced her, he kissed her with the pent up passion he had not allowed to surface for years. Amanda didn't resist and gave into him and also released pent up passion.

Morning threatened to break free as he looked at Amanda sleeping beside him in the unfamiliar bed. In the dim light he could see the shoulder that had earlier been hidden by the shawl. His lips touched that bare shoulder and she slightly stirred, but settled back into the steady, rhythmic sleep she had for a moment deserted.

Amanda struggled to remember the dream as she was pulled from sleep while something unfamiliar alerted her senses. She slowly opened her eyes to morning. Familiar, but new eyes looked at her in the twilight of early morning. Even while still in the grip of sleep, she knew the eyes were friendly. Knotted fingers rubbed the sleep from her eyes and saw him clearly. Memories of the night before came rushing back and Amanda smiled at the man she had made love to through most of the night.

The memory of a night that had changed his life forever lingered in his mind as he returned the smile. He said, "Good morning, my love." He thought how good that word felt as it rolled from his tongue.

She twisted so that her mouth found his hairy chest, kissed it, turned her eyes upward to meet his, and said with contentment, "Good morning, my love." She as well found the word easy on her lips.

As much as they would have loved to spend the day together in bed, both knew there was much to be done. Amanda asked, "What's for breakfast?"

He kissed her on the forehead and said as he slid from the bed and put on boxer shorts, "Just show up in the kitchen and be surprised." Before she could protest and confess to joking about breakfast, he had disappeared from the bedroom.

Bacon and eggs invaded Amanda's senses as she sat at the table in her pale-pink, silk robe. She curtly said, "I really can do that, you know."

He glanced quickly to her and said, "So can I." They smiled lovingly at each other.

They knew at that moment that whatever happened to one of them would happen to the other. Overnight their lives had changed, just as the world had subtly changed around them.

Chapter 6

Drip... drip... drip, the sound filled the church as some liquid dropped onto a firm surface, awakening Chandler Baptiste. He rubbed the sleep from his eyes and looked out the window to discover the sun had not yet risen. He cursed the leaking faucet and knew he wouldn't sleep until the sound was silenced. Stiff from a sound sleep, he made his way to the bathroom and subconsciously twisted the spigot handle.

Drip... drip, the sound continued.

His mind awakened enough to realize the sound wasn't near, but coming from down the hall. He listened for rain. The roof sometimes leaked if the wind blew from certain directions. He heard no rain, but another drip.

He smiled at his nervousness and decided the sound had to be coming from the kitchen faucet. He calmly walked down the stained carpeted hall until he reached the kitchen entrance. From that vantage he could tell the sound came from farther down the hall, in the chapel. His hand deftly found the switch for the hall light and turned it on. He walked toward the sound.

At the end of the hall he flipped on the chapel lights and saw something staining the carpet. He eased his way into the chapel, turned the corner, and froze in his tracks. All the things he had seen before paled in comparison to what he saw at this moment. If he had been scared before, it was nothing compared to this moment of terror.

Chandler had removed all religious artifacts from the church except for one. He felt drawn to the reprint of Victor Mikhailovich Vasnetsov's painting of The Four Horsemen of the Apocalypse. The painting hung at the back of the chapel over a hardwood table. Baptiste approached the painting and was overcome with the smell of death and sickness. His first reaction was to run when he saw the source of the dripping sound that had awakened him from sleep and cast the former minister into a world of terror.

Blood dripped from the point of the sword, which the horseman on the fiery red horse held. It dripped from the sword, ran in a stream to bodies lying on the ground, out of the painting, and onto the hardwood table—from there, onto the faded red carpet.

The figure on the white horse turned to look at Chandler and said, "Come preacher, ride with us as we do your Lord's work."

The distraught former minister shouted, "I'll go nowhere with you. I no longer serve that master."

The man on he white horse, his mouth wide with

amusement, asked, "Preacher, are you sure which Lord you serve?"

No argument could be found for what the creature asked. The horseman was accurate, he wasn't sure which Lord he served, if any. Since meeting Janice, it seemed he followed Lucifer.

All of the horsemen laughed as the rider on the white horse said, "Then you are more the fool than the rest of your humanity. You will die and rot as will the others who forsake our master."

Chandler seized the opportunity for truth and asked, "Who is your master?"

The horseman laughed at the mortal man, mocked his ignorance, and asked, "You still have to ask? That disappoints our master."

An ethereal hand grasped Chandler by the waistband of his boxer shorts and tossed him into the world of war, hunger, illness, and despair. The former minister was stunned to see he was no longer in the abandoned church, but in the world of the horsemen. This world could have been some distant alien planet or Earth in the near future. In times past, he might have prayed that it wasn't the latter. Chandler asked, not expecting a truthful answer from such a beast, yet he asked, "Is this Earth."

The horsemen looked to one another while the bowman wearing the crown given to him by Iam proudly said, "This is a thousand worlds we have taken as our own. This is your world as you will soon see it, that is, if you live long enough.

Maybe Lucifer will give you a glimpse of the horrors you have placed upon the lands as you burn in Hell."

A shudder ran through Chandler, but he wasn't sure if it was from the suggestion of an impending death for himself, or that the world would soon be in the hands of the horseman. His voice was stronger than his body and mind. He asked, "When will you be set upon the Earth?"

Evil laughter filled the decaying world in which the man stood. The four of them laughed as the bowman said, "Look to the scales of the rider on the black horse. The scales are no longer balanced. They have tipped toward your world." His lean muscular arm waved to the decay and sickness around them and continued, "Your kind has made this world. We just come to admire and continue your work." He smiled wickedly and added, "Mankind has learned so much from us in the past. "

Chandler angrily yelled, "Return to the hell from which you came."

The demon roared with laughter and haughtily said, "Define Hell, mortal. You may very well find Hell on this fragile world you call Earth." The bowman hesitated, looked entranced with the man, and continued, "In times past, mankind managed to throw a worthy opponent at me. If you are all that mankind has fighting for itself, then destruction will come easily."

Chandler angrily said, "There is one that will defeat you and your evil brethren."

The bowman leaned low off his horse as if not wanting to

miss the mortal man's words and asked, "Who might that be?"

The former minister looked at the evil entity, thought better of mentioning Janice's name, and said, "There is Lucifer, for one."

The creatures howled in unison, yet their laughter offered no clue as to what had so amused the demons. The rider slid from his horse. The bowman, who stood a head taller than the former minister, said, "Your words suggest there is another. Tell me—what other do you think may be a worthy adversary?"

Anger took control of his mouth and Chandler said, "She can see you for who you are. You cannot hide from her as you hide from the rest of us. Ja…" His words trailed off as he caught himself and realized he had almost given away Janice's identity. The minister smiled at his enemy having shown a weakness by not knowing Janice's identity.

The bowman raged with fury as he saw the smile on the man's face. He howled, "What is it you find so amusing, man?"

"You," Chandler mockingly replied.

Rage rose to the surface on a tumultuous wave as the creature demanded, "You spoke of a girl. Of what girl did you speak?"

Chandler only smiled and this enraged the creatures even more. He was unaware of the creature on the pale horse as he rode up behind him and uncorked the vial. The horseman tilted it until a drop formed on the lip of the bottle. It hung there as if not wanting to leave. It clung to the evil to which it belonged. Yet the drop longed to bring pain and suffering to mankind. The drop turned loose and set about its purpose in creation.

Chandler's shoulder exploded in pain as the drop touched, momentarily clung to the surface of the skin, before it sank beneath the flesh, and disappeared from view. The drop of bile searched until it found the steady vibration of the man's blood stream, and it slithered in and mixed with the red fluid. The drop rejoiced and knew it would soon multiply and spread among mankind.

The plague had been set loose in a new age. This time it would be allowed to run free and unfettered, and this time not isolated to a few remote villages. This new age of man had connected all the lands—While in the past, when the plague had been loosened, it had been locked within some remote village.

Chandler screamed as he fell to tainted ground inside the painting. He clutched at his shoulder, but by then the pain had found its way through his body and was already stealing life.

The bowman said to the ailing man," Give this to the girl you think can defeat us. Tell her I'll see her in Hell." He roared with laughter and then all went black to the minister.

His eyes opened to the sound of bleating monitors of an unknown description. A voice called for him to awaken, and he tried to do as asked. He opened his eyes and squinted against the bright light. Awareness slowly came to him and he looked around for the horsemen. He tried to sit up, but was too weak and fell dizzily backwards. He weakly asked, "Where are they?"

A tear hung in the corner of Janice's eye as she watched her ill friend. Somewhat relieved that he had wakened, she asked, "Who are you talking about?"

His mind cleared enough to see he was in a hospital with Janice standing at his side. He turned to see a monitor that continuously recorded his body temperature and other vitals. Chandler knew that he hadn't dreamed the horsemen and the vile creature had given him some sort of plague.

The girl took his hand. He violently pulled it way and shouted louder than intended. "Don't touch me, don't let anyone touch me."

Janice looked bewilderingly at him and asked, "What's wrong?"

Panic held him tight in its heart-shattering grasp. There was no fear for himself, but for the world. The monitor bleated rapidly in time with his increasing heart rate. An alarm at some remote nurse's station sounded. This alarm couldn't relay the true panic that had caused its trigger. The former minister's personal alarm was all that mattered. He prayed to any god that was willing to listen. He hoped someone would listen to him before it was too late.

His attention turned from Janice to the nurse who rushed into his room. She quickly grabbed his wrist to verify the heart monitor was correct and silenced the alarm. Chandler screamed in a panic to the nurse, "Kill me—burn my body and all my clothes. Get me away from these people before I kill them."

The nurse looked at Janice as if pleading for advice on why the patient was saying such things. The nurse said to the excited man as she fought to bring calm to her voice, "Sir, let me get you a sedative."

"I don't need a damn sedative. I need for you to burn me and everything that I have touched. I have the plague," he screamed. At any other time it would have been an embarrassment to use that type of language, but at this moment, etiquette no longer mattered.

Fear was pushed behind the steel curtain where the nurse hid all her emotions during work. Doctors and nurses are taught from the early days in school to compartmentalize their emotions. She said, "Sir, you have a viral infection, but it's nothing that can't be fixed with the latest antiviral drugs."

"Dammit, listen to me. Get a microbiologist to look at my blood and see if there isn't something unusual about it, and then get me away from all these people, including you,"

He turned to Janice after the nurse had disappeared in a state of confusion and said, "I may have already exposed you to this dreadful plague, but someone has to know the truth." He paused, took a deep, coughing breath, and asked, "Do you remember the four horsemen of the apocalypse?"

Janice battled back tears, nodded, and asked, "Is it true what you told the nurse—are you going to die?"

His face paled as he faced the inevitable and said, "Yes. I will die and so will the rest of the world if you don't listen closely to what I have to say."

The girl gathered her strength and listened as her friend explained about the painting and how he had been pulled inside. He told how the creature had used him to set the plague upon mankind.

Horror was the only description that could be used to convey the expression on Janice's face as she listened to her friend tell about the apocalypse that was happening. The horrible things she had seen described in the Bible were coming to pass. The world as man knew it was at the brink of death and she had no choice other than to accept that fate.

Janice thought back to her time in the dungeon and it paled in comparison to what her friend had said. The torture of the dungeon had happened only to herself, while this would happen to every man, woman, and child on the planet. Her parents, Pete, and all their friends would be dead from a hell-born plague. According to the Bible, mankind was going to pay for its sins. Many would turn to their Bible for comfort and answers. In reality, that very book was the cause of their pain and suffering. They were going to pay because of the Bible. Janice wasn't sure if even their beliefs would save them from this horror. Iam would destroy everyone if that's what it took to destroy his foe. Janice's worry was as much for the souls of mankind, as well as for their lives.

As if listening to her thoughts, Chandler said, "Listen closely to what I have to say. This is not the inevitable end of the world as written in the Bible. This is a war that you can win."

She looked at her friend with an arched brow and asked, "Do you mean 'you' as in mankind in general, or me, specifically?"

His eyes told her the answer before his lips spoke the words. He weakly said, "You, my friend... you." He told her how the creature reacted at hearing of a possible foe. Chandler explained how the creature reacted to the knowledge that someone lived who might have the ability to return them to Hell, or possibly, destroy them for eternity.

A weight unlike any that should be placed on anyone's shoulders fell heavily, overbearingly, on those of the girl. The weight was too much and she broke down and cried. The friend wanted to comfort her, but was forced by disease to sit back and watch her torment. Janice cried until there were no more tears and sat limply in the straight back chair. Clarity and a small portion of courage finally returned to her eyes. She asked, "Did they tell you who was good and who was evil? Is Lucifer their master?"

He could only shake his head to indicate a disappointing no. Offering the only advice his tired, weak mind could gather, he said, "For now, I wouldn't trust Iam or Lucifer. Lucifer has helped you in the past and maybe he will again. We do know that whomever controls the churches, is evil."

The distraught girl looked upward, more out of habit than some belief, and said, "Lucifer, save my friend as you've saved me in the past—I beg of you." She turned to look at her terminally ill friend and hoped for a miraculous recovery, but saw only the yellow eyes of a disease born from the bowels of evil.

The only voice in the world that could have brought cheer to her eyes, apologetically said, "Sorry I'm late, the traffic was horrible."

Janice looked at Pete and her eyes told him the seriousness of the matter. He flattened his voice in an attempt to hide his emotions, and said, "Mr. Baptiste, I went by your place and locked it up for you."

The conversation had taken its toll on the man and he wearily said, "Thank you, my-boy." He fought his way through the cloud of despair and sleepiness, and asked, "Was there anything unusual in the chapel?"

Pete looked at Janice as if asking permission to break some hidden alliance. She nodded and he replied, "There was one thing that I noticed. We were studying the painting of the four horsemen in school, just a few weeks ago, and I noticed something different about it."

Chandler looked up with a small amount of renewed vigor and waited for some unknown revelation. He hoped for a clue to a weapon they might use.

Pete looked painfully at Chandler and hesitated. He eventually forced himself to speak and said, "In the painting, there were several sick and dying men laying on the ground. There was an extra man and he had... well, had your face, sir."

Despair overcame the man. For the second time that day, light vanished as unconsciousness stole him from the world of awareness. He had welcomed the darkness and sleep, as well as relief from the pain he felt for the death he would bring to the people he loved. He didn't dream or have nightmares. His mind gave him peace in the darkness of unconsciousness. The respite from terror would be short lived as the nightmare of reality would begin anew once he awakened. Sleep gave him a few hours of respite from the torture his life had become.

The nurse returned to the room wearing a sterile gown and a mask that muffled her words. She commandingly ordered, "Everyone out of here. This wing is now under quarantine."

The eyes revealed fear that drove the panic in her voice. The Nurse's eyes told how she desperately wanted to run and hide from what lurked inside Chandler. The nurse had done just as Chandler had begged. She had brought in a microbiologist to study a sample of his blood. The report raised a tumultuous alarm throughout the hospital.

The two friends lingered for as long as they were allowed. Janice and Pete took a last look at their friend and wondered if they would ever again see him alive. They feared the worst, but hoped for the best. Janice once again silently asked Lucifer or God for his life. She silently offered her own life in exchange for that of her friends and the rest of humanity. She feared it just might come to that point. The prayer to God had been a desperate act, even if Janice wasn't sure if she would be ready to pay the price if he were to answer.

Pete pushed the door to leave the hospital and collided with the glass when it failed to open. He pushed harder to force it open, but it held fast. A muffled, firm, male voice commanded, "Halt there."

They turned to see a man covered in green with two large alien-like eyes. He looked as if he could have been another of hell's monsters. The National Guardsmen in his antiviral suit, his face hidden behind the mask with large, round glass eyes, said to the couple, "If you will follow me, I will take you to where you will be tested."

The tests were long and embarrassing. They were stripped by military personnel and given a battery of tests. Janice was thankful they had, at least, done the testing in small private rooms and a female medic had done the parts that would have been embarrassing with a male.

It was late afternoon before they were released from the hospital. What they saw on the outside was more shocking than what had been witnessed inside. A five feet concrete barrier had been erected around the hospital, which made the facility look more like a prison.

For a second, instead of the hospital, Janice saw a dark medieval structure that resembled the church that had been the gateway to an alternate reality—to the hell in which she had been imprisoned. Janice reached out and took Pete's arm for comfort, but knew he was also terrified of what they faced.

His arm felt good clasped in her hands. The warmth and nearness gave her an illusion of safety. Janice tore her eyes away from the building that had once been a hospital, that had been transformed into a monument to death. She said.

"If Chandler dies he might be the fortunate one in all this."

Pete feigned courage, smiled, and said, "I guess you and I will just have to save the world." The girl laughed weakly at the boy she loved, but the truth of what he said was more than she wanted to admit.

Pete parked along the curb behind Detective Johnson's car. Janice smiled when she got near enough to see Alan and Amanda sitting together in the swing as she and Pete had often done. There was a familiar sparkle in their eyes, the same one she often saw in Pete's when he was looking at her.

When the two took the last step onto the porch, Amanda and Janice shared a knowing look—a look that only females seemed to understand. Unsaid words were passed between them, which said, we must talk later and I'm happy for you. In that moment, she had told Janice that something special had happened between Alan and Amanda. After everything that had happened that day, Janice needed some light in her life. She was thankful for something that could make her smile.

Amanda asked before Alan could speak, "How is Chandler?"

Tears welled in Janice's eyes and she replied, "He's not well. They aren't sure he will live."

In an effort to not sound like a questioning cop, Alan asked, "Do they know what's wrong with him?" He failed miserably and felt embarrassed by how the question had sounded. Amanda had seemed to understand and took his hand. They smiled at one another.

Before Janice could reply, Pete said, "He has some viral disease that's very contagious. They have locked down the hospital, so I don't think we'll get to see him anytime soon."

Amanda jumped out of the swing and angrily said, "General has been locked down? I have patients there. Excuse me while I make a call." The storm-door slammed shut in an angry storm as the doctor rush into the house.

"Locked down?" The surprised detective asked. He checked his phone and saw that it was on and there were no messages or missed calls. "If they have called a quarantine, why haven't I been notified?" He asked no one in particular.

Pete offered, "I think the feds are handling this. Someone in a military uniform cornered us as we were leaving the hospital. This seems to have bypassed you local guys and gone straight to the top."

"If that's what's happened, then this is worse than we know," Alan said. He thought for a moment and asked, "Do you know how Chandler got this bug?"

Shared looks between Janice and Pete held them to momentarily silence. Janice finally repeated the story that the former minister had told. Pete continued where she left off and explained the painting.

No one had noticed Amanda standing in the open doorway. She said, "They won't let me see Chandler, or even my own patients. They referred all questions to the Center for Disease Control." The swing creaked and slightly rocked as Amanda sat down next to Alan. She looked at the two teenagers and asked, "Is the painting still at the church?"

Silence hung in the air like a thick mist as Pete hesitantly said, "No. I have it in my truck." Pete hated admitting that he had touched the vile art.

Despair filled Janice's eyes as she watched Pete for signs of insanity. It took moments before she could find her voice. She incredulously asked, "You have that evil thing in your truck? You touched it?" She collapsed into Pete and locked her arms around him, as if protecting him from the evil that lay a short distance away.

Alan retrieved the painting from the back of the truck after removing the tarp covering the evil object. It felt odd in his hands. It felt heavier than it should have been, or his imagination was placing weight where it wasn't. With all that had happened, it would have been insane not to accept that his intuition might be right. Some part of Alan told him the painting was weighted with the evil contained within.

The others stared at Alan as if he carried the plague, which he very well could have been, as he stepped onto the porch with the painting. None present doubted that the painting might hold the plague. More than one hoped it carried the cure as well.

As a doctor, Amanda wanted to believe that any virus was curable by modern medicine, but the things she had witnessed had shown her that there were powers beyond those of man. She realized that it might take a power greater then her own to cure her friend and the millions that are sure to die from the hell born disease.

Amanda was wary that a plague coming from Hell might

not be curable by man, but had to, at least, hope that modern medicines could fight the disease. In the past, entire nations had been devastated by plagues that were not much more virile than the common flu. She desperately hoped that if man couldn't find a cure, some force might.

Alan propped the painting against the wall. The work of the Russian artist somehow looked as if it belonged with the backdrop of peeling paint and the clapboard siding of a house that had gone one summer too long without new paint. They all stared at it, unsure of what they were looking for, or what words might be needed to describe it when it was found.

After an hour, they all conceded a temporary defeat. The painting was the same as when it was first painted. The body with the face of their sick friend had vanished from the many bodies lying on the ground. It looked the same as it did on any reprint or any digitized replica on the Internet.

Pete leaped to his feet, took the painting in his hands, shook it, and exasperatingly cursed, "Dammit, tell us what to do. You evil creatures, tell us what it is you have planned."

Janice wanted to help him shake answers from the demonic artwork, but instead, placed a calming hand on Pete's shoulder and said, "We'll find the answers, somehow."

He looked at her, dropped the painting so that it once again rested against the porch wall, and hugged her tightly. He whispered, "Thank you for being strong enough for the both of us."

She whimpered, "I'm not strong, my darling. I just have no choice and it's you that gives me my strength."

They gathered around the television in hopes of obtaining more information. The news had only a quick report about a contagious victim that had been taken into General Hospital, and that there was no need for concern. Pete angrily bellowed, "No need for concern? What right do they have lying to people like that?"

Alan's mind thought back to the serial killer that had killed and raped several local college girls. He had been the one who gave the order to have the press alert residents to be careful, but tell them there was no need to worry. City leaders had wanted the story down-played despite the knowledge there would likely be another body within the next week. The note had promised there would be another victim.

The powers that be decided to protect evidence and not create panic, which meant they would withhold that information. His boss hadn't wanted to tell the press anything, but Alan couldn't have lived with himself if there had been no warning. To this day, Alan remembered the blonde hair and young face of the fourteen year old girl that had been the next victim. He still saw her lying on the ground in a pool of blood that left part of the blonde hair stained red. She occasionally visited him in his nightmares and begged to know why he hadn't warned her that she was in danger. He always stood facing her with no answer. Yet there was only one correct answer, he had failed to protect and serve as his oath demanded.

Amanda noticed the change in Alan and asked, "What is it, my love?" The use of the word love brought a small smile from the group of friends, but she or Alan didn't notice.

He looked at her with sad eyes and said, "I failed someone once and I'm not going to fail Chandler, you, or the rest of the world the same way." They all looked at him with concern. He added, "We have to let the media know what we know."

Amanda roared with laughter that drew stares from the others. She looked at them and apologetically said, "I'm sorry for laughing, but if we tell what we know to the media, they will only laugh at us. They will have us committed to some asylum." After a thoughtful paused, she added, "Maybe we should be."

There was a chorus of agreement. All eyes turned to Janice as she said, "A few weeks, months, years ago, depending on the perspective, I met a young boy in the park. Since then I've been to Hell and back, literally. I'm still not sure what the truth is. I may already be unconscious in some asylum. I could accept that reality more than the one I'm facing." She glanced at Pete and continued, but not directed toward him, "He is the only real thing that's happened to me. If it wasn't for him, I might have died in that ditch. It was Pete that gave me the strength and courage to survive that night— to come out of it with, at least, some intact sanity." Janice took a deep breath and continued, "You might wonder how my sanity has remained as intact as it has. To be honest, it hasn't. I'm sure I'm as mad as the hatter, himself. It's because of Pete that I hang onto any vestiges of sanity that I can find.

Pete put a comforting arm around her, slightly embarrassed by what she had said, and asked, "What should we do?"

She kissed him, unashamedly, on the lips, turned to the waiting friends, and said, "I have been through a lot, as you know. I'm tired and just want it all to go away. This, I'm sure, won't happen." The battered girl paused, took a deep thoughtful breath and continued, "Let's go to the press. Let's shout to the world the truth. We might be labeled as lunatics, but a few will hear and listen. One ally is worth the shame and laughter. Some will laugh behind our backs, while most will laugh to our faces. The few will know we speak the truth."

They stared at her in admiration and worry, yet they concurred. The elders of the group wondered if Janice fully understood the consequences that could result from such an act. Amanda and Alan would surely lose their jobs if they were to publicly support Janice. Yet if they didn't give her their support, they would have failed a friend.

These thoughts had occurred to Janice as well. She looked at her friends and said, "I don't want anyone other than me involved in this. Anyone associated with me would be ruined professionally and socially." With the mention of socially, she looked at Pete and he knew that had been meant especially for him and how others would react at school.

"Whatever happens to you—happens to me," Pete emphatically said.

"The way things are, I can't see doing my job in the usual

fashion," Alan said.

Amanda chimed in and said, "I'm locked out of the hospital. I can't practice, anyway."

In the end, there was no arguing with Janice. She decided the information would come out in her name since it was to her that most had happened. The next question to be decided, was how much information should they tell. If the entire story was told, no one would listen. No form of news media other than the tabloids would accept the full story. That night they sat around the dining-room table where they had, unknowingly, almost been poisoned and penned a letter to the News and Reporter.

An agreement was finally reached. The letter would tell only of the plague from which their friend was dying, but it would not tell how the disease was conceived. Governments always say they are for the welfare of the people, but often only serve them with secrecy, as it was doing now with this plague. The plague that had been unleashed wasn't one that could be contained by man, his rules, or his barriers. This plague had been born in another world. The government would find, only after it was too late, that they never had a chance of stopping this disease.

Dear Readers,
This will be hard for you to believe, but I beg that you listen to what I have to say. My friend is laying in General Hospital dying from a plague he contracted from an unknown source. I would

give my life for him, yet I'm not even allowed to visit my friend. The federal government has erected a wall and is telling everyone that the problem is contained. It is my displeasure to tell you that it's not contained. This disease will spread beyond those barriers and consume every living soul around the world. Please demand that our government inform you, the public, so that you can better keep yourself disease free.

Some will tell you that I'm only a teenage girl. I am young, but I speak for some that are much older than myself.

Go now and demand that you see what's going on beyond those walls. Within a week you will see the same thing happening in the streets. The only chance of slowing this plague is to know it's there, and to use the truth to protect yourselves.

Thank   you,

Janice Carter

To their astonishment, the letter had been in the next issue. Calls began to pour in asking about the plague. Whomever answered the phone at the newspaper said they couldn't tell more than what was in the letter.

The following day, there were questions being asked by newspapers and television stations. Word began to spread around the country. Janice had planted a seed of knowledge, from which the flower of truth began to grow. Soon it would blossom and, hopefully, end the plague before it began its rampant run in the streets.

While that flower was growing, there was a knock on the door of the Carter home. Martin answered to find an austere woman in a tailored skirt-suit. Something resembling a smile formed on her lips. She asked, "Does Janice Carter live here?"

Martin protectively asked, "May I ask who is looking for my daughter?"

The woman opened a slim black wallet that unfolded into a long accordion of identification. The top card in the zigzag was an identification from the Center for Disease Control. Before he could read the others, a practiced hand refolded the collection of laminated plastic and dropped it into an overly large, black handbag that looked incongruous with her plain gray suit. The woman was neat, but it was apparent that clothing style wasn't foremost on her mind when she dressed in the mornings.

Martin found himself caught off guard by the smile, which appeared genuine. The woman said, "I am Doctor Eve Christian of the CDC. I'm sure you are aware of the letter your daughter wrote to the newspaper." He nodded agreement while she continued, "A lot of people are upset with your daughter for creating a lot of unnecessary trouble."

He reinforced his protective fatherly mode and asked, "I see. What is it you want to see my daughter about?"

A hand reached out to touch Martin's. This move changed the posture of the situation. The woman transformed herself from that of a bureaucrat to one of a woman. Her smile was disarming. She said, "I understand your daughter is a friend of the gentleman that's being held in isolation. I'm hoping she can give me a clue as to how this man contracted this disease. Any information will be greatly appreciated. "

Martin stood silent, thought of what Janice had advised in the letter, and decided this was the time to tell the truth. "She and I both know exactly how this man contracted the disease—the plague. I think she would be willing to tell you if you are willing to listen with an open mind," Martin said as he stepped to the side and invited the woman into their home with the wave of a hand.

Moments later, Janice descended the stairs after being called by her father. She became nervous the moment she saw the woman sitting on the couch. The decisive moment had arrived. The weight of the world descended on her shoulders. Atlas had held the world in his hands, while Janice was doing much the same thing with her shoulders. This was a moment when anyone other than Atlas might have shrugged and turned away. Janice knew she didn't have the option of turning and running.

The woman quickly stood at the sound of Janice's steps and turned to introduce herself before the girl reached the bottom step. She eagerly said, "I am Doctor Eve Christian from the Center for Disease Control."

Nerves had attempted to steal Janice's voice, but she weakly said, "Hi... I'm Janice Carter."

More motherly than professionally, Eve said, "This won't take long, dear. I'm not here to threaten you. We just need a few questions answered."

Janice closed her eyes and took a deep breath. Somewhere deep inside, she found the strength that fought to desert. She sat in a chair opposite the couch and confidently said, "Sit down and I'll truthfully answer all your question. I'll answer some that you haven't asked, and I hope that you have the fortitude to accept what I have to say."

Janice told the story of the painting in detail. The girl recounted the story almost word for word as it had been told to her by Chandler. The woman sat quietly and unquestioningly. Disbelief was obvious on the woman's face. Janice knew that her time had been wasted. This woman would go away and not believe anything that she had been told.

An uneasy quiet filled the room while Janice told about her encounter with Lucifer and being fatally shot. There was no reaction from the woman. Janice had wished the woman would laugh or something, but she sat quiescently.

The room exploded in sound as the front door flew open to reveal Amanda. She said while slightly panting, "I came as quick as I could. Thanks for the call, Martin."

Eve looked toward the doctor as if she had seen a ghost. She leapt to her feet with a shocked expression and asked, "Amanda, you know these people?"

Amanda smiled, but it was filled with contempt, and said, "Why... it's good to see you as well, Eve. I hope you and Henry are well."

Shock dissolved to disdain. Eve said, "I wouldn't know how Henry is, I haven't seen him since that night."

College and residency had brought the two life-long friends even closer. They shared everything, at times, even boyfriends. That is, until they met Doctor Henry Roberts. He was chief administrator at the Atlanta, Center for Disease Control. He had arrived at Mercy General hospital to interview interns for a variety of positions at the CDC. Amanda had chosen surgery so there was no need for an interview with Henry. This didn't stop Henry from wanting to talk with Amanda. The second day in town, he had asked her out and she gladly accepted. Even though the life of an intern left little time for social pleasures, she managed to find time to see him for the month he was in town.

The day before he was to leave for Atlanta, he was to announce his decision. Amanda found out his decision the night before it was to be announced, which was the night she found Henry and Eve naked in the doctor's lounge. That was the last time she had spoken to her friend.

Amanda felt deeply hurt that the man for whom she had developed feelings was having sex with her best friend. It ripped out her heart that her best friend was willing to trade a lifelong friendship for a job—not to mention her virginity. As preteens they had sworn to one another they wouldn't have sex until they were married, but neither of them had kept that promise.

Eve gathered her professional composure and asked, "Amanda, have you heard the tale this young girl is telling?"

Amanda defensively replied, "Yes. I have heard the tale. I believe that and everything else she has told me." She paused and added with dripping contempt, "I'll be more honest with you than you were with me that night."

The comment deeply stung Eve. Amanda noticed the pain and could only smile at the hurt she had caused. She said while pointing a finger at Janice, "That girl came into my hospital almost dead. I had given up all hope for her survival. Only a miracle could have saved her. That night I saw just that, a miracle. I sat with her as she was almost instantly healed and suddenly, clearly, spoke to me with a jaw that had moments before been hopelessly crushed. You ask if I believe her. I would believe her if she told me she walked on water. After what I saw that night, I might just believe that she could walk on water."

Janice looked at her friend with questioning eyes. Amanda smiled and let her anger fade. She sheepishly said, "I guess walking on water might be going a bit far."

The stunned CDC agent said, "I guess there is a lot more to this story than I've heard." The three of them looked at one another and Janice began telling what had earlier been omitted. She told of everything that had happened since meeting Lucifer, leaving out no detail, no matter the pain it might cause to herself or her family. The pain was obvious in Janice as she told of the beating and rape. Even though much of the memory had been mercifully cleansed away by the old man in Heaven, the emotional scar cut deep into her soul. No one noticed her palm as it laid flat on her stomach, or the thoughts of Angela, her daughter.

Eve's eyes filled with disbelief while staring at Janice, contemplating what she had heard. She looked at Amanda and angrily said, "I honestly think you're all mad. I have forty dead patients in the hospital across town. One man hangs onto life as if some force demands that he do so. You're right, we can never contain this disease, it's too contagious. In fact, we're not even sure how it's passed from one person to another. This virus lurks for hours or days hidden in a carrier and then suddenly springs to life in another. This disease could spawn thousands of Typhoid Marys. All this is happening while you sit here defending this insanity."

Janice jumped to her feet and angrily demanded, "Why haven't you told the world what you just told us?"

The doctor solemnly said, "If we were to tell people the truth, it would just cause chaos and there would be panic in the streets. We keep this information secret for everyone's protection."

Janice lividly screamed, "Be damned the protection. Tell those people or…" Her anger ran out of fuel and she looked to her father, begging forgiveness for cursing. Janice didn't like using such language in front of her father. He looked admirably at her with no signs of disparagement.

Eve stood and thanked everyone for their help. She walked to the door, turned, and said, "I'll do what I can. My hands are tied in this matter. The military is the one in control. You know, no one would ever believe your story. I'll try to convince them that, at least, the part about the plague is true. Just as her hand turned the doorknob to leave, she turned, and hesitantly asked Amanda with pleading eyes, "Could we talk for a moment—outside?"

The former friend hesitated, but relented and followed the woman out the door. Just before Amanda closed the door, she gave her friends an exasperated look.

When the door closed, Eve immediately said, "I want to explain about that night. I should have explained then, but I just didn't know what to say." Eve couldn't stop the tear as it ran from a single eye and down her cheek. She continued, "He told me how you had broken it off with him for Eric Boyle."

Everyone inside the house heard Amanda's laugh. This was the type of laugh that comes from hearing something very incredulous. It's the type of laugh that Eve should have released after hearing Janice's story. Amanda said, unforgivably, to her former friend, "So, you slept with him after hearing the news I was seeing Eric Boyle. Anyone working at the hospital knew I couldn't stand that man, yet you believed it? You would have done anything for that CDC job. You had told me many times that you would sleep with the devil for that job." The disconcerted woman paused for a moment and continued, "It's unforgivable that you slept with him for the job. If you had fucked him for the raw sex just because you wanted him, it might have been forgivable. You stabbed your best friend in the back for a job."

Tears mixed with the different colors of makeup as they ran down Eve's cheek to form a narrow multi-hued furrow.

The despondent woman gave one last attempt at salvaging an old friendship and said, "I swear on all that's holy that I didn't sleep with him only for the job."

Anger replaced the earlier sarcastic laughter and Amanda said, "I guess that's as much of a confession that I'll ever get from you. As for the holy part, I'd be careful with that word, these days. If you want to make amends for that night, spread the word of what we told you, today. Make them believe." With that, she walked back into the house without looking back at her former friend, and closed the door.

Eve stood on the porch crying and for a moment thought of knocking on the door to beg her former friend for forgiveness, but she knew it would be of no use. Instead, she went back to the disease-ridden hospital and its formidable barricades. At one point, she wished the cursed disease would take her from this world.

Inside the house, Amanda's strength deserted her and she collapsed into tears. Martin watched as his daughter comforted her friend. They had heard most of the conversation through the door, but no one would ever mentioned it until Amanda did, which she never would.

Eve donned a yellow bio-contamination suit, entered the hospital, and went straight for Chandler's room. When she entered his room, he lay in bed with closed eyes. His face was covered with raised, bleeding boils. The doctor rested a forearm on the bed-rail, stared at the man, and thought of everything she had been told. "Could this disease be born in

Hell?" She thought. No one in the CDC had ever seen anything that came close to this disease. Just when you thought there was a predictable course, the disease would mutate and send everyone rushing in a different direction. AIDS—Acquired Immune Deficiency Syndrome—was much the same, which is why no direct cure had ever been found.

Chandler had been in this bed for a week and his condition never seemed to get worse, or better. It was as if the devil himself held this man in his grip. Eve smiled to herself and dared to believe that might just be the truth in this case. If any part of Janice's wild story was true, then the devil did have him in his evil grip.

Something nearby roused a sense deep inside the sleeping man. He awakened from a sound sleep. Dreams still hung elusive and distant. His eyes hurt when he opened them to the dim, sterile fluorescent lights in the room. He saw a figure in a contamination suit and said with as much humor as he could muster, "Beam me up, Scotty."

The woman's smile was mostly hidden from the man by the helmet, but he managed a glimpse. She said, humoring him in a fake Scottish accent, "Aye, I would captain, but I don't think she can stands no more." He smiled thankfully at the woman for the momentary respite from his living hell.

Her hand carefully wiped bile that oozed from his forehead with gauze that had been left for that purpose. Her smile wasn't the practiced smile that the medical staff used everyday when they were tired and wanted to go home. Hers was the type of smile given to a friend or a patient she truly liked. Her hand found his bandage-clad hand and she said, "I met some of your friends, today." He looked up at her questioningly. She smiled and continued, "I met Janice and Martin, as well as Amanda, who I have known all my life. They told me how you became ill."

He looked up at her in surprise and weakly asked, "Do you believe them?"

"Amanda would never lie to me no matter what has happened in the past. Still, you have to admit, it's a difficult story to believe," she replied.

His smile was bright in contrast to eyes that were hollow and weak. He said, "I wish it was make-believe. I wish this was some horror movie and I was sitting with my arm around you in the theater, eating popcorn."

Her smile brightened. She said, "I'll make a deal with you. You get well enough to walk out of this hospital, and I'll date you every night for a week. Every night we can eat popcorn while watching a movie, and I would welcome that arm around me."

Sickness was pushed away for a moment, his eyes momentarily cleared, and from somewhere deep within a hidden strength was found. He said, "You do offer a lot of incentive to get well. For that wager I now have a new goal for living. I hope you like Italian."

She smiled brightly and said, "Italian is perfect for the first date. We can discuss the next date over a glass of wine."

A polyester covered hand touched the side of his face. She desperately wished that the promised date could come to pass. The man that had once been a minister, who dared to fight the true evil of the world, was someone with whom she suddenly and urgently wanted to have that special date. Eve knew she would use every tool at her disposal to see that this man lived.

Chapter 7

On the top level of the parking garage, a command center had been erected from a tractor-trailer load of prefabricated components. For protection, it sat perched on a million tons of concrete that had served as a parking garage. The command center had its own power source, as well as a filtered air supply. Around it, stood a dozen men covered by bio-hazard suits, carrying automatic assault rifles.

Inside the small fortress sat four men and one woman. Two of the men had on military uniforms, while the other two wore the unmarked uniform of Washington, DC, a black, tailored suit.

Doctor Eve Christian sat watching these men and knew they had been waiting on her report so they could each swing their own prodigious department into action. The men looked at her and waited impatiently while the woman ran Janice's words though her mind in an effort to turn them into something these men would understand. With all her effort and carefully chosen words, Eve knew these men would think she was insane. In fact, Eve thought she must be insane for even considering the things she had been told. The waiting men wanted something practical and tangible on which they could put their hands, something Eve couldn't offer.

The gentleman at the opposite end of the table from Eve impatiently asked, "Well... doctor, you have something for us?"

She contemplated their questions and knew that she could sit there for hours talking of possible medical causes and even some credible prognosis. In her heart, she knew it would all be a deception. There was only one logical answer, the illogical one she had learned that evening.

Fingers unconsciously played with a pencil that had been laying on the table. She looked at him and lied, "I have no tangible information for you. The victim did have an encounter with some foreign blood-born pathogens at his home. We analyzed the substance and have yet to determine a source." Eve thought back to how she had been told about blood coming from the painting and of the four horsemen. She envisioned herself saying this to the gentlemen seated in front of her, then being handcuffed and locked away in some place for the criminally insane.

One of the Washington men gruffly asked, "Is that all you have?"

Eve knew these men would tear her apart if she showed any sign of weakness. She went on offense, bore her ire into the man, and said, "I have been in town for only twenty-four hours. You gentlemen called me in only after the letter appeared in the paper. That information is more than your combined staffs have been able to contribute." Anger had taken over her mind and she no longer controlled what came from her mouth. She asked, still in attack mode, "Did your people know that Doctor Amanda Evans was a close friend of the girl that wrote the letter?"

The military men looked at each other in stunned surprise. The older man from Washington asked, "Who is this doctor, and what does she have to do with this case?"

Eve calmed and said, "She is chief of surgery at General."

The general at the end of the table said, "Maybe it's she we should have in here to answer our questions."

Uncontrollable laughter poured from the doctor and she sarcastically said, "Yes, that's exactly what you need to do. I know word for word what she will tell you and I can guarantee that it will not be what you want to hear."

The younger Washington man sitting to her left showed the same austere look, but there was a certain softness that could only come from being new in Washington. He, as the others around the table had done as they spoke, leaned slightly forward with hands clasped in front of him on the table and asked, "Would you care to inform us of what this good doctor would tell us?"

She looked at them incredulously and said, "Surely you jest. You want me to tell you the same story I was told by the girl and Doctor Evans?"

General Anderson, the man at the opposite end of the table said, "I think that is what he was asking. If you feel you cannot tell us what you learned in your interviews, we can have you dismissed from the CDC and a replacement here by midnight. "

This job had cost Eve the friendship with her best friend, and she had sacrificed most of her life for the job. Now it hung on the precipice between logic and fantasy. If she told them what she had been told, she would probably lose her job. If she lied, she would lose her job. Exasperated, she relented and told them the entire story as it had been told to her by Janice. The men, surprisingly, listened attentively to what she said.

When she finished, the General said, "I think its time your colleague and her friends seek counseling." Eve nodded as if in agreement.

Just as Eve pressed the elevator's down call-button, a hand caught her arm. She turned and was startled to find the younger of the two Washington men. Before she could speak, he asked, "Did you believe any of that story your friends told you?"

Eve felt like the doe that had accidentally stumbled upon the hunter. She pulled her arm from his hand and asked, "Did you?"

The man replied, "Maybe... some of it."

She sized up the situation and asked, "Is this an official interview?"

"No," he hesitantly replied

Unsure of why she was smiling, the woman said, "Let's talk about this over some of that god-awful coffee in the doctor's lounge."

The agent was hesitant about walking into the plague-infested hospital, but he capitulated and followed.

He sipped the hot substance that the staff jokingly said substituted for coffee. He said, "You were right, it is god-awful."

She smiled uneasily.

The lounge was busier than usual. Everyone was too tired to notice anyone other than themselves. The doctors found they could do little for the dying patients, other than spend tiring hours making them as comfortable as possible and hoping to find a cure. Their precious free time was spent in the lounge or an adjacent area filled with small uncomfortable bunks. The agent leaned close, as to not be heard by others, and said, "I'm Steve Parker with the Bureau of Civil Affairs. My mother is a devout fundamentalist protestant. As a child, I often went to church with her and we were told at least once a year about the apocalypse. Do you think this is Revelations coming true?"

Eve laughed and said, "I'm pretty much an atheist and don't believe there is some biblical Apocalypse happening. I'm not sure how much I believe of the things that were told to me. I don't think I'm going to be much help to you if those are the questions you want to ask."

Steve apologetically said, "I'm sorry to have wasted your time. If you could give me the number of Doctor Amanda

Evans..."

He was cut off by a voice from behind, "Who is it that wants my number."

He turned to find a weary woman with unkempt auburn hair. He quickly stood and said, "I wouldn't have expected such a lovely woman. "

In a time when the world wasn't about to destruct, and she was less tired, Amanda might have been flattered. She shrugged off the comment and once more asked, "Who is it that wants my number?"

"I'm sorry," he stammered as he fumbled for his official identification and flashed it to the doctor. She looked no farther than the state department seal.

Amanda cut a sharp look at Eve. Her former friend just shrugged to indicate that she had nothing to do with the man asking for her number. The doctor asked Eve, "Did you tell him?"

"Yes"

"Everything?" The surprised doctor asked.

Eve nodded affirmation while Amanda welcomed the relief that the extra chair at the table offered her fatigued legs. Eve stood and asked, "Fresh coffee for everyone?" They nodded.

Amanda's eyes bore into the strange man as if she hoped to see something other than the obvious, which was just an annoying government bureaucrat. His dress was complete Washington attire, but his manner showed a freshness that you didn't see in seasoned agents. Amanda had known enough bureaucrats in her time to know this man hadn't fully reached that status. She curiously asked, "You're too young to be here. How did you get assigned to this mission?"

He said with a sincere smile, "No one wanted this assignment. I'm still young enough to believe I'll live forever, as well as believe the world will survive this and I might merit some promotion and raise."

Her smile was as unpretentious as his answer had been. She asked, "Do you believe what you were told?"

He looked down at the empty coffee cup and slowly brought his eyes back to hers and replied, "Officially, no. Unofficially," one corner of his mouth rose in a half smile, and he added just above a whisper, "I guess I do."

Careful not to give her question the weight of hope, she asked, "Can you help us... them?"

He asked quizzically, "How could I be of help when the best scientific minds in the world are at work on this disease?"

Desperation was a powerful force and at that moment it pushed aside Amanda's fear. She said. "It's not the plague we seek help with, it's the whole of the problem."

The perplexed agent said, "I don't understand."

The aroma of fresh coffee arrived with the presence of Eve. She sat the coffee down and drew only glancing looks. She sat quietly as Amanda said, "Janice is alive only because she was able to see the reality—the truth around everyone. She seems to think that the only way to help these people is for them to have knowledge of what's happening, even if it's only the facts of the plague, itself. The fact that it might be the most virile plague ever released on the Earth is what they must know. Tell Janice's story to anyone that will listen. Eve took a chance with you, and you believed, at least in part."

A sullen look spread over his face and he said, "I'll do whatever I can to help." He gave her a card with his phone number and said, "Call me if you need me."

She smiled at him and lightly touched the back of his hand in thanks as she stood. Amanda looked at her old friend with a friendly, thankful smile and said, "I need to get back to rounds. I'm behind after being locked out for a while." As an afterthought, she added, "Thank you, Eve, for being so kind to Chandler. He mentioned that you spend a lot of time with him."

Her old friend tenderly said, "No need for thanks. It's been my pleasure getting to know him."

The CDC agent took the hand of the state department agent and said, "Here is a plan. You buy me dinner somewhere crowded and we can talk really loud." He smiled knowingly and amiably followed her as she led him from the lounge. They had to push away the fear of being thought insane if they were to save humanity. It was that kind of fear that Iam uses to control people.

Chapter 8

Someone shouting outside the window startled Janice awake. Her mind clung to sleep like a drowning man to a life-ring. She couldn't grasp what the voice was saying, but knew to whom the voice belonged. Even with sleep still fighting for control of her eyes, she smiled at the sound of Pete's voice.

She sleepily stood before the open window. He stood below her window holding a newspaper so that she could see the headline. Her eyes slowly focused on the far away object to see the words, "Is There A Plague?" Accompanying the headline was a picture of the fortified hospital.

Down the street she could see early risers going to the paper box, pause to read the headline, and slowly walk a few steps back toward their houses, often pausing once more to read further.

(API news) General Hospital has been quarantined for the last seven days because of an unknown disease.

From an unknown source at General Hospital, it has been said there is an incurable plague that has caused an extreme quarantine of the facility. A source was quoted as saying, "We do not, at this time, know the origin of the plague. We do know that it is extremely virulent."

Until there is more information, the source urged everyone to remain calm and to stay in their homes.

The official hospital spokesmen, when asked about the plague, would only say that they had the situation in control and the quarantine would soon be lifted.

Police commissioner Albert Davidson had this to offer: "If there are any discrepancies in the hospital report, we will be the first to take action. I have personally been in contact with the CDC and can assure you that there is nothing to worry about."

This paper will continue to follow this story and keep you informed to any new developments. We urge you not to panic and to remain calm until all the facts are in.

People began drifting over to their neighbors, discussing the article. It didn't take long for word to spread. People spilled from their houses to form a writhing mass on neatly manicured lawns. Panic hung just below the surface as they pondered the article... and their lives.

Janice was still wearing her nightgown, covered by a pink

quilted robe, as she joined Pete on the porch swing. She said while watching the neighbors milling about with crumpled newspapers, "It looks like my letter has caused quite a stir."

His smile was brighter than she thought it should have been. He said, "I think it's more than your letter." He handed her the newspaper.

She read it intently, looked up with more of a smile than intended, and said, "I think our friends have been busy. Other than the lady from the CDC, my letter seems to have drawn little notice." Janice looked at Pete as if she had an epiphany. She asked. "Do you think the lady from the CDC went to the press?"

He thought for a moment and said, "I'm not sure if she went directly to them, but I would be willing to bet she had something to do with it. Someone important has caused a media buzz."

After several minutes of watching the neighbors, Pete asked, "What do we do, now?"

She mournfully replied, "I'm not sure if there is more that can be done."

A police car rolled slowly down the street. The article in the newspaper had put police agencies on high alert for any problems. Across town, similar scenes were unfoldng as the morning paper arrived. Within view of Janice's house, a throng of people stopped the police cruiser. A short, squat, balding man held up the paper so the officer could see the headline and asked, "Is this true?"

The officer shrugged and replied, "You know as much

about this as I do."

A woman pulled a tattered, faded blue, quilted housecoat close to her chest and shouted, "You're not telling us the truth. Your guys threatened my husband when he went to the hospital to see about his brother. Tell us what's going on."

People began to press against the cruiser in an angry circle. The officer, only a year out of the academy, was beginning to panic. "This is suburban America," the officer thought, "not the center city scum that he had been trained for in these circumstances." He looked at his partner and they silently agreed to ease their way out of the crowd to find safety.

They had waited too long. The throng of people had become too compact around the blue and white cruiser. The veteran officer used the public address feature of the two-way radio and authoritatively said, "Ladies and gentlemen, please step away from the vehicle." This seemed to only infuriate the middle-class crowd even more, causing their shouts to became louder.

A loud voice was heard over the shouting crowd. Martin admonish the crowd and demanded, "What are you people doing? I have known some of you for twenty years. I have never seen you act this way."

The pack of angry citizens quieted and turned to look at Martin as he stood in front of them, still wearing his pajamas and a plain cotton robe. The squat, balding man fought his way through the crowd and faced Martin. He angrily said, "All we want is the truth about what's happening over at that hospital."

Martin stood firm and calmly said, "If it's the truth you seek, then ask me your questions."

The woman with the faded housecoat said, "He might know something. That cop and woman doctor have been spending a lot of time at his house, lately."

Like a pack of wolves that had found fresh prey, they descended on Martin and abandoned the police cruiser. The officers, as hungry for information as the people, joined them on the street. Martin looked at the gathered mass of angry neighbors and wondered if he had done the right thing. He wondered if he could tell these people the truth, and if he did—would they believe such a far-fetched tale? If they did believe him, Martin could only wonder how they might react.

The people stopped short of Martin and seemed to slightly settle. The hope for news was like the wolf after a fresh kill. The wolf will hungrily feed and then lay contented for as long as he isn't threatened. The moment that threat is near, the beast will pounce with all its fury.

Martin watched the intense eyes of his friends and neighbors, and said, "I know the truth and will gladly tell it to you. I ask only one thing from you, and that is you have an open mind. What I'm about to tell you is impossible to believe." He paused to collect his thoughts and continued, "My daughter was in an accident and was nearly killed. Through some miracle that I don't pretend to understand, she lived when she shouldn't have. I am thankful to whatever entity that took care of her and gave her back to me. Today, I am going to offer you the truth as I know it. Unbeknownst to you, a battle has been raging in this town between good and evil. My daughter and our friends have been at the forefront of this battle."

Janice watched the commotion and froze with fear when she saw her father confront the angry mob of neighbors. She tried to dash to her father's side, but Pete grabbed her arm and said, "It's not safe. Those people are scared."

She shouted at Pete for the first time since they had become a couple, "If it's unsafe for me, then it's unsafe for my father. Let me go, dammit."

The boy felt a sting as her words cut deep into his soul. Pete relented, released his grip, and she ran across the lawn to where her father stood."

Martin stopped talking and looked at his daughter. The concerned father said, "Go back to the house."

She obstinately replied, "I'm staying with you. Finish telling the people how evil is out to destroy all of mankind. Tell them how they poisoned our friend."

The two stood in the bronze morning sun as it began to evaporate the dew that had given the grass tips a coating of sparkling wonder. Janice and Martin looked upon confused faces and the father told how Janice had been beaten. Together, they told how most of the world had forgotten the events of that week.

Sympathy flowed from the once angry crowd as they looked at Janice. The squat, balding man asked, "How could we have forgotten such a thing?"

The crowd hung in limbo and wanted to believe, but they couldn't cross the boundary of disbelief to give up the tangible world they could see and touch. They clung to the things they had been taught all their lives. The father and daughter knew they were losing them and at the end of the day, the neighbors wouldn't believe. Even if they believed for that moment, their minds would fight against that belief. The mind would leech onto normalcy, the world with which they were familiar. Even those who truly believed in the Bible couldn't accept the truth.

Risks would have to be taken to win these people over. Janice had an epiphany, but did she dare take the risk? If she was wrong, the people would never believe anything from her or her father again. Indecision tore at her and clutched her heart in its vice-like grip. The world around her seemed to pause as if waiting on her to reach a conclusion. Her heart raced as she stood in the vacuum that had consumed time and space. She stood alone in that void and fought with her choices.

The air collapsed on her like a sudden weight as the world around her returned to its normal motion and she said, "Listen to me like you have never listened. Your very life could depend on what I have to say." There was a sudden intake of air as they turned their attention to the young girl who spoke with strength beyond her chronological age. The time spent in the dungeon had not aged her chronologically, but it had mentally. She took a deep breath and the gathered neighbors did the same. She continued, "I need one of you to believe what you heard today—you have to believe it with all your heart."

She and her father searched the crowd for eyes that didn't show confusion. They begged to see eyes with a flicker of hope and belief, but saw only the shallow eyes of despair. Janice pleaded once more, "I beg that you see the truth as I have seen it. I want everyone here to see the truth as my family and friends have. You have known my father for a long time and know him to be an honorable man. Do you think he would come before you with some wild tale about some battle between good and evil if it wasn't true?"

Janice wanted to cry as she watched the sullen crowd standing before her in disbelief. Hope was evaporating quickly when she heard the whimper of a baby to the left of the crowd. She saw a young woman only twenty-three years old holding a small newborn. The woman looked at her baby and then to Janice. Janice smiled because in the young woman's eyes she saw hope. Janice walked over to the young woman, took the baby's tiny fingers between her own, and said to the woman, "Do you believe me?"

Her eyes looked once more at her baby, then back to Janice, and desperately said, "I have to or my baby will never have a chance to live a normal life."

All eyes turned to the two girls. They waited and wondered what was going to happen. Janice raised her voice so that all could hear her ask the woman, "Do you have any newspapers from the past few weeks?" She turned to the crowd and asked the same.

The ones that held the current paper looked at it thoughtfully. The squat man that had assumed leadership of the crowd said in a near whisper, "I can't remember reading a paper for the last few weeks until today."

The girl pulled the baby close to her bosom and thoughtfully said, "I should have most of them. Since the baby came, I just never seem to have the time to read them. I should have thrown them out by now, but I haven't had time for even that."

Janice was grateful that the girl had been too busy to toss the old papers and said, "Could you go and get them? I would love to hold the baby for you."

The woman looked nervous as she pulled her baby protectively close, but eventually relented. Something in the eyes had told the woman that Janice could be trusted with the baby. The women gently handed Janice the warm bundle that contained the baby. As the woman walked away to retrieve the newspapers, Janice thoughtfully called out, "What's the baby's name?"

"Angela," she replied before disappearing into the house.

No one noticed the tears that welled in Janice's eyes. She stared at the baby and thought of her own that lay in a world far different from the one in which she stood. Janice hoped her own baby was safe and at peace in a place where there was no battle waging, or had no plagues to cause pain. The disconnected mother kissed the infant's forehead as a tear fell on the child's cheek. The baby that had moments before been antsy from being held by a stranger, smiled and drifted off to sleep.

Janice noticed that something had captured the attention of the group of disconcerted neighbors. She looked around to see the baby's mother with an incredulous look while standing at the foot of her steps, holding a stack of unread newspapers. The woman with the faded bathrobe said as she rushed to the girl holding the newspapers, "Let me see those."

Moments later, everyone was reading a newspaper. Sometimes there would be three straining to read the same paper. They would read for moments and then stare up at Janice who was still holding the baby. She felt a quiet uneasiness and wondered what was going through everyone's mind. Martin went over to stand with his daughter, ready to protect her if need be, but said nothing.

A frail woman with gray hair haphazardly splayed over her head shouted, fell to her knees, began to pray, while others dropped newspapers to hang limply at their sides, and stared at Janice. The squat, balding man confoundedly said, "This really happened to you? This is some kind of joke. You had those papers made up to back up your preposterous story."

Janice or her father didn't say anything as the man dropped his head and reluctantly accepted the truth. The young mother went over to Janice, placed her arms around her, and said, "I'm so sorry for you. It had to have been horrible."

Janice closed her eyes and hoped to conceal the pain that

191

she constantly battled to keep hidden, even from herself. She clutched the sleeping infant tightly and thought of her own. Janice returned the baby to her mother and stood by them with an arm around the mother. She surveyed the people and said, "I wanted you to know the truth about what's happening around you. The truth is the only weapon we have found, so far. Doubt will take you back behind the veil of illusion. I ask you to be strong. All evil depends on lies and deception to survive."

The squat, balding man said, "This has to be a dream that I'll wake up from, soon."

Martin painfully said, "It's a nightmare, a living nightmare."

Nervousness from the events that had just transpired settled in on Janice and she felt weak. She saw Pete standing on the sidewalk and remembered the look on his face when she had cursed him. Her heart ached at that image and she reached a hand out invitingly in hopes of seeking forgiveness. Pete walked to her and took the offered hand. The tearful girl looked at him and asked, "Can you forgive me for speaking to you like that?"

A bright smile radiated from his face and he said, "There is nothing to forgive. You did what you always do, and that's protect those you love." He pulled her close to him and was content with her nearness.

Delores watched the happenings on Credence Drive from the window. She showed no acceptance or disdain for the things she witnessed. The woman went back to her room and prayed that the world receive the just punishment it deserved. "All of mankind must pay its debts and accept the retribution that is upon it," she thought. Delores had heard her husband and daughter talk about the truth, but she was sure neither of them knew the real truth.

Her husband had always been a sinner and she often wondered why she had married the man. The pious woman had worked hard to make sure her daughter had taken the correct road to God and had indoctrinated her into the church. Where she had gone wrong was no longer of importance. Her daughter must pay her debt, as must all of mankind.

Elsewhere around the country, people gathered on their lawns just as the people had on Credence Drive, yet they had no one to tell them the truth, no calming voice. Fear of an unknown deadly plague gripped the people and they panicked. It started out as disagreements over nothing, and then came fear of each other while accusing life-long friends of having the plague when they had only a simple cold. One family burned their own children alive for having the same allergies they had since birth, while others killed their enemies because they, now, had an excuse. In a single morning, madness had broken out all over the country. Law enforcement had, as well, succumbed to the insanity as they divided into self-empowered groups.

Somewhere a rider on a pale horse laughed and handed

the country into the hands of the rider on a fiery red horse. He held his sword high in the air and rode off into the rising sun as if he were charging toward some sworn foe. The pale rider trotted along, reveling in the sickness and despair he had brought to the world of man.

The rest of the world had fared no better. Circumstances were different, but the outcome was the same. Some people around the world died by the plague, while others died by the sword of a conqueror. God had, at last, unleashed his wrath on mankind. The world as man had known it for two thousands years was coming to an end. Iam had decided to rescind freewill.

Chapter 9

"Repent and you shall be saved," the derelict of a human said as he stood on top of an abandoned car. The old and tattered suit he wore had become a symbol to the travesty of mankind. He wore it with pride. The Bible had taught that passion for money was a sin. Years spent on the streets had robbed him of his mind and left him a peripatetic preacher.

He misquoted verses from the tattered Bible he always kept clutched in his hand. He survived on the alms that people occasionally tossed at his feet. He would keep only enough for food. When his belly hurt from hunger, he knew the Lord had blessed him for his devotion

Three teen gang members walked past where he stood sermonizing. The derelict said, "Repent, for the apocalypse has come. Death rides the street and touches each of you with its diseased finger. "

The apparent leader of the three teens picked up a discarded liquor bottle and threw it at the man. It landed a glancing blow on his right temple where it ripped the flesh and let loose a small trickle of blood. They laughed at the startled look on the aging preacher's face. "How's that for touching you, old man?" The gang-banger humorously asked.

The preacher touched his fingers to the open wound and wiped the trickle of blood as it threatened to run down his face. He held the bloodied fingers out to the boys and said, "The blood of man shall flow like wine into the streets. Repent and accept the glory of God and ye shall be saved."

One of the gang members started for the man, but the leader held him back. He looked at the ruin of a man and saw something in his eyes that scared him more than meeting a rival gang in a dark alley. Trying to hide his fear, the boy said, "We don't have time for this fool, let's go." They walked silently away, but the leader turned back several times to stare at the vagrant. Each time the vagrant was staring at him and smiling as if he saw some fate for the young gang member.

Harold Friendly's face glistened with hot beads of perspiration. Fingers tugged at the suddenly too tight tie that he had worn everyday since graduating college. The knees of his expensive suit were torn where he had, at some point, fallen. One hand clutched at an expensive leather briefcase. He felt the bile rise from his stomach. When it reached his throat, he dropped the briefcase and covered the expensive leather with the rotten bile that had come from his diseased stomach. He gagged as his body rejected the croissant he had eaten for breakfast, and the coffee his secretary had brought him as she had done every morning for the past ten years.

Harold Friendly wiped the clinging bile from his lips with the starched French cuff and saw the bum standing on the car. The derelict held out his hand with the coagulating blood on his fingers. The panderer dropped to one knee on the car's hood and unremittingly said, "The rider on the pale horse has come to you, Harold Friendly—repent or succumb to the apocalypse."

Even in a weakened state his awareness was rocked by the man's word. He swallowed hard to try and control the next wave of rising bile. He asked, "How did you know my name?"

His laughter was mocking, while at the same time pitying the man before him. The vagrant preacher sanctimoniously said with an upward pointed finger covered with dried blood, "He tells the true believers what we must know. He has told me that you and a thousand more just like you would be falling at my feet. He told me to beware of the girl. You must beware of the girl that claims to know the truth. She lies, as does the devil to whom she kneels."

"You're insane, you decrepit man," The sick man weakly said.

The laughter returned and the vagrant could tell that Harold Friendly hated this laughter, so he let it go on longer than he would have otherwise. He said with disdain, "Your kind has always thought of my kind as insane. You sit in your crystalline towers and look down on the world, when in fact, you should have been building monuments to God and looking up to him."

Deep within, something gnawed at Harold. It might have been a memory from some long abandoned church activity, or something in his soul. Still, he mocked the preacher and said, "I'm too sick for your crap, go bother someone else."

Harold would never make it home that day. In a nearby alley the teens that had earlier confronted the derelict on the car, saw the man near death and attacked the weakened prey. As with any predator, they saw weakness as a reason not to live. They saw the man no different than a lion sees an elk as its dinner. They pounced on him, smashed their youthful fist into him, shattering his face. They took joy in the destruction of this man and felt no pity for him. They felt no pity as they took the wallet from the coat pocket of his expensive suit. They felt no pity as they tore past a picture of his three daughters to reach the credit cards. They kicked him as he lay bleeding on the ground because he only had the ten dollars he carried for snacks at work. It no longer mattered that he commanded a dozen people, or that they followed his direction without question.

The next day those same people who followed his direction would learn of Harold Friendly's death. They would pretend to mourn and then the next day a new man with another leather briefcase would be at the desk with a different nameplate. A secretary would open a small tin box that contained the flower fund money. She would take out the prescribed amount, call a florist, and order an arrangement for the twenty-five dollars on which they had all agreed. None of them would attend Harold Friendly's funeral... they all had previous plans.

In their plunder, the gang members didn't see the largest of the bounty they carried away that day. The blood that had sprayed them as they hit the man was the unwitting prize. That blood carried the unseen plague that had belonged to the rider of the pale horse. The disease took comfort in the confines of a new warm host. It multiplied quickly so that it would be ready for when the flesh of this boy was broken and it was allowed to escape to another. Somewhere the horseman smiled.

Chapter 10

Sirens wailed as police rushed to an unusual call. The wailing of sirens had once meant to gain the awareness of those hearing it, to warn them of impending danger. Times had changed so that now the sound of sirens was an everyday occurrence, which most never heard through filtered ears. The only ones that cared the sirens were near, were the ones gathered in the square. Mothers pulled their children close, but stood and watched the scene that was unfolding before them. Vagrants climbed from their underground hiding places that kept them isolated from the world they had, for a variety of reasons, escaped.

The poor, the rich, and the infirm gathered on the streets and sidewalks to stare in wonder. Heads dotted open windows of surrounding buildings as the normal sounds of the world were replaced with those of whispers and wailing sirens. Somewhere the cry of a baby broke that pattern and a fearful mother fought frantically to quiet the cries of the feverish child. The woman had been to every hospital, clinic, and medical facility, only to be turned away. Hospitals had given up any hope of treating or containing the deadly plague. Despair had fallen on the witless woman. With no hope, she stood and watched the things happening in front of her—she watched as the world would forever be changed.

Shopkeepers stood outside their forgotten businesses and didn't seem to notice or care that some customers were stealing from the shelves. Other than the events in the street, the world didn't seem to matter to any of the people watching.

The vagrant preacher still stood on the abandoned car and smiled at what he saw. He looked to the sky and said, "The time has come for me to take my rightful place in the world."

An authoritative voice came, not from the sky, but from the street, and said, "Come and stand at the right hand of your king."

In the middle of the square an elegant, bearded man with silver robes swirling from his shoulders sat on a white horse. He held a bow high in the air and waved to the people as an ancient conqueror might do to the conquered. His horse danced in circles as a wave of police cars encircled the strange man. Police officers knelt behind open car doors and brandished weapons of varying design. An officer bravely stepped up with a bullhorn to his mouth and said, "Surrender your weapon and no harm will come to you."

The man on the horse laughed contemptuously at the man in blue. He lean over on his horse to face the policeman and said, "I do not offer you the same promise."

He nocked an arrow in his bow. There was a sudden rhythmic clattering as policemen cocked and readied their weapons, prepared to disperse deadly projectiles into the strange perpetrator.

The bowman was the first to send his instrument of death on its set course. It seemed to hang in the air as policemen fired their weapons at the entity on the horse. Empty casings clattered musically to the paved surface below the men. A rhythmic, smoking hell rained down on the innocent white lines of the street as shell casings continued to fall.

The arrow shattered the bullhorn the officer held inches from his face as it forced its way to its intended target. The arrow came to a rest once it had penetrated the man's head.

Silence once again found its way into the streets as the policemen turned to see their commander with an arrow protruding from his head. He stood screaming in torment, but didn't collapse as expected. The man on the horse rode closer to where the commander stood and said to the surrounding policemen, "Your weapons cannot harm me, but as you can see, I can harm you. Pledge your allegiance to me, your new king, and I will let your leader die. If not, he will live for an eternity with the pain I have given."

The man's hands tore at the arrow that rested within him, but couldn't pry it loose. The horseman said, "I am feeling kind today. If one man will come and kneel before me, I will release this man from his torment."

As if on cue, the vagrant dropped from the car and onto the street. He pushed his way past stunned policeman. He walked until he was within a foot of the rider and said, "My king," and humbly knelt.

The best friend of the commander dropped his weapon to the asphalt surface with a clatter that was nearly lost in the commander's screams. He nervously walked to the horseman and said, "Help my friend and I give you my life."

The bow tilted to touch the police officer on the shoulder as if anointing some knight and said, "I accept your offer and withdraw the pain of your friend." The policeman collapsed dead onto the street, as did the commander.

Confusion began its spread among the policemen and they turned to look at the next officer in charge, a young captain that had advanced, not through hard work, but through a multitude of golf games. The reluctant leader looked at the thousands of empty shell casings that littered the street and then to the man sitting tall on his white horse wearing a crown of glittering gold. He then looked to the fallen bodies of his companions and knelt.

The king rode the circumference of the circle of humanity that had moments before surrounded him and said, "Follow me and I will protect you from the plague that has besieged your city. Follow me and I will give you immortality."

In the beginning, there was only one that came forth and knelt before the king. With each succeeding one, it became easier for the next. One became two, two became four until there was a steady trickle of humanity coming forth. When they knelt before the king they gave away any chance of turning back. People that ran giant corporations knelt and gave themselves to this stranger. They knew only that the creature held a power greater than their own, or that of any living man. Some sought to make deals with the new king. They saw new power and thought to share that power. Most of those were struck dead. The king had long ago decided who would be at his side. The street preacher had also known that he would, someday, be at the right hand of the king.

The woman that held the feverish baby wove her way nervously through the crowd of kneeling bodies, approached the horseman, and asked, "Can you help my baby? I would do anything."

The horseman said to the air around him, "Brother, take back your potion from this young one so that she may belong to me." He looked to the woman and said, "Know that your child is well. Now it is your time to do duty to your king."

He held out his hand and took the woman's. The bundle in her arms felt cool and the eyes of her babe had cleared. She knew that she would go with the man who had saved her daughter. The woman was pulled onto the white horse and sat behind the king with the healthy baby held protectively in her arms.

Those that chose not to kneel, backed away to stand behind those who did. They watched as life long friends and colleagues gave themselves to the stranger on a horse, both of which looked to have come from another time. They gave themselves to a man that called himself king. They knew the man would rule, but weren't sure they would follow.

The king worked his way through the throng of kneeling

followers and rode silently with the woman that sat on back of the white horse, clinging tightly to the stranger. A massive parade ensued as those that had given themselves to the king, followed. The curious brought up the rear of the strange parade. For the first time in a hundred years, a horse gained preference on the street.

Soldiers surrounding the fortress-like hospital turned to see the parade of people coming toward them. They saw the man on the horse leading and confusion overruled the soldier's training. The soldiers didn't close ranks as they had been trained—instead, they watched and whispered to one another. Beside the horseman was a vagrant in a tattered suit, and behind him was a police captain. Sight of the police captain caused the soldiers to relax their guard as the rider approached.

The soldiers saw family and friends in the throng of followers and sought them out in hopes of gaining information. Commanders barked orders, but few heard them in the ensuing chaos. Word spread rapidly around the city and more people packed their way onto the street to see what would unfold.

The rider dropped the reins of his horse, placed his hand on the thigh of the girl behind him, and said, "With a salvo of my arrows and with the help of my unseen brothers, I can destroy the world. I command all warriors to surrender unto me their allegiance." With an authoritative wave of his hand at the hospital, he continued, "As an act of faith I will take back the plague from everyone in that structure. This is the first and only time I will take back my brother's poison from anyone other than those who follow me."

Amanda stood in Chandler's room watching the scene through the window. She couldn't hear the words, but knew from seeing the man on the horse that the world was in deep trouble. Chandler weakly said, "You see something out the window. I see fear in your eyes."

She looked to her friend and said, "The time has come—the bowman has arrived."

Chandler tried to sit up, but only manage to roll onto his right shoulder, and said, "Go to Janice, you must protect her."

An excited nurse burst into the room and shouted, "They are healed... all of them."

Amanda said to the nurse in the voice she often used to calm excited patients, "Now slowly tell me who is healed."

The nurse exclaimed, "The patients, the plague patients... everyone in the damn hospital! Even Bertha that was to have the hip replacement is up and running around as if she was twenty years old, again."

The doctor looked at her friend, who still lingered near death, and sadly said, "Not everyone."

The nurse didn't want to hear anything that would dilute her cheer. She rushed from the room to spread the news to anyone that would share her excitement. Chandler smiled and said, "I guess I'm not on the bowman's favorites list." He sullenly added, "There is going to be a high price to pay for this token of good will."

Amanda dropped her eyes to the floor and said, "I think it's going to be a higher price than they will want to pay, except, now, there will be no choice."

Alan burst into the room and said, "What a madhouse out there. Most of the police force has given this creature their loyalty, and those that haven't were fired and ostracized." The detective turned on the television and said, "If you thought things were bad... watch this."

A bright smile lined the face of the field reporter as she stood before a changing television screen. It displayed city after city around the world where millions had been cured of the plague, and the mass of people offering their allegiance to the king who had briefly appeared to them. One reporter proclaimed this the greatest day in the history of the planet. Another compared it to the second coming of the Messiah. The excitement had escalated to the point that no politician or leader dared speak against the miracle and the self proclaimed king.

It would take no more than two days for the total collapse of all the power structures around the world. Armies slaughtered those within the power structure that wouldn't join them in their homage to the new king. The desire of man since the beginning of time had come to pass, the world would be ruled by one power. Man had fought and died for thousands of years and never came close to world domination. Wars had raged for centuries in pursuit of this honor, yet this horseman had managed it in only two days.

Chandler used all his strength to sit up and said, "Take me down to see him."

They looked at the man incredulously. Alan said, "You're out of your mind."

Weak laughter escaped Chandler and he said, "I'm insane beyond reason, but I need to see him." He looked at his friends with determination and showed more strength than he had in a while. Chandler asked," What's he going to do, kill me?"

A nurse was called to bring a wheelchair, but no one ever came. Everyone was out in the streets with former patients cheering the new king. Amanda went to the nurse's station and found all the monitors quiet and deserted. She found a wheelchair and returned to the room. Chandler had, somehow, found renewed strength as they helped him into the chair. They pushed him to the entrance of the hospital, looked up at his friends, and said, "I'll go alone from here."

"You're too weak, "Amanda dissented.

Just as Chandler was going to offer an argument, the crowd parted and out stepped a man with a bow slung over his shoulder. An invisible force rolled Chandler to within feet of the horseman. The king's voice was jovial, as if greeting an old friend. The king asked, "How is my old friend the preacher doing?" He leaned down with mocked concern and continued, "Oh, I see you are ill, is there anything I can do to help?" He roared with laughter, as did those behind him, even though they didn't know why he laughed.

The man in the wheelchair said with disdain, "I'm glad you didn't cure me of the plague. I would hate to have owed you anything."

Again, the creature laughed at the man and said, "You have no plague, fool."

Alan couldn't stop Amanda before she rushed angrily to her friend's side and said, "I did the test myself—he has the plague. If it's not the plague then do tell me what is wrong with him."

She was shocked when the creature said, "Amanda, it is so good to meet the honored doctor. I have heard many wonderful things about you." He smiled, as a man would smile at a woman, and said, "This man has no plague, he only carries it. My brother fed him from the vial so that he would carry and spread the plague to mankind. His body will, in time, adjust to the poison inside. In time, his body will regain its strength, but will still carry my brother's potion unless he submits. In that case, I would have my brother remove the poison from the preacher's body."

The wheelchair bound man spat at the creature and said, "I would die first."

"You have threatened that so often it's getting boring," the creature said. He leaned in close. Chandler could smell the foul breath of the creature as it threateningly said, "It's not death that you must fear."

The three thought of Janice and knew the truth of the

creature's words. Amanda whispered in Chandler's ear, "Let's get back, there's nothing we can do, here."

Where is it you can go that you can do something?" The creature asked. If it had been anyone other than the king speaking, they might have caught the concern in his voice.

Smiles spread on the faces of the three friends when Chandler replied, "You're starting to bore me with that question."

Rage sprang from the creature at the man's defiance. He turned to the police captain and commanded, "Arrest these three. Lock them away so that no one will ever see them again."

Former friends and colleagues of Detective Alan Johnson handcuffed the three, forced them into police cruisers, and whisked them away from the creature. The confrontation had not ended as Chandler had anticipated. He had let his temper get the better of him. He had sought only information or any knowledge that could be used against the demon. He had learned that his own illness wasn't permanent, but the price had been too high.

Three hours after being booked with no explanation of charges, Officer Ryan brought a food tray to the detective and said, "It sure is strange seeing you in there."

The detective weakly laughed and said to the young officer, "Not half as strange as it is seeing you out there."

The young officer leaned against the bars and said, "I'm not sure I agree with what's going on around here. I'm not sure I trust the man that has been named king of the world."

Alan saw the uneasiness in the young officer and asked, "What can you tell me about my friends?"

Ryan said, "I was told to keep you separated." He hesitated and continued, "I just came from feeding them and they are okay. Since the man on the horse took over things, there is almost no crime and all of the prisoners have been released." He paused thoughtfully and continued, "Even the guy who killed three cops suddenly asked for forgiveness and was released into the king's custody. My father had been about to die from the plague and is now miraculously healed." Something inside the young man forced him to talk more than he really wanted.

The detective, if he could still be considered such, asked, "Why are you still a skeptic?"

He sat on the floor outside the cell, crossed his legs and took comfort in finding someone with whom he could confide about the things that troubled him. His fingers toyed with a button on his blue shirt and he said, "I have always gone to church regularly and believed in God. I've read Revelations countless times, but never really believed anything like that could happen. This isn't exactly as the Bible said, but it's close enough to make most people blindly follow." He paused for a moment, looked momentarily at the detective before returning his attention to the button that his fingers had found so mesmerizing, and continued, "If this king was sent by God, why punish those that believe in God with all their hearts? My father was nearly dead until the man rode into town and cured everyone that would follow. My father is out

211

there worshiping that thing just like everyone else."

Alan could see the young man was near tears. He moved from the bunk on which he had been sitting to sit in the floor facing the young man and said, "The man on the horse isn't the only one that can protect you from the plague."

These words captured the young policeman's attention and tempted the officer from the pit of despair into which his depression was sinking him. His eager eyes forgot the button and he asked, "Please tell me."

The detective thought that if he could keep the boy talking, he might learn if he was loyal to the king or if this was only a trick to gather information. The king had taken the most loyal with him to convert the church into a palace for him and an unnamed queen. This boy was left alone to guard the jail. Alan could only wonder why the boy had been chosen for that task.

If this boy truly had the doubts he professed, then he might be an ally. The eyes of the lad told the older cop that he was worth the risk and said, "I have a friend, a young girl I think can protect us from the plague."

"How?" The officer inquisitively asked.

"Let us out and we'll take you to her," Alan hopefully said.

Ryan emphatically said, "No."

Everyone at the station had often called him boy because his age in relation to most of the officers was a lot younger. He might have been younger, but he wasn't naive. The young officer wasn't about to take for granted anything a prisoner said, not even if that prisoner was a detective.

A tired, aging hand grasped the cold, blue steel of the bars. Alan pulled himself closer and whispered, "Tell my friends that I'm well. Then go to 2215 Credence Drive and tell anyone there that the others and myself are here." He thoughtfully added, "I beg of you not to tell anyone about this other than the people at this address."

Jason Ryan had been out of the academy for two years, but everyone in the department still called him boy. At first it had bothered him, but he soon accepted it as the endearment for which it was intended. The lad was well liked by everyone in the department and most thought he had a bright future. His assignment to the cell area was typical for new recruits, but it was obvious to everyone that he would soon be on patrol. He had said since day one that his goal was to be chief of detectives. Few doubted he would achieve that goal.

Night had fallen when his shift ended. He started the ancient Chevy and sat listening to the rough idle of the engine. The address given to him by the detective stuck in his mind. He had purposely tried to forget it, but it held fast in his thoughts. A decision had been made, whether it was a reckless one or not. He drove south toward Credence Drive.

When he turned onto Credence Drive, he immediately noticed something strange. Most of the town had been dark since everyone was either working to help build the palace or worshiping the new king, yet the homes on Credence Drive were lit and active with life. Ryan eased down the street and heard a baby cry. It wasn't the cry of desertion or pain, but one of hunger and a mother near to see to its needs. The cry stopped and he knew the baby was being fed. It was the cry he had often heard from his younger brother and sister when they were babies.

He stopped in front of 2215 Credence Drive and sat staring at the house. He saw the same as he had seen in all the other houses on the street—normalcy. He welcomed it into his life and never wanted to leave this street.

Before he was halfway up the walkway, a man met him and guardedly asked, "Who are you?"

The off duty officer still had on his uniform, but it hadn't made a difference to the man blocking his path. Again, the man asked, "Who are you and why are you here?"

The young officer added some caution to his voice and asked, "Do you live at this address."

"I do," he replied.

Unsure of what would happen, the officer said, "I'm here in an unofficial capacity. Detective Johnson sent me. I have a message from him."

Martin approached cautiously and noticed the officer's youthfulness in the dim light of the street lamps. Concern filled his words and he asked, "What is it that you have to tell?"

The young cop said, "He's in jail at the Twenty-First Precinct." As an afterthought he added, "Two of his friends are in custody as well."

Martin didn't want to give the policeman any knowledge he might not already have and asked, "What are the charges?"

"Sir?" The officer asked.

Martin's anger elevated and it was evident in his tone. He said, "Charges, the reasons you arrest someone and lock him or her behind bars."

At a loss for words, the officer shrugged and said, "There are no charges."

Anger unfurled from where Martin kept it hidden away and lashed out at the young officer. He demanded, "Then, why in hell is he in jail, along with our friends?"

Jason simply stated the truth to the aggressive man. He said, "He pissed off the new king."

A cloud of doom and despair descended on Martin as he stood in the dimly lit walkway. "Tell me," he asked, "are my friends unharmed?"

"For now," replied the young officer.

The officer said with no hint of consternation, "Detective Johnson said there is someone that could protect people from the plague without selling their soul to the devil, so to speak."

Martin smiled brightly and said, "That's an interesting way of putting it, officer."

"Call me Jason," he said, and thoughtfully added, "Ryan."

Martin felt the young man was being truthful, put an arm around him, and said, "Come with me, Jason Ryan, and let's find out if you want to see truth."

Jason looked at the man, and was puzzled by what he had meant by the truth.

Janice had watched the scene from inside the house. She hadn't heard what had been said, but knew from her father's reaction that the man was safe. As they stepped on the first step, she opened the door and stood watching the two men. With the men standing on the top step, Janice appeared slightly taller. Martin removed his arm from around the stranger and said, "Meet my daughter, the truth."

The baffled officer looked at both of them and asked, "What do you mean—the truth?"

Janice looked to her father with a questioning look, and he explained to her how the officer had come to tell them about their friends' plight. Fear for her friends rose in Janice. She confronted the officer and said, "You have to help me get them out, right now."

He looked at her incredulously and said, "That's impossible, miss."

She pounded the side of a fist on his chest and screamed, "There is a damn way, and you had better find it, now."

Martin pulled his daughter away from the man and said, "Let's sit down and talk about things and try to understand everything. Pounding your fist on him won't accomplish much." This brought a small smile from her and she collapsed into the swing. Martin sat beside his daughter, comfortingly laid a hand on her forearm, and said, "Tell him the truth of what's happening."

The officer pulled a chair close and sat listening to Janice tell about her kidnapping and miraculous healing. He often stared at her in disbelief. Since joining the force, he had seen and heard a lot of things, but the things he had seen in the past week weren't of this world. He knew he would awaken someday and find it all a horrible nightmare, yet he watched the girl while she talked and saw the pain in her eyes. For the first time, he had seen someone honestly pour out their pain and fears in unadulterated truth. He wept for the first time since he was a child.

Janice saw the emotion well in the man, leaned to grasp his hand, and tenderly asked, "Will you help my friends?"

"Yes," he weakly replied.

He gathered his composure and said, "This neighborhood, it's different from the others in town. In fact, it might be different from any in the world." He stopped talking, looked around, and added, "It's so normal." The boy desperately wanted things to be normal. Normalcy was something he had little of in his life.

Martin laughed at the sound of the word normal. He thought how it had been a long time since he had thought anything was normal, especially this neighborhood. Yet he knew that compared to the rest of the world, this may be the most normal place on the planet, and that scared the father.

Janice said, "We have to form a plan to set our friends free."

Martin looked sternly at his daughter, a look that only a father can give a daughter, and said, "Whatever plan there is, you won't be a part of it."

She loudly protested, "You need me to go for whatever protection I can offer. You know you might need my help."

The young officer interceded and said, "The king was trying to force Chandler to reveal who it was that might defeat him." He smiled at his own small epiphany and said, "I think that someone was you."

She blushed, even though Janice wasn't sure what she could do to defeat anyone, especially someone as powerful as the king.

Jason was beginning to like the father and daughter and knew he couldn't allow either of them to risk themselves. He said, "The police station is almost deserted since that thing came to town. I could probably walk them out of the jail, unnoticed."

Jason sat on the floor in front of the cell and said, "I talked to your friends last night and they are very nice. They told me everything that has happened and I believe them."

A sigh of relief escaped the detective and he asked, "Then you will help us?"

"I will," Jason replied.

"When?" Ask the detective.

He stood and said, "Let me make my rounds. When I feel it's safe, I'll return with the key and unlock your cells. When I make the last round of the night, you follow me and, hopefully, we can all walk out of here together."

The plan had so far gone well. Alan sat on the bunk where he stared at the unlocked door of his cell, resisting the temptation to burst through it and go after his friends. If he did, there might be more risk than needed. There was always a chance the young cop was deceiving him, and if he waited, he would fall into a trap.

On the officer's final round of the night, Alan slipped silently from the cell. They walked down a maze of twist and turns until they came to Amanda's cell. She leapt to her feet and nearly screamed with excitement at seeing Alan. He held a finger to his lips and put an arm around her as they made their way to Chandler's cell. They were both surprised and happy to see him sitting alertly on the bunk. His strength had returned just as the creature had said. He followed them down the corridor to a door marked "Exit Only." Jason opened the door, stepped out into the cool night air, and said once they were all outside, "You go ahead. I have to get back inside for some last minute duties. I'll see you all soon, I promise." Something in the officer's words sent chills up Chandler's spine and he nodded an acknowledgment.

The small room contained a wall covered with security monitors that constantly scanned the hundreds of cells in the massive facility. The man sat with his feet propped up on the desk and watched every movement in the building. The door of the office opened, Jason stepped in, and said, "I have done as you wished, my king."

He dropped his sandal clad feet to the floor, sat up, leaned forward, and said. "If the young girl is truly my adversary, we will soon know. You have done well and will be substantially rewarded for your loyalty." Jason bowed and took his leave from the room.

After the officer left the security room, he took the stairs that carried him to the same exit that he had earlier taken the escaping prisoners. The guilt of betraying such kind and strong people tore at the young officer. Silence followed him as he walked down the dark alley beside the police station. He looked out of the darkened alley to the dim lights of a changed city. He thought of the life he had planned for himself, and for the millions out in that dim light that had planned the same.

A trucked passed the alley and echoed loudly against the dingy bricks shaping the alleyway. The truck was one of hundreds that still carried plague infected dead bodies to some forgotten grave in the landfill. Everyone who hadn't followed the king had died, or so he thought until that night. There was the father and daughter on Credence Drive, and their neighbors who had survived without giving loyalty to the king.

Guilt tore at him when he thought of Janice in the hands of the king. He pressed the cold steel of the service revolver to his head and pulled the trigger. No one cared to notice the explosion of sound that echoed through the dark alley. If anyone had happened by, they likely wouldn't have cared.

Chapter 11

The massive cathedral had been built in the eighteenth century by the hands of Irish immigrants that labored day and night to feed their families. It rose into the night sky like some giant white guardian of the city. Every year, millions prayed in the church. Many Bishops had resided over the cathedral, but none before could have imagined the change it was undertaking. In two days time, the magnificent church had been reclaimed and turned into a monument of honor for the new king. Where the pulpit had once sat, now resided a golden throne. It sat empty, waiting on the time when the king would address his flock.

The new king sat upstairs in a smaller version of the golden throne in one of the maze of rooms. This room was magnificent in its own right. Priceless religious art lined the walls. The most prominent of the art, was the painting of the four horsemen of the apocalypse. No one noticed, or didn't want to notice, that the man sitting on the throne was the same man who sat on the white horse in the painting.

Bishop Carson had once been a leader of the city, but now was no more than a doorman and secretary to the newly crowned king. The former religious leader felt glorified in his new role because the Bishop thought he served the Messiah.

The bishop heard a knock on the massive front door of the cathedral and slowly opened it to reveal a middle-aged, blonde woman. He smiled the practiced smile of his former job and asked, "May I help you?"

She looked at the bishop and then to the changed church. The church wasn't one she would have attended. The woman knew from watching television that it had been changed to something other than a church, but she knew it still served the Lord's purpose. At one time the woman would have called the changes an aberration, but not on this day. Her eyes returned to the man before her and said, "I have come to see the king."

The bishop laughed mockingly at the woman and said, "No one walks in here and just asks to see the king."

A voice from behind the bishop who stood blocking the door, sternly said, "She can."

He turned to see the vagrant street preacher that had become the king's number one. The faithful bishop backed away from the door, bowed ceremoniously to the man, and waved the woman through the open doorway.

The woman approached the former street preacher, knelt on the floor, and said, "I am here to serve my Lord."

He smiled and said, "You owe me no fealty. Call me Obadiah—please stand."

She stood and firmly said, "I wish to see the king."

Obadiah smiled at her innocence and said, "The king also wishes to see you. He has been expecting you."

The woman followed the street preacher up the wide, elegant stairs with polished mahogany handrails. They would have been more suited to a palace than a church, but had been a part of the original structure.

They climbed the stairs as others had done for three hundred years. Religious paintings worth a king's ransom lined the polished marble walls. The woman let her fingers drag along the frames of the paintings while genuflecting her future, the one that had been set by God.

At the top of the stairs, she was led to a pair of large doors. The man opened the doors, letting both swing open wide, stepped aside, and waved her through. The sight before her was like some dream come true. Even though the room was decorated in priceless treasures, she saw only the king. She never noticed the silver cape that glimmered around his muscular shoulders, nor did she notice the maiden washing his feet with a soft cloth—she saw only the man of her dreams.

The woman fell to her knees in adulation. Her eyes looked to the floor while her soul fought to stare at the magnificence she had only glimpsed while entering the room, yet the vision was etched into her mind. Her mind was filled with images of the man in all his glory sitting on a golden throne and the shimmering of the silver cape that hung from broad, immortal shoulders. A hand went to her lower abdomen and the woman tried to suppress the tingling she felt within. There were feeling she hadn't felt since the first year of her marriage.

His voice was strong and as magnificent as his looks. He said to the woman, "Rise and come to me."

She tried to do as he commanded, but her legs failed to move. He had, somehow, sapped all of her strength. She looked up to see him standing only inches from her and weakly said, "I'm sorry, my king, my body has failed me."

His hand reached down for her, she took it, and the instant there was contact, the woman knew she belong to this man. God had given the woman to the king—and she was thankful. Her life now belonged to the king. That night he took her to his bed and she became his concubine. Her church teachings said she should have been ashamed, but she wasn't.

As the sun rose through the stained glass windows of his bedroom, the king said, "Delores, we have much work for today."

The married woman laid her head on his naked chest in reply. The moment she had given herself to the king, she had promised to forever forsake her husband and daughter.

Chapter 12

The knock was loud and panicky as Janice awakened from a sound sleep. The fog of sleep slowly dissipated and she heard a weak, urgent voice behind the knock. Martin asked, "Janice, are you awake?"

Sleep was washed away by the mild panic that came with her father's voice. She said, "Come in, dad." The look in his eyes said as much as his loud, panicky knock.

He sat on the bed and she looked at him questioningly. He said as his voice trembled, "Your mother is missing. She left last night and hasn't returned. She has never wandered off like this, before."

"Did you call the church or the pastor's house?" She hopefully asked.

He nodded and said, "They haven't heard from her in days. She missed last night's prayer service and were worried about her, themselves." The only time Delores missed any church service was if she was extremely ill, and this apparently wasn't the case.

The father and daughter heard a faint knock in the distance, not unlike the one Janice had just received on her bedroom door. Janice threw on the light blue cotton housecoat that matched her gown, while Martin rushed for the front door. Their nerves were on fire and they feared that whomever was behind the knock had brought bad news about Delores.

Martin reached the door first with a painful smile that was filled with despair. When he opened it, Amanda threw her arms around Martin said with relief, "God, it's so good to see your face."

Alan smiled and mockingly said, "Careful, I might get jealous." They all laughed as Janice came down the stairs in a rush and tore Amanda from her father's arms. She hugged Amanda with one hand, while reaching out the other to Alan and Chandler, who stood weakly behind. Janice said. "I was so scared for you all."

"I'll just collapse out here while all of you hug." Chandler, with mock derisiveness, said.

They all closed in on him and apologized for their carelessness. Janice said, after they were all seated and had tea or coffee to drink, "Jason helped you, I guess."

Alan said, "He really came through for us. We might have died in that place if it hadn't been for him."

"Thank goodness—I've been worried sick for you all," the relieved girl said.

Amanda smiled reassuringly and said, "We were treated well. In fact, I saw only the men that brought us our meals.

We seemed to be the only prisoners in the entire building."

"Chandler, you seem to be looking much better. I guess you were cured with all the others in the hospital." Martin said.

The three looked at each other and Chandler said, "It's not as simple as that. I wasn't cured."

"But you're alive and appear to be getting better. If you weren't cured, how could you be up and walking around?" Martin asked.

"According to our self-proclaimed king, I won't die anytime soon, at least not from the plague," the former minister said, unperturbed.

"I don't understand," the man and daughter chorused.

He swallowed hard and said, "The creature told me I never had the plague." A sad look came to his face and he continued, "It's actually worse. I'm the carrier. I'm the Typhoid Mary of the new world. I probably shouldn't be here. I'm putting all of you in danger."

Amanda comfortingly touched his arm and said, "I don't think any of us have to worry about the plague. If we could catch it, I think we would have it by now. Look at all the time I spent with you and the other patients in the hospital. Before the king cured everyone, half the staff had taken ill. The ones that weren't ill had begun to show symptoms."

Alan's mind wasn't on the conversation in the room. He asked, "Is it me, or is there something different about this neighborhood. No matter where I've gone, everything looked dead and lifeless. This street looks like it's sealed off from the rest of the world. People are outside talking to their neighbors. In fact, some actually seem happier than normal."

Janice looked at her father proudly and said, "My father is the greatest man I've ever met."

Martin blushed and said, "Oh no, you're not laying all this on me, it was you that did the real work, out there."

A bright smile lit Alan's face and he asked, "I hate to disturb this mutual admiration society meeting, but what are you talking about?"

They both laughed and Martin indicated that Janice tell them what had transpired that day. She told how her father had confronted the disturbed crowd of neighbors and calmed them, and how he had pointed them toward the truth. With less enthusiasm, she told of her own part that day.

Amanda had tears in her eyes as she hugged the father and daughter. She said to Martin and Janice, "We all have so much to thank you both for. We might not be here right now if it wasn't for the two of you. You have never failed us when we needed help."

His daughter's sad past came to mind and Martin said, "You have done so much more for me than I have for you. My daughter might not be here if it wasn't for the both of you."

"I want to add my kudos as well." Pete said as they all turned to see him and his father standing at the opened door. Pete had spent so much time with Janice that he often just opened the door and announced himself instead of knocking.

Frank apologetically said, "I hope you don't mind our dropping in without calling." He hesitated and added, "Things are getting weird in our neighborhood and we weren't sure where to go. Pete suggested here. I hope you don't mind."

Alan and Amanda looked at one another and silently inferred to the other that they might be in the same predicament. Martin empathetically said, "I think everyone needs to stay here until we can come up with a better solution, or this horrible thing is over."

"I think we are safer as a group than separate." Janice added.

Relief appeared on Frank's face and he said, "I should go get the bags," he added with embarrassment, "I packed just in case." Everyone laughed harmoniously.

"Alan and I weren't as prepared as Frank and Pete. I don't have any extra clothes or anything to sleep in," Amanda said.

Excited at having all her friends, especially Pete, staying, Janice said, "Alan can wear some of my dad's clothes. She saddened at the thought of her missing mother and added, "Amanda can wear my or mom's nightgown."

The mention of Delores brought a pall over the father and daughter. The first to notice the change of emotion was Amanda. She asked, "Is there something wrong with Delores?"

Martin sadly replied, "She's missing. She left sometime yesterday and never returned home." Facing the truth, he added, "She's been acting strange since all this started." His eyes begged for forgiveness as he looked at his daughter, the pain evident on his face. He said," I'm kind of glad she's gone." He quickly corrected, "I don't mean to say I wish her harm. The last few years we've not been as close as we had once been, and since all this started we've grown even farther apart. Sometimes she even scares me with how she would stare at me as if I was something evil."

Martin expected a tirade from his daughter and visibly shrank away from her. He was pleasantly surprised when she said, "I understand, dad. Every since the night of the fire, I've been afraid of mom." They hugged and comforted one another for the thoughts they harbored for the woman they both still loved in their own way. Martin might not love Delores as a wife, but he still loved her for being the mother of his child.

In an effort to dissipate the sad moment, Martin said, "I guess we need to work out the sleeping arrangements." Martin looked at the doctor and Alan, and said with slight embarrassment," The two of you can take the guest room, if that's okay."

Alan and Amanda thanked him appreciatively. The couple exchanged looks and were glad they had been saved the embarrassment of having to ask to share a room, as well as a bed.

Martin looked at Pete and said, "You and…" A sudden quiet settled over the room in anticipation of what he might suggest for the boy. Martin noticed the looks and said to them, "Oh no, not in my lifetime. My daughter is sleeping alone in her room." They all laughed while Janice blushed awkwardly. Her father, expecting her reaction, smiled, and continued, "Pete, you and your father can sleep in Delores' room."

His words were an admission that he and his wife didn't share a bedroom. They hadn't slept together since Janice's birth. After the difficult pregnancy, Delores had declared that sex was dirty and not something God would approve of since they didn't planned to have more children. Martin had only told her that they would wait before having more. His wife had used that as an excuse to avoid any amorous advances.

In some ways, it had also been an admission that he didn't expect her to return home. Something told Martin that he would never see his wife again, at least the same woman he had married.

The detective had felt a gnawing feeling in his gut since their escape. Until now, he had hesitated to voice that feeling out loud. Everyone's mood was better than it had been in days. He hated to do anything to destroy that mood, yet he knew he must share his trepidations with the others. He stuttered weakly, "I need... to... say something."

Everyone in the room could see the seriousness on his face. They waited with bated breath. Alan said, "I think our escape was too easy—I think we were let go for a reason. I've been a cop most of my adult life, and there is no way a jail could be as empty as that one."

What little cheer had been in the room evaporated. Amanda said, "I think he's right. If that king had been so mad at us, he wouldn't have let us live, much less escape a jail with only one guard."

"You think Jason was working with him?" Janice asked.

Alan nodded and said, "Yes. He had to, to have let us go. The question is, why?"

"To follow us?" Amanda queried.

The detective said, "Bingo, but why would he want to follow us. Where would we go that could be of use to him?"

Martin looked at his daughter, perturbed, and said, "He would follow you here to find my daughter."

Pale and distraught, Chandler said, "He would come looking for her because of me. Of all the stupid things I could have said, I had to taunt him about someone being able to defeat him."

Amanda comfortingly said, "He doesn't know who it was you were talking about."

"He might not know who, but he now knows where," the detective said.

Janice wearily said, "My father and I told Jason everything. If he was working for the king, then your coming here is unimportant."

Alan said, "The king might not have believed the boy, but did want to see where we would go. If nothing else, we confirmed everything that Jason might have told him. I do believe Janice is partially invisible to the king's power or she would already be dead."

Martin said to no one in particular. "What do we do? How can we battle him if he does come here?"

Janice's eyes were steady, clear, and emotionless. "We do nothing," she said

232

Fear grasped Pete as he thought of what might happen to Janice if she was to face the king. He asked, "How can we do nothing? When he comes, we have to fight him with everything we have. I'll fight him as long as there is life in me."

Janice kissed him on the cheek and sternly said, "No one will risk his or her life for me. If and when he comes, I'll go with him. If anyone is hurt trying to protect me, then I'll be gone and someone I love will have lost their life for nothing." She looked directly at each person as she surveyed the room and added, "Promise me that you won't risk yourself for me when the time comes."

Words were choked back by the emotion of the moment. Every eye was on Janice when Martin, near tears, said, "Honey, you know I would willingly die to protect you from harm."

She looked at her father and said, "As I would for you, dad."

"This man is not going to do anything foolish. How would it be to his advantage to rush this house and take Janice? He would have to take us all to be sure he had the right person. I think he will take his time to be absolutely sure which one is his enemy. As far as the king knows, everything Martin and Janice told Jason could have been misdirection," Chandler said analytically

"Chandler," Amanda took a thoughtful breath, and asked, "This king came from God, didn't he?"

Janice anxiously waited for Chandler's answer. He said

with the authority of years of study, "The Old Testament tells us the horsemen will be unleashed on Earth during the apocalypse. From everything that has happened to me, this king is no doubt one of the horsemen. This is true only if the Bible is accurate."

He took the Bible that he kept in his pocket as a constant reminder of his past, opened it, and stared at the words that had once comforted the fallen minster. Since meeting Janice, the former preacher began using it as a reference book. Now it was to be used as a demonstration. He opened the Bible, ripped a page from it, and said, "This is the page where God tells us he is a loving god. He ripped out another page and said, "This is where it says that if you believe in him, you will have eternal life." He tossed the Bible onto the floor and continued, "It's all lies or half truths. Look at what's happened to Janice. She has endured torture we cannot fathom. Whether it was God or the devil that tortured her, it doesn't matter. One of them could have spared her. We have watched loved ones tortured to death. For centuries, those like me sat back as the world crumbled around them and said, It's God's will… he is testing us."

They all looked at the former minister in astonishment. Man has followed the Bible religiously for a thousand years, yet a former minister suggested it was all a lie. Scholars and laymen have debated the Bible for centuries, while much of the world followed it blindly. Yet the Bible was the only reference book they had for the problems the world was encountering. They knew from Janice's experiences that parts of the Bible were wrong, but to suggest that it was completely flawed left them blind to the things they might face. Knowledge was power and the minister was ripping that power from them page by page as he tore them from the Bible. They could only hope that the minister was wrong and there were things in the Bible that could be used against Iam or God, if they are one and the same. At this point, they couldn't be sure if God, Iam, or Lucifer was the enemy.

A rapid knock on the door tore them from the moment that had approached despair. Martin opened the door to expose the one who had chosen that moment to interrupt their lives. It was the squat man that had been the self-appointed spokesman the day Martin had delivered his speech to the neighbors. The man respectfully said, "Mr. Carter…" He hesitated and looked embarrassed.

Martin asked, "Are you alright? You look pale."

The man searched for the words that he hoped would soften the truth, except there were none. He simply said, "You should turn on the television." The man turned and trudged away, sad that he had been the bearer of bad news.

Janice turned on the television and settled back on the couch before looking to see what had caused the neighbor such concern. The king smiled brightly as his face was electronically reproduced all around the world. He looked more regal than any king in all of history. He wore his silver robe and the golden crown that had been placed on his head by the hand of God.

He looked directly at the camera, spread his arms in a

welcoming gesture, and said, "People of Earth, I welcome you to my kingdom." In Germany they heard him in their native language: "Völker der Erde, ich heiße euch in meinem Königreich willkommen." In France they heard him say, "Peuple de la Terre, je vous souhaite la bienvue a mon royaume."

He leaned slightly forward, looked warmly into the camera, and said, "I come not to do harm, but to save you. Through carelessness, your former leaders have killed millions of your loved ones. In their secret laboratories they grew germs that our god never intended when he created this world. Man dared to play god and created abjurations."

He paused for his words to be analyzed by those listening. He somberly said, "Your leaders steal your children from you, leads them to war, and then, eventually to their deaths. They proclaim to do this to defend your freedom, while at the same time chaining you to the government though taxes and healthcare. As your king, I have ended all wars. All of mankind will live as one, as it was intended before Adam and Eve sinned—before the idol of the golden calf when man was sent to the corners of the Earth and forced to speak different languages."

The king paused, looked around at the million people assembled in the square, and said, "Those that follow me and give yourself to helping your fellow man, will prosper and find the happiness you deserve." His expression hardened and he leaned forward with his forearms resting on the podium that had previously been reserved for the President of the United

States. A golden cross had replaced the familiar presidential seal. He continued, "Those that seek to stand in the way of me and my followers will invoke the wrath of God onto them. There will be no mercy for those who defy me. She will suffer at my hands."

Janice watched and knew as this man stared coldly into the camera that he was speaking directly to her. It was at this moment that she knew he was aware of her watching the speech. She looked at her father and said, "He knows for sure who I am."

"How?" He emphatically questioned.

Truth, once an ally, had become a bitter enemy as it slammed against the father. Martin said, "Jason did betrayed us as we had guessed."

Alan retrospectively said, "I knew it, the officer had only been a trick. He told the vile creature everything."

No one doubted what the king said wasn't the truth. Their minds searched for a solution to the problem while watching the king. He said, "I am sending the police to those who seek to destroy me. I will offer them as a gift to you—my people. I will bring them before my people so you can witness the destruction of my enemies."

There was a large cheer. The mass of people had not only accepted their new leader, but embraced him. This king had told them everything they wanted to hear. The people of the world were happy to finally have a leader that was action and not just empty words. This was a blessing come true. In the past, they had lived with leaders that promised everything, but gave nothing—leaders that spoke bravely of conquering enemies, while cowering behind patriotic words.

The king turned to smile at someone hidden out of the camera's eye and then turned once more to address his people. He said, "As an example of the things I have to offer, and the graciousness of my love for mankind, I want you to meet the woman I have taken as wife. This woman has suffered a terrible pain to be with me. She had to escape a man that had, for years, forsaken her. He had pushed her from his life, as well as his bed. He had not only forsaken her, but the god that created the universe."

He turned, bowed to a woman as she stepped forward, and took her place at his side. She wore a white gossamer material as thin as air, which draped over and around her lithe form. The dress covered her, but still managed to accentuate her curves. She was a middle-aged woman who had not aged with grace. Everyone watched and wondered why he had chosen such a woman. They thought a king might choose a young nymph, not someone who was still beautiful, but displayed the wear of time.

Behold the power of your king. He kissed her long and passionately. When he broke the kiss and revealed her face, she had suddenly changed to a woman no older than twenty-five. There was a harmonious gasp from the crowd.

By this time, no one was sitting at the Carter house. They had all stood with their mouth's hanging open. They watched the television with unbelieving eyes. The woman that stood with the king, and would become betrothed to him, was

Delores Carter.

"How can this be?" Martin asked with bewilderment and pain. His legs finally gave way and he fell backwards onto the chair. He said with tears forming in his eyes, "Never in my wildest nightmare could I have seen this coming. This has to be some trick."

No one thought much of the sound of something hitting the floor until they looked down and saw Janice sprawled unconscious on the floor. The shock of seeing her mother in the arms of that creature was more than her tortured mind could stand. The girl had been through a lot of pain and torture, but nothing had compared to this moment. Her mind had searched for a grain of sanity in the thing she saw, but it found nothing. When there was no thought process that could make sense of the things her eyes saw, and her ears heard, it sought the solace of unconsciousness.

When Janice tried to open her eyes, all she could see was spinning faces hovering above. She quickly closed her eyes to reduce the nausea created by the spinning faces. A soft voice finally coaxed her from the darkness. She slowly opened her eyes and saw the worried face of Amanda. The doctor said, "It's about time, you had us all worried."

"Was it all a dream?" She asked while looking at her father. He shook his head but avoided eye contact because he felt guilt for what his daughter had just witnessed.

They helped Janice from the floor and onto the couch. In the distance, they heard the sound of sirens. It was as if the creature had timed their arrival to coincide with what he said on television, "Come to your mother, child of darkness, and let her lead you to the light."

Tires screeched as half a dozen police cars slid to a halt in front of the house. A gunshot made everyone duck for cover. Detective Johnson said, "That shot came from farther way than the police cars." Confused by the sudden gunfire, he asked, "Why would the police be shooting?"

Crouched low, Alan worked his way to the window and peeked out in time to see a flash from the muzzle of a gun. It had come from the house across the street. The woman that seemed to always be wearing the tattered, faded blue housecoat had shot at the police from a window. She had been watching television and knew what was happening. The woman didn't need to think about which side she would choose, those decisions had been made the day Janice spoke to them on the lawn.

Moments later, multiple shots rang out as other neighbors began firing. Astonished, Alan said, "My God, your neighbors are shooting at the police."

Chandler smiled and said, "That might not be such a bad idea." He looked at Martin questioningly and asked, "Do you have any guns in the house?'

Martin hesitated for a moment and said, "I sure do, come with me." Martin stopped with one foot on the bottom step of the stairs and said, "The rest of you get some things you might need and go out the back door. I'll keep them pinned down while you get Janice away from here."

"I'm not leaving without you, dad," she determinedly

shouted.

Martin was half way up the stairs when he shouted sternly," Get her out of here."

He came back down with an old, rusting, pump shotgun and a small caliber revolver. He looked at them apologetically and said, "Sorry, I'm not much of a gun person. Delores wanted me to get rid of even these..." His voice trailed off at the mention of his wife's name.

Alan took a position at the front window with his service revolver, which the young cop had managed to retrieve for him upon their escape from jail. He looked at Martin and said, "You go with your daughter." He looked at Chandler questioningly and continued when the preacher nodded affirmation, "Chandler and I can manage here. Besides, your neighbors are keeping them pretty busy."

Chandler was familiar with firearms, even though, for the most part, he had detested them, but he was prepared to fight, or even die to save Janice. He said, "Go, get her out of here."

The father saw the eyes of the two men and knew there was no arguing with them. They had made up their minds.

Amanda looked pleadingly at her lover and wished she could kiss him one last time before leaving, but she knew there wasn't enough time. She managed to get close enough for her fingers to momentarily brush against his as he reached out to her. At that moment, an overzealous policeman fired a shot into the house and shattered a vase, missing Amanda's head by mere inches.

Alan looked at Amanda longingly and emphatically said, "Get the hell out of here, now!"

Janice, still in shock, was slow to leave the house. Amanda took her hand, led her out the back door, and into the shroud of darkness. She looked around to see Martin following them, with Pete and Frank bringing up the rear. Janice regained her composure, pointed to a thicket of bushes, and said, "Go that way. There's a broken board in the fence that we can slip through."

Her father looked at her and wondered how she could have known about the loose plank and asked, "How in the world?"

Janice snickered despite the tense circumstances and said, "It's a long story for another time."

He smiled at the impish side of his daughter that he hoped to, someday, know better in the future, if there was such a thing as a future.

The board had been loose just as Janice had promised. The gunfire had become more frequent, and more distant as they slipped through the narrow opening of the fence. They cut across the neighbor's yard and found themselves in a densely wooded patch of trees. Janice looked around in the dark, tried to find her direction, and finally said, "The park is that way, I think."

The sound of distant gunfire trailed off to small pops as they broke out of the underbrush into the park. Time spent walking silently through the park gave Janice and the others time to think. Janice said, "We should have stayed with our friends."

Everyone had been thinking the same thing, but it was Frank who had reason with him, and said, "We did the correct thing." He looked questioningly at the others and asked, "What do we do, now?" No one had an answer.

When Alan was sure the others were safely away, he said to Chandler, "Its time to end this before someone gets hurt." The former minister nodded in agreement.

The detective opened the door a few inches, tossed out their weapons, and shouted, "We are tossing out our weapons and coming out with our hands up."

The sounds of their surrender silenced the neighborhood. The police rushed the two men as they exited the house with their hands placed on top of the head. The first policeman, angry from being shot at, approached and shouted at the two men, "Lay on the ground, face down." They silently complied.

Two other officers arrived, one a detective. He looked at the two men on the ground and asked with surprise resonating in his voice, "Alan? Detective Alan Johnson?"

Alan looked up, grinned, and sarcastically said, "So good to see you, detective."

The detective angrily asked, "Why the hell were you shooting at these officers?"

The prone man pointed to two weapons laying on the ground, and said with a smile, "Check those weapons, neither has been recently fired. The pistol is standard force issue. If you check the serial number, you'll find it belongs to me. Canvass the neighborhood for slugs and casings, and if you find one that matches either weapon, I'll plead guilty to any charges you can dream up."

The detective in charge looked despondent, turned to the officer in charge, and asked, "Who the hell was doing all that shooting?"

The officer said in defense, "We arrived on the scene and took fire from several directions."

The investigating detective's eyes surveyed the area and noticed no obvious signs of a gun battle, other than the broken windowpane in the Carter house. He asked the officer, "That window is broken, do you know how?"

The officer could see that there was no glass lying on the outside of the house. He knew there was only one plausible answer. He hesitated and said, "It came from weapons fire, detective."

"Very astute, officer—What was your name again?" The lead detective asked.

"Jenkins—sir," the officer rigidly replied.

The detective pulled a notepad from his pocket, not unlike the one that Alan carried. He scanned it, and then asked, "Officer... Jenkins, this random fire that you took upon arriving on the scene, could that have broken this window?"

Cornered, the officer replied, "It could have," he hesitated and reluctantly admitted, "but it didn't. One of my men had a weapon to misfire."

He rubbed his three-day growth of beard and said, "Hmm… yes… a misfire. Let me carefully sum this for up. You fired on a private residence from which you had not received gunfire. You have a detective of this police force face down on the ground because your man… err… had a misfire."

The officer could only offer an embarrassed nod, and said in defense, "We had orders to bring in anyone in this house. I had no idea the detective was in the house. He never identified himself."

Alan looked up mischievously and asked, "Can we get up, now? I'm too old to be laying on the cold ground at night."

The detective offered his hand and Alan used it to pull himself up. Chandler stood as well.

A sense of duty brought the officer back to why he had come to this place and asked, "Where's the girl and her father?"

Alan feigned ignorance and asked, "What girl?"

"The girl that lives here," the officer angrily replied.

"Ohhhh… that girl," Alan said to the officer," I was going to ask you the same thing. I came to arrest her and she was gone. And then you guys started shooting at me."

The officer shook his head and walked away in disgust. He knew Detective Johnson was lying, and also knew there was no need to challenge the deception.

Alan put a hand on the detective's shoulder and said, "I owe you one."

"You owe me a lot more than that. The least you can do is

offer an explanation as to what in the hell went on here, tonight. That would be a good first payment," he forcefully said.

"You will get it and more, I promise," Alan graciously said.

Police cars began to untangle as the officers drove silently from the embattled neighborhood. When the last car had gone, neighbors stepped out of their houses and waved triumphantly at Alan and Chandler. The two waved back, but didn't feel nearly as triumphant as the neighbors.

The neighbors had only shot into the air in an effort to prevent anyone from accidentally getting shot. They new there would be a risk to their own lives, but they also knew their lives would have been a small price to pay for Janice's safety.

The sound cut through the night like a dagger. It could be one of the most ominous sounds, or one that brought peace. On this night, the ringing phone was the latter. Chandler rushed into the house and grabbed the phone from its resting place. He waited nervously for a voice to speak from the other end. A smile brighter than a sunrise covered his face when he heard the nervous tone of Amanda's voice on the other end. He tried to hided the excitement in his voice, but failed miserably and exclaimed, "Amanda!"

She cried at the sound of his voice and couldn't hide her emotions. She worriedly said, "I was so scared—there were so many gunshots. Is Alan alright?"

Alan took the phone from the preacher and comfortingly said, "The police have gone. A detective friend of mine happened by and helped smooth things over. I convinced the police that I was here to arrest Janice and it was the officers that had bungled the operation."

She wanted to laugh at his ploy, but was still too shaken to do so. "Thank God," she cried.

Alan asked, "Where are you? We can come and get you."

Just for an instant, she wondered if Alan had been taken by the police and was being forced to have her reveal Janice's location. The rational side of her mind knew the man she loved could never be forced to hurt anyone he loved, or his friends. Paranoia gave way to reason and she managed to find calm in her voice. She said, "We're at the park"

"We'll come get you," Alan said

"Be careful," she pleaded.

Alan reined in his emotion and said, "I'll be there in five minutes." The detective had faced danger many times in his career, but in the past there had been no one like Amanda sharing that danger. Alan would give his own life before he would let any harm come to the woman with whom he had fallen deeply in love.

Alan looked at his old clunker and knew he would need something better and bigger. He spotted Delores' mini-van parked in the drive. He found the keys hanging in the kitchen. Moments later, he eased his way through the park and looked for his friends. He rounded a curve and the headlights reflected off an object. Alan slowed the car to a stop and strained to see into the underbrush. Relief washed over him when he saw Amanda emerge from the bushes with the others following close behind.

When they were all seated, Alan turned and inquired, "Where to?"

No one had an answer to the question. Janice said with disappointment, "Home was the safest place we could have been. He has forced us from that safety. No matter where we go, we are at a much higher risk. Those that believed in the truth protect our neighborhood. Out here, we're at the creature's mercy."

"I have a suggestion as to where we can go," Alan said. They all looked hopefully at the detective. He continued, "Across town there is a safe house that we use for protecting witnesses, as well as criminals who might have really displeased someone."

Everyone caught the meaning that it was used to protect criminals from being murdered by their associates. It was a safe house for the witness protection program, and they surely needed protecting.

The mini-van blended in with traffic as they approached the square where the king had made his television speech. The massive, newly erected stage still sat in the street like an ominous idol. Across the street, in what had been Saint Peters' Cathedral, the king's palace stood looming over the square.

Martin leaned toward the front of the mini-van and angrily asked, "What the hell are you doing, defecting and turning us over to that creature?"

Alan laughed while everyone looked at him incredulously.

He turned left and eased the van down a street one block from the church. He pointed to a modest apartment building and said, "There is home for as long as we need it."

"You have lost your mind," Amanda said first, but the others chorused the same.

He turned sideways in the seat, looked like the cat that had just eaten the king's canary, and said, "What better place to hide than under his nose? We're close enough to keep a close eye on what the king might be up to, as well as so close that he would never look for us here. He will have the police scanning every motel/hotel in the state. He won't bother with the ones in this areas since only a fool would attempt to hide so close."

"Fool is the perfect word for this," Amanda said.

"This is just crazy enough to work," Martin said while shaking his head at himself for agreeing with the lunatic cop.

Janice hopped out of the van and said, "Let's hurry inside and unpack, I'm starved." They all laughed at her remark, since they had only the clothes on their back.

The king was angry that the police hadn't returned with Janice. He sent them back to Credence Drive. Twice as many police filled the street as there had been earlier. They stormed the house to find it empty. The k-9 team was called in to search for the elusive residents. They found one of Janice's dresses in the dirty clothes hamper, which they had the dog sniff. Once the dog had the scent, the animal barked excitedly and jerked his trainer out the back door of the house and into the backyard. They found the loose board in the fence and crawled through the tight opening. The policeman ripped his new shirt on a nail, the one about which Janice had warned her friends. The trail ended the in the park. The dog ran in circles after losing the scent. The dog's howl would pale in comparison to that of the king when he found out they had, once more, failed.

After the police rushed into the Carter house, the neighbors had gone back into their homes and locked their doors. Once the police were leaving in search of their prey, the neighbors trickled out of their houses. The old, as well as the healthy and infirmed, stood in their yards and stared at the remaining officers. A rookie officer shouted at his captain and demanded, "Let's arrest these people. They shot at us."

The older and more experienced officer turned to the rookie and sullenly said, "Go right ahead. Then you might as well start thinking of an explanation on how a group of seniors and cripples helped the suspects get away. Then you can explain how one of our detectives helped the perpetrators escape. Son, this is one incident that we just want to go away."

The steely eyed neighbors closed in on the officers. The trained police circled back to back as if they were pioneers circling their wagons for protection against marauding Indians.

The squat man approached the captain, who stood between the people and his officers, and held out his hand as a peace offering. The captain shook it nervously. What had the officers nervous, was that not one person showed fear of any kind. They looked as if they knew something that would protect them. The squat, balding man calmly said, "We have a lot to talk about."

The balding man told the officers, nearly word for word, everything Janice and Martin had told them. The young mother produced the newspapers from the missing week. Mistrust was thick among the officers. Everyday they met con-men, thieves, the insane, and knew this could be no different, especially since the things they said sounded truly insane.

When the man first began talking they were sure he was the latter, the insane, yet they wondered how the entire street could have gone mad at the same time. As Iam's fog clouding the officers' minds slowly faded, they began questioning their own sanity. They stared at the proof as the newspapers were passed around.

The clatter of metal against asphalt sounded out of place as an officer dropped his weapon. Slowly it became a symphony of sound as others began dropping their own. Reason had found a place in their mind. Once it was in place, they knew the man calling himself king was evil. The officers saw how they, and the rest of the world, had given into evil without question. They, at first, felt ashamed, but that was soon replaced by anger.

One of the younger officers remembered something he had once read in school. At the time he had given it little thought. As the words replayed over and over in his mind, they finally poured from his lips in a near whisper, "May the truth set you free." Everyone looked at him and nodded.

That night the officers drove home to their families instead of the station as they had been ordered. They had an overwhelming need to be with the ones they loved. They left their weapons laying on Credence Drive. The men knew they had no more use for them. Their greatest weapon was now their minds. The truth had truly set them free.

Chapter 13

He looked at the soft form lying beside him in the massive, elegant bed that had been taken from a nearby five-star hotel. Her blonde hair spilled onto the pillow as he watched the slow rise and fall of her average breasts. She had given him what only a woman could give a man, yet she couldn't give him what he truly desired most from this world full of humans.

His thoughts were of the young girl that dared to stand against him, the immortal king. He had no idea what she looked like, other than she look much like the mother that lay next to him. The officer had told him her name was Janice and offered to show the king a photograph, but he didn't trust such things and wanted to see her for himself. That name was burned into his soul. For as long as he had known existence, none had possessed him like she did. The king had asked his creator for the reasons, but the only answer was silence.

Bed-covers slid silently from him as he slipped from

beneath them. He walked to the window and gazed up at the full moon. Something touched his senses. He smiled and knew that Janice was near, too near. The king decided he would have the entire city searched for the threat, especially the nearby area. A laugh escaped his lips and he said aloud, "It's been a long time since I had a worthy adversary. Only the brave or the foolish would have dared hide so close to their enemy. He knew that she was anything but a fool."

Guards could have been alerted to begin an immediate search, but for the moment, he chose to feel her nearness, to bask in its warmth. He turned to see the face of Janice's mother as the moon shed a soft glow on its features. The thought of soon having the girl, instead of the mother, in his bed made him content, yet eager.

The night air wafted into the room and he sniffed it as a wolf might sniff the night air in search of its mate—or its prey. He could smell her scent on the cool, damp air and knew she was near. He leaned out the window and whispered, "Janicccce."

The sound floated out the window and onto the night air where it searched each building. It drifted and sought the recipient for which the message was intended, the one whose name it carried. If the girl could not be found, the wind would carry the message around the world, and for an eternity it would search anytime there was the slightest breeze on which to travel.

The wind found a window that appeared to be closed, yet there was a crack beneath that only the wind could have found. It slipped downward and through the unseen opening to find a sleeping girl. The wind was so gentle that it was barely noticeable. The wind released the name it carried, "Janicccce."

The girl stirred as her name was released from the wind, but she didn't awaken. The wind dissipated and became still—and it was no longer wind. What had been the wind was inhaled by the girl and was transformed into life.

Strong hands held her as she tried to escape. She wanted to flee, but desire held her in its grasp. His eyes were like flaming candles in the night and they brought her fear, but she desired him more than she had ever desired a man. His lips touched hers and she heard him whisper her name.

Janice thought of the one she loved and reluctantly pushed the man with dark piercing eyes away. His eyes filled with rage and then pulled her back into his arms. The girl slipped from his grasp and rushed to the waiting arms of the only one she had ever loved.

A scream of pure rage reverberated on the night air. The rejected king ran from the window, opened the heavy door, nearly ripping it from its ornate hinges. The guard looked stunned and worried. The king screamed at the trembling guard and said, "She is near, find the girl that looks like the woman lying in my bed. I want her before the sun rises twice more."

The guard looked past the king and saw the naked woman that lay sexually spent and sleeping. Her nakedness held his gaze for several moments until the king impatiently asked,

"Well… what are you waiting for?"

The guard bowed his head and rushed down the regal hall, shouting orders as he ran. In less than an hour there were ten thousand police officers and civilians canvassing the city. Search and seizure warrants were no longer needed in the new world. The only authority needed was that of the king. The posse took into custody any young girl that resembled Delores, or simply had blonde hair. By sunrise there were over fifty girls lined up on the stage where they waited for the king's inspection.

Janice awakened bathed in sweat. She laid on the bed that sat in one of the apartment's bedrooms, remembering the strange dream and the voice that had called her in the night. She touched fingertips to her lips as she remembered the dream-man's burning kiss. The girl could still feel the heat from his touch as if he was still there. She pushed the memory from her mind and looked toward the window. Fear made her want to stay in bed, hidden under the covers to avoid facing the world that wanted to consume her soul.

A siren screamed angrily as it passed her closed bedroom window. Janice slid from the bed and looked out in hopes of finding the source of the chaos. She saw police cars and angry mobs that moved quickly from door to door, knocking. When there was an answer, they would enter, look quickly around, and move on to the next door.

The door nearly shattered from the force when Martin exploded, unannounced, into her bedroom. He saw his daughter looking out the window and jerked her away. She looked at her father in shock and asked, "What's wrong?"

He said, his voice shaking with panic, "They are looking in every house and apartment searching for a young blonde girl. They are taking anyone that fits your description." He trembled, protectively held his daughter in his arms, and said, "They are looking for you."

Alan rushed in and slammed the already tortured door against the wall. He grabbed Janice's wrist, tore it from her father, and said while he half dragged the girl behind, "We have to hide you."

He stopped at a normal looking bookcase and pushed at it with his free hand. The bookcase, at first, resisted his efforts and then gave way. Behind it was a small room. He shoved Janice into the small space, followed, and said, "Close it, now! Tell them anything, but get them to leave, quickly."

Her father and Pete looked longingly at the girl they both loved and closed the bookcase, sealing them off from the rest of the house. Pete had wanted to go with her, but there wasn't enough room for three in the small space. There was no choice who stayed with Janice because Detective Johnson was the most capable of protecting her if something went wrong. The last thing Pete saw as the book-laden structure closed was the worried look in her eyes as a hand reached for him, pulling him away.

No sooner than the bookcase closed, there was a loud, ominous knock on the door. A voice filled with commanding authority said from the other side of the door, "Open up or we will break the door down."

Amanda went to the door and looked back at the others as her hand closed on the doorknob. She took a deep breath and turned it slowly. Before she could remove her hand from the knob, the door flew open, knocking her backwards.

Three men dressed in police uniforms stood with their hands on the weapons at their side as if to intimidate. One unconsciously said, as he had repeated dozens of times that morning, "Stay where you are and don't move. We are looking for a girl approximately sixteen years old with blonde hair. Remain calm while we search the premises and no harm will come to you or the girl."

Men wearing black body-armor rushed into the room and began a thorough search. The policemen looked anywhere that was big enough to hide an adult person. While the others searched, the officer in charge stood staring at Martin. For a moment, the father thought the officer recognized him from some earlier event.

The search only lasted a few minutes and they filed out the door in a hurry. The lead officer took one last lingering look at Martin and then said as he closed the door, "Sorry to have bothered you, ma'am and sirs."

No one moved for several minutes. They listened as footsteps receded down the hallway. They counted the pairs of steps to be sure all the police officers had left.

When they were sure all the officers had gone, they waited five more minutes before sliding the bookcase to the side, revealing the man and girl standing nervously in the small space. Martin smiled when he saw two pistols pointed at him, one by the detective, and one by Janice. Alan smiled and said, "We keep a spare gun in here—just in case."

No one commented on the fact that he had given a gun to the young girl, because they knew it was for her own protection. They also knew that her true age was great than the sixteen listed on her driver's license. Janice would have been eager to point out the fact that she would soon be seventeen. With an unknown time spent in the timeless prison, Janice guessed her true age to be much more than seventeen.

To ease the tension, Amanda said with mock sarcasm, "I'll have to be careful of our bed when we're married. You might have a gun hidden there."

Marriage had not been discussed, but despite blushing, the detective was pleased to see she was thinking about the possibility, even if it was in jest. The woman realized what she had said and blushed profusely. Janice tugged Alan's arm to gain his attention, and when he looked at her, she rolled her eyes to make fun of his embarrassment. This caused Alan to blush even more. They all laughed and were glad to have something to relieve the tension of their near escape from disaster.

Throughout the night, angry shouts and screams could be heard as police continued their search with the occasional arrest of a teenage girl. When parents protested too aggressively, they were beaten or arrested, sometimes both.

No one would have recognized these men as the same police officers of the past. Men who only a week before had sworn to uphold the law had turned into a gang of marauders. During searches, some took women and abused them sexually as they forced their husbands to watch. If one of his fellow officers protested, the officer was castigated. Sometimes the complaining officers just happened to get caught in the line of fire. Things such as that were no longer questioned. Evil ruled the world and was welcomed by most of the officers. They felt the world had achieved its true nature. Evil brought out some primal instinct in men that didn't seem to exist in most women, but there were many exceptions. A few women were as bad, or worse than the men.

When the police were out of sight, gangs filled the streets and the night air came alive with the sounds of partying and sex. Only the brave and the foolish dared to venture out at night. From above, the king watched all the chaos and smiled at his world.

That morning, officers lined up one-hundred and thirty young, blonde girls on the stage for the king's inspection. He walked down the steps from his palace to the stage with Delores on his arm. Delores had a dazed, blissful look on her face. She was doing God's work and was content. She didn't care that most of one breast had spilled from the gauze-like material of her long, elegant dress that would have been suitable for an ancient Greek queen.

For several minutes the king walked back and forth inspecting the young girls, but seemed unaware of their varied states of dress or undress. He saw only their faces. He occasionally stopped to look at Dolores and then to a girl. The king finally stopped and turned to Delores. She smiled at having his attention. He asked, "Is one of these girls your daughter?"

The woman had a confused look on her face as she looked at the girls. Her eyes then returned to the king and she said, "No, my king, none are my slut of a daughter."

He turned to squarely face her, roughly grabbed her shoulders, and angrily said, "Look again, she has to be there."

Once more she scanned the lines of scared females and said, "No, my king, she is not here."

Everyone within hearing distance expected an explosion of anger, but the only look any of them saw on the king's face was that of contentment. The king said to the police officer in charge, "Bring me a knife." The policeman stood waiting for further directions. The king shouted, "Do it, now!"

The stage was too small to have all the girls on it at once for what he intended. He had twenty girls lined up on the stage with the rest waiting nearby. The king stood at the microphone that been quickly setup, with Delores at his side, and asked, "Is this thing working?" His voiced boomed over the square, bounced around corners, and echoed down dead alleys to reach every apartment and store within three blocks.

He stood erect and scanned the mass of windows

surrounding the stage. His strong hand grasped the microphone and lifted it from its metal stand. He walked slowly around the stage, while the cord of the microphone following like a trained snake. He took a deep breath and distinctly said only one word, "Janiccce." It was the same way he had said it the night when he set her name adrift on the wind.

Janice trembled when she heard the booming sound of the voice as it rattled around the brick and concrete buildings. Her name carried the same tone as she had heard in her dream. Janice shuddered and remembered the sensuousness of the tone. Her mind recalled every detail of the moment when his arms embraced her, and the warmth of his kiss. The girl realized that it had been much more than a dream. Even though she had been asleep and nowhere near the creature, it was now apparent that this had been much more tangible than a simple dream.

Janice shook the image from her mind, ran to the window, and looked down to see the king's head turning in search of his prey. Moments later, the girl was joined at the window by her boyfriend and friends, where they silently watched.

The king appeared to look directly at Janice and said, "Come to me and take your place with your mother and your king-lover."

Janice had a confused look as she and Pete stared at one another. The voice of the king was that of a father calling to his long lost daughter, while also carrying the tone of a lost lover. He seductively said, "I wish you no harm. I want to give you the life you never had. I want you and your mother to once again be happy. Come and rededicate your life to God."

Fear ran through her body as she clutched Pete's arm and hand. Janice kept her eyes locked on the king and said, "He knows I'm here, he's talking directly to me."

Too many years on the force caused Alan to suspect that someone had betrayed them. He had been through a lot with the people in the room and knew them well enough to know they would never do anything to harm Janice.

As if reading the man's thoughts, Janice said, "He doesn't know exactly where I am, but he can, somehow, sense that I'm near. Last night I had a dream where he called me and I went to him." Janice left off the part where she had desired and kissed him wantonly.

His booming voice interrupted them and asked, "Don't you want to be with your mother like you once were? Don't you miss your mother?"

The girl remembered her mother and the happiness they had shared while attending church together. During those times it had been her father who had been left by the wayside. Janice had always loved her father, but had never been as close to him as she had been with her mother. The world had reversed. Now it was her father who stood at her side and her mother at a distance as if not caring for anyone other than her god. The girl wanted to rush to her mother and have things become as they had once been.

Impatience crept into the king's voice and he said, "There is nowhere to run, nowhere to hide. Let's make this easy for everyone. You come to me and we can work out some kind of compromise."

Silence had taken over the negotiations while the king scanned the tall buildings in hopes she would appear in a window or walk out a door. His heart beat in time with each waiting second. This king had fought many men, women, and children since he came into existence, but none had puzzled him like this one. She was always at a distance and unseen. Even at a distance she had managed to leave stumbling blocks and set traps.

Patience ended and he angrily said, "You refuse to settle this in a civilized manner. Let's see how tight your lips will be by the end of this day."

He waved a hand and one of the girls was brought to him. He pulled the girl so that her back was against him, wrapped an arm around her, and held her face up in the general direction where he thought Janice might be hiding. He held the girl firmly by the head, with pain and fear clearly etched across her face. In his grasp her face become a contorted caricature of the pretty girl she had once been. The girl whimpered. He smiled as he slit her throat. Blood sprayed everyone on the stage as he held the struggling girl up by the head and turned in a slow circle to ensure that everyone had a good view.

He said antagonistically, "Another girl will suffer the same fate every half hour that you refuse to join me on the stage." He dropped the twitching girl onto the floor, stood with bloodied hands on his hips, and waited.

Janice screamed in horror as she watched what the evil creature had done to the girl. Alan was the first to her, but instead of offering comfort, he clamped his hand over her mouth to stifle the screams. Pain tore at Janice. She felt all the pain that had befallen the murdered girl. Janice broke the grip of the much larger man, ran toward the door, her soul tormented by the violence she had witnessed, and said, "Nooooo, I have to stop this."

Martin nearly tackled her as her hand touched the doorknob. She twisted in his grip and he saw the anguish on her face. She screamed at her father, "Those girls are going to die because of me. I can't let this happen."

No one in the room had a counter argument, not even her father. They felt the same pain as Janice, but knew she would be sacrificing herself with no guarantee the girls would be saved. Martin held his trembling daughter and said in an effort to replace torment with reason, "More lives than those of the girls on that stage are hanging in the balance. If you fall into his hands there is no one left to fight him."

Tears streamed down her face. She said in stuttering sobs, "I... can't let those... girls die because of... me."

For a moment, her tears slowed and her voice cleared. She said to her father, "How could I live with myself if I sit here safe and watch those girls die because of me? I would gladly give my life to save theirs."

Martin held her face to his chest as tears soaked his shirt and said, "I would give my life for yours. If you recklessly give your life for those girls, I would have to give mine for you."

The girl eventually relented. Janice went back to her position by the window and watched the girls. They all knew that when the next girl was murdered she would fold and it might be impossible to stop her from leaving.

Pete pulled a stool so that he could sit with the girl he loved as she stared mournfully out the window. He looked down to see the first girl killed, still laying on the stage. It was obvious that the king would stack them up to increase the terror. Pete wasn't sure if he, himself, would be able to take the onslaught of depravity, yet he had to offer comfort to the one girl he must protect at any cost.

Her hand was sweaty and clammy when he took it into his. Pete wished he could take her from this evil to a world of laughter and fun, the type of world she, or any other teenager deserved. He saw the sadness in her eyes that silently pleaded for the creature to understand what he was doing is wrong and to spare the other girls. Pete softly said, "Come away from the window, you're only torturing yourself."

Fury rose in Janice, she turned to him, and said, "What right do I have to not be tortured? That girl is dead while I sit here safe and sound. I should be laying there, not her. That girl did nothing to deserve death, other than being born in a wrong year with the wrong color hair."

The creature took another girl from the line.

Janice watched the silent scream of the girl as the creature, with no fanfare, slashed the throat of a second girl at exactly half an hour after the first. Janice closed her eyes and relived the fear and pain she knew the girl had felt. Her eyes opened to see the second girl lying on top of the first. The king hadn't said anything since killing the first girl. He was letting the blood bath do his talking. He only stood looking upwards in hopes of seeing Janice.

Amanda sat on the sofa where she watched Janice sitting by the window. She solemnly asked, "Alan, is there nothing we can do?"

He sullenly said, "There are too many guns down there for us to make any kind of rescue attempt. I think Pete is doing what none of us could do, easing some of her pain. If she was to give into that madman, then we all might be lost. I'm not sure what she can do, but she is the only hope mankind has."

The doctor empathetically said, "Someone has to get her away from that window. If she continues to sit and watch those girls die, she will go mad. If it was me in her place, I would have already lost it. Shit, her mother is down there with a creature from Hell that's going to kill a young girl every half hour. We have got to do something to help her… to help those girls."

A knock on the door froze them all. They all looked at one another as if seeking an answer on how to react. Alan walked softly so as not to alert whomever was at the door. He looked through the peephole at the disfigured world beyond and saw a man in a blue uniform. He turned to the others and silently mouthed, "It's the police."

"Detective Johnson?" the officer asked conspiratorially from beyond the door. He waited for an answer. When he received none, he said, "I was one of the policemen that searched this place earlier. I once guarded a prisoner here and know about the secret compartment. I could have given you away, but I didn't." The officer searched for the correct tone in an effort not to sound threatening and said, "You have to let me in. I might be able to help."

Martin tried to stop him from opening the door, but he arrived too late to place himself between the door and his friend. The officer entered and quickly closed the door. He turned to see the tormented Janice sitting and staring out the window. He turned his attention to his fellow officer and said, "So, that's the girl this new king is hell-bent to find."

Protectively, the detective steered the conversation away from Janice and said, "Thank you for not exposing us. What is it you think that you can do to help us?"

The officer looked around the room at the assortment of people who were willing to fight for what they believed was right and couldn't help but smile. His attention returned to the detective and he replied, "When the world... began to go crazy, I stashed some weapons on top of one of the buildings near here. In that stash is a sniper rifle. That was my assignment in the army."

The detective asked, "What is it you intend to do with these weapons, and in particular the sniper rifle?"

"Kill the demon," the officer confidently said. He paused and added, "I know he's been shot at, but I don't think the bullets ever touched him. If I catch him unprepared, it might work."

They all looked at the man incredulously and Frank asked, "Is that possible—I mean to kill him with a simple bullet?"

Pete managed to tear Janice's eyes away from the window long enough to look at him and asked, "Is it possible," he waited until he was sure he had her attention and continued, "to kill the king?"

Somewhere in the depths of her despair the boy saw a glimmer of hope. She said, "It might be possible if we can weaken him." Janice rose and walked to where the officer stood just inside the door. Her eyes were red and swollen from tears. She said to the policeman, "If it comes down to having only one chance to shoot, and this creature has made me do his bidding, use that one shot on me."

Pete shouted, "No!"

She looked at the boy she loved and said with seemingly impossible strength, "You would never want me to belong to that vile creature and you would never want me to do anything to harm you or our friends."

He knew what she had said was the truth, but to face a future without her was more than he could bear. The air in the room seemed to thicken as he tried to walk close enough to take her into his arms, and to hold and protect her from all that is evil.

As Pete put his arm around Janice, the officer said, "I need to get in place." He looked at Janice and sadly said, "There is no way to know when the opportunity will arise. He seems vulnerable, now, but if he can't be harmed by a bullet, I'll have given away the small advantage that weapon gives us."

The amplified scream cut through the air like lightning taking its revenge on the Earth. The king's voice was calm and ominous. He said, "That was number three. How many more must fall before you come to me and save them?"

This time Janice didn't cry, but stared toward the window and imagined the scene of a young girl having her throat sliced open like a pig gone to slaughter. She was barely aware of the police officer as he exited and headed for some unknown rooftop. They had decided it was better not to know his exact position. Everyone was well aware that his bullet might, in the end, be for one of them, especially Janice.

Alan looked down at the three bodies as they lay crisscross on the platform. He felt the tug of his profession, the desire to charge the man and take him into custody. No matter his origins, this man was no more than a street thug. During his long years on the force he had brought many like him to justice.

Police surrounded this perpetrator, yet they weren't there to arrest him, but there for his protection. The police, like most people, had willingly, with no trepidations, given into the creature. They followed him through blind faith. Detective Alan Johnson wanted to bring them to justice just as much as he did the king. All of mankind had failed him except, Janice, Amanda and the rest of his friends, as well as those on Credence Drive. On some rooftop sat a lone cop willing to sacrifice his life for the world. That was the kind of cop Detective Johnson wanted in his world. The kind he could respect.

No one noticed as Alan slipped from the room and made his way to the concrete sidewalk. He looked around the jagged skyline and knew a rifle might be trained on him, ready to steal his life at any moment. He worked his way, unseen, through alleyways to get as close to the stage as possible. He found a small niche behind a garbage dumpster, which was within hearing distance of the stage. He was close enough to see the congealing blood of the young victims as it ran from the stage and formed a small pool on the asphalt beneath.

A scream filled the apartment, but this time it came from within. Amanda ran to the door, tore it open, and screamed in anguish, "Alan!" She exploded out the door, ran to the stairs, and looked down them in desperate hope that he would be standing somewhere safe. The stairs were as empty as her hopes.

A hand caught Amanda from behind, she jerked around, and hopefully asked, "Alan?"

She disappointingly found Frank, instead. The devastated woman collapsed into his arms. She needed comfort even if it couldn't come from the arms of the man she loved. Her mind knew where Alan had gone and why, but her heart greedily wished he was there holding her and saying all the things that he knew would calm her fears.

"Maybe he's only gone for a walk. This place is stifling me as well," the man reassuringly said. They both knew Alan hadn't just gone for a walk.

The devastated woman regained the composure that years of being a doctor had instilled in her and said, "Let's go back in before we're spotted or arouse suspicion."

When Amanda entered the apartment, Janice rushed to her and closed her arms around the woman as they shared their grief. The younger girl took Amanda by the hand and led her to the window where she had sat vigilant over the slaughtered girls. Pete could see Janice and Amanda wanted to be left alone, so he left to join his father in another room. Janice smiled at him thankfully.

Everyone had given them distance, and that gave Janice the time she needed. She covertly said to the other woman, "We have to do something to help Alan... and those girls."

In a conspiratorial tone, Amanda asked, "How? What can we do?"

Janice glanced at the men who had congregated to talk about some sporting event that might never happen, but it was a much needed distraction. She was grateful they were considerate and had given her this time alone with Amanda. She leaned close to the woman and secretively said, "You have to help me leave this apartment."

The woman shouted, "You want to what?" Everyone turned to see what had caused the outburst. The girls smiled apologetically at the men through the open door in an effort not to arouse suspicion. The doctor adamantly said, "There is no way I'm going to allow you to leave this apartment, alone."

The girl impishly asked, "Does that mean you want to go

with me?"

Anger filled Amanda's voice, but she kept it contained and softly said, "Neither of us are going anywhere. If you go out there, you will end up dead like those three girls."

Janice's despaired and said, "It's better for me to die than those girls down there. Those girls have done nothing to deserve the fate they face. I can give myself to save them." She looked at her friend and emphatically asked, "Wouldn't you do the same for them?"

The doctor replied in protest, "That would be different."

"Oh," she questioned, "how might that be different? Is your life worth less than mine? Would my life be of greater value than yours? The answer is no on all accounts."

Amanda couldn't come up with a valid argument to Janice's arguments. With a worried look she lifted a finger, pointed it at the girl's father and boyfriend, and asked, "Do you think they could ever forgive me if I helped you leave and something happened to you?"

Janice said unequivocally, "Do you think I could live with myself if I continue to sit idly by and watch more girls die because of me?"

Amanda had no reply because she knew her friend was right. If faced with the same situation, Amanda would have gladly given her own life for the girls who would surely die by the the king's hand.

She sat with Janice and looked out the window at the line of girls waiting to die. Fear, or possibly some power, kept the captive girls silently standing as they stared at the three dead girls. Their minds thought of ways to fight or flee, but the king's power kept them in a thrall, which prevented movement. They had stood in place for hours with no water. The sun beating down on them caused the girls to begin collapsing from dehydration, fear, and fatigue. When they fell, the vagrant preacher, who had become the king's right hand, would whip them with a riding crop until they were once again on their feet.

Amanda stood and said loud enough for everyone to hear, "I need to get some air, do you want to join me, Janice?"

Martin eyed the woman suspiciously and asked, "You aren't going to do something stupid, are you?"

She gave a dismissing laugh and replied, "Of course not. Janice and I have talked and we've decided that Alan can take care of himself. I just need to get out of this apartment for a few minutes and I think Janice needs to as well."

The men could understand the feeling of being imprisoned, but Martin had a sinking feeling in his stomach. He looked at his daughter and wondered if this would be the last time he saw her alive. Martin's thoughts went back and forth over whether he should allow her to leave, but he knew he had no say in the matter. He could see in her eyes that her mind was made up. He hugged his daughter, kissed her on the forehead, and said as if he would never see her again, "I love you with all my heart."

She looked at her father and forlornly said, "I love you too, daddy," something Janice hadn't called her father since she was a little girl.

Janice shared a look with Pete and smiled weakly at him and almost lost her resolve to carry through with her plan. Pete wanted to rush to Janice and take her in his arms, but he remained at a distance and acted as if she would return in a few minutes. He wanted to believe that she really was just going out for a moment of fresh air. He knew that if he took her into his arms the facade would collapse and they would all be faced with the truth.

The scream of another girl being slaughtered froze everyone except the two females as they closed the door behind them as they left for a date with fate. Martin fully cried for the first time since he was a child. Pete placed a hand on the shoulder of the father of the girl he loved and shared his grief. Pete knew the immensity of what had just occurred.

No traffic ran on the street that just days ago had been packed with thousands of motorists as they wandered about on self-important errands. The blacktop gave off rising waves of heat as the sun beat down on the inky surface. Heat rising from the street made buildings on the far side appear to have a ghostly shimmer.

Amanda took Janice by the hand and said, "Let's get this over with."

Janice jerked her hand away, turned to face the older woman, and sternly said, "You're not going with me. You give me a lead, then go back up and tell my dad and Pete that I ran away from you."

"Oh no," the doctor declared, "you are not going anywhere without me."

Janice pleaded, "If you go with me, it will mean your life. I don't expect to return. "

"Then we won't return together," Amanda said in an effort to sound much braver than she felt.

Janice sighed and walked toward the large opening of the square and possible death. The doctor hesitantly followed. The woman tried to think of every possible reason there was to convince Janice there were better options. There were none. Logic dictated only one course of action, and that was to face the enemy and to stop the slaughter of innocent young girls.

Pete stood with his hand on the door knob and said, "It's time for me to go." His sad eyes said more than his words.

The older men looked at one another and walked to stand behind Pete. Martin said, "Yes, it's time for us all to go, my daughter awaits us."

The men stood on the street where only moments before Janice and the doctor had stood. Frank asked, "What are we going to do, march up to that thing and introduce ourselves?" That invoked a small laugh from the other men.

Pete sullenly said, "I just want to find Janice and make sure she's safe." The men agreed and started in the direction of the square. They kept close to the walls and avoided eye contact with anyone they met as they made their way down the sidewalk. Fear knotted the boy's stomach when he thought of the girl he loved in the hands of the evil creature.

He worked his mind feverishly to find a way to prevent that from happening, but he knew that might have already come to pass. Janice's fate had been decided the day the king arrived, even if they had tried to deny the truth.

The king's voice boomed while he slit the throat of another girl, "You sit and let others die for you. I thought you might be a worthy adversary, but you are nothing except a frightened child. You cower in fear as others die in your place."

Her voice was surprisingly strong and steady. She said to the creature, "It's true, I am frightened, and I might not be much of an adversary, but I will not let anymore die in my name."

The king scanned the silent crowd that had momentarily forgotten the executions. The crowd would sometimes thin, but when time came for another execution, the mass of people would once again expand. Mankind was hungry for the death and violence they found on the stage. It showed in everything they did in life. It showed in the movies they watched, the books they read, the sports they watched, and the games they played.

The king searched until he found two eyes that were strong, unlike the mindless followers that stood in the crowd. He smiled and cheerfully said, "It is so good of you to come to my party, Janice." He reveled in the moment and then politely asked, "Would you come join me on the stage?"

Janice fought to keep her voice steady. She had never

been so scared, but dared not let the creature see the fear. He, like any other creature on the face of the Earth, would leap to take advantage of such fear. She looked coldly at him and said, "Let the girls go."

Janice's demand was answered by a laugh that chilled her to the bone. It was the laugh of unspeakable evil. Men closed in around Janice. One grabbed her roughly by the upper arm.

The king said, "You are in no position to make demands. A girl will still die every half hour until I have been satisfied that you are the one I seek and are of no threat to me." He smiled at her and added, "Now, come join me on the stage."

Another man grabbed Amanda's arm and the men half-dragged her and Janice onto the stage. The grip was so tight that their arms immediately began turning a sickish purple. The men let them go when they were within reach of the creature. An imprint of the men's hands was left in the form of a bruise on the arms of both women.

Janice saw the handsome man, remembered the dream, and began to perspire. The creature seemed to read her mind and said, "So you found our little midnight liaison exciting."

She spat at him and lied, "I find nothing exciting about a vile creature such as you."

His hand touched her cheek, while another pulled her to him and embraced the girl. She was back in his arms as she had been in the dream. Even as she fought the urge, she still wanted him more than she wanted any man. She lusted for his touch and his kisses. Her trembling hands searched his massive arms and chest. She basked in his animalistic male scent. The feelings swelling within were not something she had anticipated. She fought to reclaim the revulsion that she held for the king.

"That was not a dream, my love. That was the present, as well as the future you saw. That was the future for you as my wife as we rule this world together," he presciently said.

The sound of her hand hitting his face was like a gunshot as it echoed off the tall buildings that surrounded the the stage. Rage filled the king as his face reddened. He called one of the men that had brought the girls onto the stage and said, "Tie her hands until she learns their proper use."

He let the rage slip back to its hiding place just beneath the surface and said, "I think you just need inspiration." He nodded to one of the men who grabbed one the girls on the stage and slit her throat."

Janice thought the image had been horrible from her distant vantage point, but to see it close-up was unbearable. She collapsed to the floor and welcomed the darkness that protected her from the horrible sight.

Awareness returned and she tried to focus on the hand stroking her hair as her mother had once done. She felt sick to her stomach when her eyes focused and found the hand belonged to the king. He smiled in mocked worry and said, "I am glad to see you are well—we have all been so worried."

His eyes moved from Janice to something behind her and said, "You missed the late arrival of more guests."

Janice looked around to see her father, Pete, and his father standing with their hands tied behind their backs. The haze rapidly dissolved and she screamed, "Let them go or I'll never do as you want."

Confidence rang in his voice. He said, "Ahh... but you will do what I say either way. When they are no longer useful, I'll add their bodies to the existing pile on the stage."

Janice looked at the boy she loved, her father, friends, and asked, "What is it you want of me?"

"To be my wife, of course. Didn't you realize that from the vision I gave you?" He asked.

Pete screamed, "If you touch her I'll kill you, demon."

The king laughed and said, "I admire such loyalty. I may keep you alive as a servant."

Martin whispered to Pete, "Calm down, don't antagonize him."

The creature laughed and said, "Yes, let's not antagonize me. You might not like me when I get angry."

A woman approached the king and the familiar voice angrily said, "I thought I was your wife."

The caring words didn't sound as if they should come from such a vile creature. He said, "You are my wife, as will be your daughter."

The girl's mother contemplated what the man said and hated him for it, yet she knew there was nothing she could do. She obediently replied, "Yes, my love, if that is your wish."

He demandingly said to Janice, "Kneel before me and offer yourself to me before another has to die."

Tears ran from her eyes and down her cheeks to leave

small, glistening drops on the stage as she knelt and supplicated herself to the king. She could no longer watch others die because of her stubbornness. The girl knew that she, now, belonged to this creature, but she vowed he would never have her mind, or her love that belonged to Pete, even if she could never be with him.

The crowd was focused on the stage when Alan slipped from his hiding place. The cop made his way, unnoticed, through the crowd. Ahead of him was a group of policemen. The compactness of the crowd forced him in their direction. He tried to hide his face, but also didn't want to look suspicious. One of the policeman stared at him and Alan froze in controlled panic. He was sure the officer had recognized him as one of their own. His mind calculated every move he could make to free himself, but none ended in freedom, only capture or death. Just when he thought capture was imminent, the officer turned his attention back to the show on the stage. Alan took that moment to disappear into the crowd.

Her small hand wiped tears from her eyes and she said, "Before I swear my fealty to you, I wish to ask a question. Who sent you here, Lucifer or Iam?"

He looked thoughtfully at her, rubbed his bearded chin, and finally replied, "Both... neither."

"I don't understand," she said.

Bemused, he said, "I would not be here if not for the

creator, nor would they."

More confused than ever, she asked, "God sent you?" He didn't reply. She rephrased and asked, "Who gave you the crown? The Bible says the lamb, who some think is the son of God."

He smiled at her and said, "You ask questions I am not allowed to answer. You have read your Bible and you know that I was prophesied. I'll not answer anymore of your questions." He called for one of the men to bring another girl.

Janice stood, faced the creature, and angrily said, "Since you didn't answer my question, I would like to speak to these people."

He roared with laughter and mockingly asked, "What are you going to do? Beg for your life? Beg these pitiful fools to help you escape?"

Her single word carried magic that shook the king to his core. She simply replied, "Yes."

She stared at him and saw something akin to fear in his eyes. The look was fleeting and was quickly replaced by amusement. He said, "Go ahead and beg these lambs. This should be amusing." He thought for a moment and added, "Just remember that your friends' lives are in my hands. If at anytime your words are not welcomed, then one of them will die. You have little time before another girl dies. To halt that execution, you must have, by then, convinced me that you have freely given yourself to me."

Fear nearly silenced her, but Janice knew she had to risk the lives of her family and friends, as well as those of the remaining girls. There was only one way for any of them to leave this place alive. Janice stood and faced the gathered crowd. She glanced at her father, friends, and her mother who stood with a scowl at the side and slightly back of the king.

Janice fearfully walked to the microphone, her legs barely able to maintain her weight. She touched the metal object and spoke, but nothing came out. Nerves were reined in and she opened her mouth again and said, "I have a story to tell you. It's how a girl came to be standing on this stage, today. She was a God-fearing girl who went to church at least three days a week. That girl loved her mother very much, and still does." Janice turned to look at her mother, but saw no reaction to what she had just said.

She took a deep breath and tried to ignore the creature that stood behind, so close that he was almost touching. She could almost feel his hot breath on her neck. Janice said, "The god in whom I had put all my faith, made my parents take me to this church. There, I was taken to a place that wasn't a part of the church, or of this world. I was kept in that place for months or years."

Her eyes scanned the crowd and she was pleased to see they were at least listening. Janice continued, "That place was worse than any hell anyone could have endured. Day and night no longer existed because there was only darkness. With each day, constant hunger gnawed at me like some savage beast. This was a place where death was welcomed, but could never come. Can you imagine being trapped and not allowed to eat... or even die? Can you imagine starving with no chance of death? In this hell, even standing would have been a simple pleasure. The only sounds, other than my own sobs, were those of small creatures that scurried about in the darkness."

Janice turned to point at the king and said, "That vile creature and his god did that to me." She turned back to face the crowd and continued, "Darkness and my thoughts were the only companions during that time. I thought of my family and how I longed to be with them. I thought about my family and knew I would never see them again."

Once again she turned to glance at her mother and said, "It was my mother who put me in that place. Even for that, I don't hate her. I want to see the smile on her face that has been lost since that night. I would give anything to see that smile again."

The next words were directed more at her mother than the crowd, "I still love you and forgive you. I hope you can forgive me for distancing myself from you." The girl waited for a reaction from her mother, but none came.

There was a commotion in the distance, but she paid little attention as she once more faced the crowd and said as her hand waved in an arc, "This world you hold so dear is not always the one you see. Around you are alternate realities. Look on this stage and see it with an open mind. Look at us with open eyes. See the truth as I can sometimes do."

Pete said, "She's telling the truth, Janice has shown me how to see," before one of the guards crashed a fist into his face.

A tear trickled down her cheek when she saw the boy she loved in pain. Blood ran from his nose, lip, and cheek. Janice wanted to rush to comfort him, but he gave her a look that indicated her attention was needed elsewhere.

Janice fought back the urge to be with Pete, and more determined than before, said to the people, "Turn and look at the church behind you, the one that your king now uses as a palace. See it for what it is." She saw heads turn. She continued, "See that structure for what it is, a monument to evil. It's not my place to say what religion is good or bad, but I am to say that man has distorted the truth while this creature behind me has perpetuated that distortion."

"You do amuse me. I'm glad that I decided not to kill you." The king laughingly said. He rested a hand on her shoulder, pointed to the crowd of people, and said, "Those people can see only their own selfish greed. They cannot think past their own wants and desires."

Janice turned to face the creature and said, "Your kind can survive only with the faith of others. When that faith is removed... you have no power."

He roared with laughter and said, "You are wise for someone so young. Having knowledge of something, but defeating it is another matter. You can stand here and tell these idiots the truth until you collapse, but they will not believe. They will not believe you because you have nothing of value to offer them."

She turned in desperation to the crowd, dropped to her

knees, and pleaded, "I beg for you to think of what I have told you. This may be your last chance. This creature and its master have tortured me beyond belief. Don't let this happen to you. For centuries the church and politicians have lied to you. They use lies to lead you around like sheep. This animal is right, I have nothing to offer you except the truth." The girl collapsed onto the stage, crying fitfully. She looked up at the people through tear-filled, pleading eyes.

No words were spoken from the crowd amassed around the stage. They had watched the girl plead with them, but no one stepped forward to offer support for her words. It might have been for fear of reprisal, or they just didn't believe what she had said. Maybe the king had been right, and people only cared about themselves or the golden calf.

The king looked down at the sobbing girl and said, "Come to me, wife."

She twisted to look at him and all hope evaporated. The girl had placed all her hopes in mankind, and her friends would die for her stupidity. Racked with grief, she turned to look at her father, Pete, and friends. Janice mournfully pleaded, "Please forgive me—I have failed you."

They stood, helpless to comfort the tortured girl. Their eyes forgave the girl, but they knew she would never forgive herself. Pete cried unabashedly for the girl he loved. The boy looked to the sky and said, "Dammit, Lucifer, you started this, now help her." His plea for help went unheard.

Janice stood and faced the king. She said, "You have kept your word, and now I will keep mine. Let my friends go and I'll become your wife. I will lay with you in your bed and bear your children, if that's your desire."

The king didn't act as a man would after having won a battle. He acted as if he had known the outcome from the beginning and had waited patiently for the scene to play out. He pulled his new wife to him, wrapped a strong arm around her, and said, "That is what I desire."

She stood with him, not as an enemy, but as a wife. Fighting back tears, the girl began to resign her fate to life with the creature.

There was a scream of rage from behind. They turned to see Delores running for the two. Her hand grabbed an arrow from the ever-present quiver on the creature's back.

Everyone stood frozen and watched the scene as if it was happening in slow motion. Pete forgot his own safety and ran toward Janice. She saw Pete and shouted, "Nooooo."

It had sounded like no more than a firecracker as it echoed through the buildings. The bullet raced from the barrel of the gun a microsecond after the policeman perched on the roof pulled the trigger. The bullet spun as it followed a perfect trajectory to its target. The air crackled as the bullet passed the sound barrier. People tried to look toward the sound, but too much was happening at once. The king tried to understand the crackling sound, while at the same moment, Delores raised the arrow in the air. He sensed danger from more than one direction. He had no choice other than to target the most apparent danger, and that was Delores.

The king moved to grabbed Delores, causing the bullet

intended for the king to hit Delores in the back just below the right shoulder blade, knocking her forward. The impact added to her previous momentum and threw her forward into the king with the deadly arrow pointed at its target.

Janice watched as the arrow momentarily came in her direction, but knew she wasn't its target. She happened to see the the king's face and smiled. He was showing intense fear—the great king was afraid. Janice knew she had to live long enough to at least pass on how to kill the creature.

The only sound to be heard was that of ripping flesh and shattering bone as the arrow tore into the king's chest. It had been driven in with near inhuman force. Rage had been the force that propelled the arrow. The love of a mother's hand had chosen the target. The king collapsed and lay on the stage, bleeding profusely, with Delores lying on top of the creature. Blood ran from his massive chest as he pushed the woman away.

Janice rushed to her mother and cradled her head in her arms. The stricken woman looked at her daughter and said, "Please forgive me for everything I've done. I should have stood with you no matter what. I was foolish to have followed so blindly." The mother gagged and blood ran from her mouth. She pulled her daughter closer and said, "I love you."

"I love you too, mother," Janice cried.

Martin rushed to join his daughter and wife. Delores touched her fingertips to his cheek, smiled at him, and said, "I have always loved you, my husband. I won't bother to ask for your forgiveness, but I hope that some day you may find it in your heart to do so."

The dying mother's hands gripped those of the two she loved. With each beat of her heart, life-giving blood ran from the gaping wound onto the already bloodied stage. She closed her eyes for the last time. Janice knew that whatever afterlife there might be, her mother's soul would be safe, there. Whatever role Lucifer had played in all this, his prediction of the Janice's mother's soul being doomed would not happen. She knew in that instant that everything could be changed. Nothing was preordained. The love Delores had for her family had made her see the truth.

The creature howled in pain and fury. His muscular hand grasped the shaft of the arrow, ripped it from his chest, and threw it onto the stage floor. He growled angrily and said to the dead woman at his feet, "I'll see to it that your soul is damned for eternity." He jerked Janice by the hair from her dead mother and said to the lifeless, prone figure, "I hope you are watching when I take your daughter at night, and when she howls from pain as I rip into her."

The wound on the king closed as it healed almost instantaneously. All hope of killing the creature evaporated. Janice hoped the man on the rooftop would take another shot and have the bullet take her life so that she would never have to spend a night with the demon. Death would be the only thing that could save her from the hell that she would endure at the creature's hand.

A gunshot rang out and Janice froze, sure that she was the

intended target. At that moment, she heard a scream and saw the police officer tumble from atop the building behind the stage. The stage shook noticeably when his body crashed into the concrete sidewalk. Janice turned away from his limp, tangled body and despaired.

"Listen to what the girl has said. She spoke the truth," a man's voice said from somewhere in the crowd. It was then that Janice noticed the circle of police that had enclosed the existing line of police that were loyal to the king. Those in the outer circle began talking to those in the inner circle. Conversations began between officers that had once been loyal to each other.

This caused a ripple effect as the chatter worked its way through the crowd. The low rumble of talk became a roar as that ripple came to those nearest the stage. People began to turn and stare up at the stage and point. Janice had seen the same look on the faces of her neighbors. She saw faces in the crowd as they change from fealty for the king to one of disgust.

She turned to look at the king and saw nothing special, although she could tell he was somehow weaker. It was then she realized they were beginning to see the king for what he truly was. Janice had avoided seeing him in his true form. Janice knew if she lost this battle, life with the king would be hard enough without having to see his true face of evil. The girl closed her eyes and thought of only the truth. She slowly opened them to reveal a contortion of what had been the king. Gone, was the handsome muscular face. The once strong king had been replaced by something that could have never been mistaken as human. His once tall frame was bent and twisted like the spires of the church in which she had been held captive. The creature's eyes were like those of a cat and glowed a sickly yellow. There were no horns as depicted by fiction, but wouldn't have looked out of place on top of his head.

The creature repulsed the girl as much as it did the people in the tumultuous crowd. They saw the creature in its true form and were sickened by the image. Everyone was stunned and frozen in place when Alan ran from the crowd and onto the stage. He pushed the creature and a guard that had stepped to block his way. He grabbed Janice and nearly tossed her into the hands of her father who had managed to free his hands after the distraction.

The king howled in fury, a sound that was befitting its true form. It had come to realize the people were seeing its true form. The place where Delores had impaled him with the arrow reopened and a brown fluid began running from the wound, filling the air with a foul stench. For the first time, they saw true fear in the eyes of the beast.

It lashed out at Janice in retaliation for turning the people against him, for allowing them to see him in his true form. His hand closed on her throat as a shot rang out.

The creature turned to see Alan holding his gun with smoke still rising from the warm barrel. The detective angrily said, "Go back to whatever place you come from and tell your master that you are not welcome here." He fired the service revolver once more, but the creature still stood, unwavering. But it was enough for the creature to release Janice.

Janice shocked her friends and family when instead of fleeing, turned to face the creature and took his deformed hand in her own. She glanced at the unusually long reptile-like fingers and nails that looked more like talons. The girl looked back to the creature's distorted face and said, "Let's see where you belong."

She closed her eyes and willed herself to see the truth. Janice opened them to find only darkness. At first, she thought something had happened to her eyesight. Janice then realized that she was in a place similar to the dark cell in which she had been imprisoned. The familiar feeling of Hell made the girl tremble and she tightened her grip on the creature's hand. She said, her voice filled with pain, "This is your home. You're no more than a prisoner yourself."

The king said nothing, but she could feel his fear. Janice knew the creature didn't want to return to this dark world and would do anything to avoid that fate. The next moment, they were once more standing on the stage where the bright light was momentarily blinding. Pete asked through his swollen lip, "Where did you go?"

Janice ignored her boyfriend and said to the creature, "You know I can't allow you to stay here."

He laughed and said with forced bravado, "Little girl, I don't think you can stop me. The power to momentarily take me from this world was impressive, but it will take much more than that."

292

Janice pointed to the confused mass of people gathered in front of the stage and said, "You're right, I alone don't have the power to change Iam's will, but those people do. The collective power of those people is stronger than any god. Their will tells me they want their world back. People want one thing in their life, and that's normalcy, something you can't give them. They want to go to work and then come home to have dinner with their family. Those people want to sit around at night in front of the television. They want the world where they know the bills are paid and their children are healthy. They want all the things you aren't."

Janice looked at her friends and family once more. She still held the creature's hand when they once more disappeared. A moment later, Janice reappeared on the stage alone and said, "It's over, at least for today.

At the same time, the three remaining horsemen disappeared into wisps of mist. In the blink of an eye they were torn from the world they had desired to own. The horsemen had been created to possess worlds. This was their first loss, and it angered them. They would someday try to return and complete their task.

Her family and friends circled the girl and hugged her as the confused people in the crowd began to slowly wander away. Mothers went home to their children, while fathers went home to their wives as they wondered why they had cheered this beast on as it slaughtered young girls. That night they would have nightmares about the things they had supported and done. Because of this, many would take their

293

own lives.

A group of policemen made their way onto the stage. One of them went to join Detective Johnson and said, "I can't believe all of you are still alive. I thought for sure you would have been killed before we could arrive."

Before the detective could reply, Janice asked the officer, "How were you able to convince those people when I had failed?"

The young officer smiled and asked, "Why do you think you failed?"

She sadly said, "I told the people about the things that had happened in the world and they didn't listen."

He smiled and said, "They heard you, but a few police officers and rogues that hadn't believed stood in back holding guns, ready to shoot anyone that left. When the people saw friendly police, they opened their eyes and saw the truth, just as we had after visiting your neighborhood."

Martin arched a brow and asked, "What did our neighborhood have to do with it?"

The officer told them how they had gone there to arrest Janice. He said, "She had apparently slipped out the backdoor, along with the rest of you. Your neighbors confronted us with everything the girl and you had told them. They showed us the newspapers." The officer laughed and continued, "The people here became brave when they saw that we were with them. If they had only known that we left our guns laying on the street in front of your house."

Everyone laughed, as much from what the officer said, as

from the realization that the end had come. Relief washed over them like a warm summer rain. Pete took Janice's hand, looked at her, and said, "I'm so glad you're safe."

She contently said, even if worry filled her eyes as she touched Pete's swollen cheek, "Not near as happy as I am to have you safe."

The girl looked at her dead mother and what cheer there had been was gone. She looked at her father and said, "We have to..."

One of the officers interjected, "Don't worry about her, ma'am. We'll take care of any arrangements that need to be made."

She hugged him and said, "Thank you."

Trees passed rapidly by the car window as she sat with her father on the way home. Janice allowed herself to relax for the first time in weeks. She knew home would be different. Her mother would be missed, but she knew that with all the friends they had made, in time it would once more be a happy place.

She looked out the window as they passed by a church and her heart sank. Janice saw the truth of the brick structure, the twisted spires and dark gray stone. The girl knew then that she had won only a battle and the war would rage on.

Continued in Heavenly Deception book 2.

ABOUT THE AUTHOR

T.L. Crain was born and raised in rural South Carolina. T. L. has always been curious about all things, whether it's science, theology, or politics. Born in 1952, T. L. has many interests, such as politics and science,
Writing is a passion and not a choice. There are always ongoing projects, such as an autobiography, nonfiction supernatural, and a sci-fi novel about a girl with incredible mental capabilities.

Check out www.booksbytlc.com for more info about T. L. Crain's writing.

Also visit www.thechosen-tlc.com for more info about **The Chosen.**

Visit www.heavenlydeception.com to learn more about this novel.